COMING FROM THE SEA

alking up the steep slope from the harbor, Yeolani felt like a fool yet again. His father, coming up behind him from the boat, certainly reinforced that notion having found yet again nothing good with his son's work on this latest fishing trip. Of course, Yeolani had been sea-sick. He had made it a tradition, ever since he was nine and deemed old enough to join his father's crew, of losing his breakfast over the side.

"Feeding the fishes," his father had called it.

But, this voyage, Yeolani had been so ill on the three-day trip that he hadn't even been able to keep down water and so had passed out, leaving the rest of the crew to do his work. His father, the captain, couldn't rouse him and instead threw the rations of ale at his son, leaving none for the crew which led to a near mutiny onboard. Left with only the water barrel, they had sailed back into port with only half a hold full. How was Yeolani expected to inherit his father's boat if he couldn't tolerate being out at sea? Every trip, the moment he stepped onto the gangplank Yeolani invariably ended up losing whatever he'd managed to eat. It was so bad that the sixteen-year-old had taken to eating only after they'd come back into Simten's port and carrying only water with him for the three-day voyages.

If he looked scrawny and wasted, it was Yeolani's own fault, his father insisted, but the boy had better figure out how to endure or someone on the crew, if not his own father, would slit his throat just to be rid of him, and someone else could inherit the family business. Now, after another failed voyage, Yeolani could feel his father's anger like a hurricane brewing just offshore, waiting to reach their home on the bluff where the thrashing could occur and not be witnessed by his crew. His father would probably get good and drunk beforehand, but Yeolani knew his anger didn't need liquid encouragement.

However, as he topped the bluff and turned up the path, Yeolani stopped cold, knowing something was wrong. In the fading light, he could see the village not far down the path, and he struggled to identify the changes to his expectations. Laundry flapped in the constant wind, not brought in for the evening. No smoke tore from chimneys. Even the woodcutters usually coming from the Fallon Forest just beyond the town were absent. It was all wrong.

Father, still grumbling and huffing after the climb up from the docks, didn't notice a thing. He swatted Yeolani on the back of the head for not moving along and then went around his son who remained rooted in the sandy footpath. The older man noticed nothing and had stomped all the way to their home that clung like a barnacle to the cliff on the southern edge of the town. Somehow the act of opening the door broke through the boy's frozen study, and he staggered the fifty yards to his home. He felt weak-kneed and unsure if it was the lack of food or his sudden fear.

Yeolani threw open the door and almost plowed into his

LIFE GIVER

THE WISE ONES BOOK 3

LISA LOWELL

father's back, where the captain stood frozen, now drinking in the scene he had ignored before. The blackstone hearth was cold. The usually carefully cleaned table still bore the wooden bowls from the morning breakfast. Mother would never allow that to remain. She kept an impeccable if humble home. In the corner, Yeolani saw his mother on her knees beside the rush bed, draped over the still body of his nine-year-old sister, weeping and moaning. Mother's hair was unkempt, her apron dirty and her haggard face puffy with her grief and deathly pale. How long ago? Yeolani could not bring his mind to finish the thought, let alone speak aloud.

"What have you done, woman!" Father bellowed, though it came out as a growl. Before Yeolani could react or his mother could duck, Father reached out and backhanded his wife, throwing her against the hearth. "You've killed the child!"

"No, Da," Yeolani gasped, reaching for his father's arm to stop the second blow, but weakened as he was, Father simply shrugged Yeolani off onto the floor and used his momentum to slug the boy before returning to his unconscious wife.

Desperately, Yeolani looked around the single room home for some weapon and found the knife his mother used in her cooking. He snatched it from the wash tub and leaped at his father, climbing onto his father's back as the man continued to beat his wife. The boy carefully placed the knife at his father's throat, and the man stopped his swing, slowly straightened up, and lifted his hands.

"Da, you will stop now," Yeolani hissed into his father's ear. "She's not to blame for Nevia's death. There's a sickness in the village."

With the full weight of his son clinging to his back, the captain moved carefully, deliberately, and from behind Yeolani couldn't see his movements, so when the captain's calloused hands wrapped around his son's knife hand, he wasn't prepared. He grasped the boy's wrist and, with a tremendous tug, threw Yeolani sprawling into the cold fireplace. Stunned, Yeolani only just managed to remain conscious as his father grabbed him by the leg and pulled him from the ashes. He knocked his head on the hearth as he landed on the floor rushes and dizzily couldn't roll to absorb the blow when his father's kick caught him in the ribs. But he still held the knife.

"You," kick, "were never," kick, "my son," kick, and this time, Yeolani rolled toward the descending boot and stabbed at the foot with what little strength he could muster. Blood and shrieks barely registered, but the momentum of the next kick stopped as his father hopped around on his undamaged foot. Yeolani staggered to his feet to defend himself and his mother who still remained unresponsive on the floor.

Enraged and careless of his wounded foot, the captain rammed himself bodily into Yeolani, pinning his son up against the wall with one arm under his chin, and began beating him about the head with a free fist. Yeolani realized then that his father would murder him and had probably already murdered Mother. If Yeolani did nothing, he would die. His pinned body allowed little movement, but he pried his hand free and, without any thought or hesitation, sank the knife into his father's side. The blade cut deep into the liver. The arm across Yeonlani's throat eased, and his father's bloodshot eyes, a hand width from his own, widened in sudden pain. The restricting arm fell away. Then his father collapsed sideways along the wall.

Yeolani stood against the hearth a moment, still in his shock. How had this happened? It took him an eternity, it seemed, before his legs crumbled beneath him and he landed with a thump between his parents' bodies. With trembling and bloody hands, he reached over to feel for his mother's pulse at her neck and found none. In his wake, Yeolani left his father's blood there on her pale skin. He felt sick again at the sight and would have thrown up if he could.

Then, with the shakes making it almost impossible, he reached for the knife still in his father's side and tugged it free. How was he doing this? His mind was a haze, as if he were again on the ship, going through the motions of drawing in the fishing line without his awareness. Again, he left a bloody mark on his other parent's neck. No pulse. He couldn't look at what he had done and instead crawled wearily toward his sister's body. She had been dead for half the day, Yeolani estimated, so he resisted leaving his bloody mark on her neck as well.

In a matter of moments, Yeolani had lost his entire family.

Carefully, the boy lifted his sister's head and sat down on the bed with her body in his lap, brushing her fine hair back from her forehead, and let his mind drift. He might have died himself, and it would not have mattered in the least.

2

BURYING THE DEAD

The next morning, the young man came into the heart of town pulling the cart his father used to load fish and to bring wood from the forest. Yeolani had eaten a dried fish and a bit of bread and felt much better for it, though he avoided the water his mother had left in the pail. Something had killed his little sister, and from the sounds in the village, some sickness was afoot, probably cholera, and he didn't want to add himself to the toll, even if he felt he deserved it. Someone from his family had to survive just to carry on.

After a night of drifting on sour dreams and panicked thinking, Yeolani had made his decisions. So, he could avoid questions about what had happened, he laboriously wrapped his parents' bodies in the bed linens so that their injuries didn't show. He intended to blame the plague for all three deaths. There wasn't enough linen to complete the job for his sister, but he placed her in their mother's shawl and laid Nevia gently between the adult bodies. Then he struggled to put them on the cart. Still nursing his bruised ribs and lingering seasickness, Yeolani pulled the handcart into town where the cholera outbreak filled the square with other plague victims.

As he suspected, he wasn't the only one bringing dead loved ones into the square that morning. He recognized two crewmen from the ship who must have been spared because they also were on board when the illness struck but were now burying their wives and children left behind. Now, he studiously avoided looking at them. How was he to explain his father dying when he had been on the ship with them? Instead of worrying about that, he went to the bonfire, as was the requirement, to add his family to the burning pyre. Everyone knew you couldn't risk burying when disease could spread so quickly. The bodies must be burned immediately before the entire village was consumed.

As he stood in line waiting for the priest, Yeolani spied a woman he didn't recognize. She had a long, honey-colored braid and a huge pack. She scurried about like a baby goat, trying to meet all those that brought bodies to the pyre. She seemed vibrant, young, though she was probably in her late twenties. She moved with authority and stopped anyone who came in bringing a body. Yeolani thought he knew everyone in Simten, but he didn't know this woman. The priest who oversaw the speedy funerals didn't object, for she only pestered the living, so he left her alone. And when it was his turn to face this insistent young woman, Yeolani swallowed a pit of fear. Would she notice the blood seeping through the sheets covering the bodies he was bringing?

Of course, she did. "I'm sorry for your...loss," she petered out, looking him in the eye, flicking her green eyes to the bodies and back toward him, widening a bit in surprise.

"Your whole family?"

"Mother, father, and little sister," he mumbled, hoping his voice didn't crack, as it often did under stress.

"From the cholera?" the woman queried. By the tone of her voice, he could tell she didn't believe him.

"If that's what's going around. I was on board our fishing boat until last night, and when I came home, I found them dead," he lied.

The healer pursed her lips knowingly. "You shouldn't try to lie," she whispered. "You're not very good at it. Tell me what really happened."

Something about her command made his tongue loosen. Yeolani looked around to be sure the magistrate wasn't nearby to listen in and then confessed to her frankly. "My father and I got off the ship last night, and when we got home, my little sister was dead and my mother was probably dying. He was so upset that...that he began beating my mother. I tried to stop him, and a lot of good I was at that. Then he started beating me..."

To his surprise, the lady, without asking, flipped Yeolani's tunic up to see the bruising on his ribs. "Hey, warn a body!" he barked in alarm but stopped himself when her amazingly warm hand rested on his side where it hurt the most.

"Three broken ribs, a bruised liver, and internal trauma. You're lucky he missed your kidney," she murmured as her gentle hands moved over him with alarming thoroughness. Yeolani didn't protest, for wherever her hands rested, a warm loosening of the pain and tension soaked into his body. He felt like he was melting and floating at the same time. How was she doing this?

Her bold, unexpected actions began drawing attention from other townsfolk, and the healer abruptly straightened up and pulled his tunic back into place before she was done. "What's your name?" she demanded, now continuing her interview.

"Yeolani, ma'am, and you can keep going. That felt like Jonjonel's own welcome flame."

The healer's green eyes widened slightly, and the freckles on her nose suddenly stood out as she blanched beneath her tan, but Yeolani was more worried about the townsfolk noticing her examination. His customary flippancy must be reasserting itself now that his pain had eased.

"Not here, Yeolani. You may call me Honiea. Just burn your dead, don't drink the water, and come see me here at dusk. I'll see to the rest of your injuries, then."

Dusk seemed a long time away with nothing but his thoughts to occupy him. Yeolani couldn't settle until he knew what he was going to do. He didn't want to go back to his empty house, so he resolved to visit the crew members at their various homes and inform them of his father's demise. Despite Honiea's admonition to not lie, he skirted the truth by claiming his father had committed suicide when he saw his wife and daughter dead. When Yeolani went to the first mate's home, he found the man grieving for three of his four children as well as his wife. Only the eldest son had survived.

"It's not all a loss then," Yeolani explained, "because I'm giving you the boat, and good riddance to me. We both know I'm about as fit a sailor as a short-tailed cat. Your boy can take my place and you can take my father's."

The first mate looked grim but grateful. "What will you do instead?" he asked frankly. The new captain never suggested that Yeolani could stay on with the crew. They both knew better than that.

With a sigh, Yeolani shook his head. "Anything but the sea.

The fish are fat enough without my help. Good luck," and, abruptly, Yeolani left.

Now, faced with several more hours before his rendezvous with Honiea, Yeolani forced himself to return to his empty home. There he had to again acknowledge the bloody murder and the ghosts he imagined there. Rather than wallow, he began packing everything he felt he could carry and fashioned a bag out of his father's winter coat. Hopefully, Yeolani would not need it for several more months, and with luck, by then he could make a better bag once he needed the coat for warmth.

Yeolani was resolved. He was leaving Simten.

He took the last remaining stores of dried fish and potatoes, a brick of cheese, and the one jug of ale his father had left, though Yeolani had not drunk any before. He then placed the best of the kitchen tools: flint and steel, a hatchet, pot, pan and a spoon in his pack. He dearly wanted a knife but couldn't endure the thought of taking that knife. Instead, Yeolani buried the weapon under a loose stone in the hearth and used the cholera-infested water to wash the stones free of blood. And then he was done.

Yeolani sat in the hut, memorizing the shape of the simple furniture and watching the shadows pass across the room, fighting tears. He felt like a little boy now, with his eyes aching and a burning down his throat, wallowing in his loneliness until, finally, he gave in and wept. His tears took him to the point that the western window glared at him with the sun at sea level before he wiped his nose, took a final shuddering breath, and mastered his emotions. He was over it now. He stoutly rose and walked out the door of the only home he knew, never to return.

The bonfire still burned in the square, a glowing ember in his mind, reeking and evil in his eyes. The glow provided the light to see his way as he returned for his meeting with Honiea.

In a way, it seemed alien to come meet her just because she had requested it of him. His side didn't ache anymore. The bruises had shifted to gray and yellow blotches rather than the angry red and purple swellings they had been before her touch. Maybe that was it – magic. She had done something mystical to him undoubtedly, and now she was luring him back into her web. For what purpose, he couldn't guess; but even as he acknowledged the magic she had wielded, he still had no desire to miss the appointment.

Honiea stood by the well, the main source of water for most of the town and therefore probably the cholera. It had been capped off by someone, and barrels instead lined the pedestal and a wagon team unloaded yet another full barrel to add to the supply. Honiea supervised this effort but caught sight of him and waved him over.

"I've put a treatment in the well, but it will take another week before the water will be fit to drink again. Thank you for coming." Then she bent to pick up her sizable pack, but Yeolani stopped her and hefted it instead. It was heavier than his own, and she smiled her thanks.

"Come with me," she ordered since he was offering to take both packs. "I'll buy you supper at the inn. That's where I'm staying, and we need to talk."

Obediently, Yeolani followed the lady toward Simten's only inn, swallowing his excitement. He'd never been inside the public-house, always considering it his father's hideout where he grew drunk and learned where the best fishing could be found. However, somewhere within, Yeolani also knew this was where travelers stayed and where the townsfolk could always come for news, like cholera. The inn had always been the denizen of adults, but at this point, carrying his father's ale and giving away his inheritance, Yeolani realized that yes, now he could consider himself an adult.

He had expected the inn to be crowded with men who had been away fishing and now came to drown their sorrows after spending the day burning bodies. However, the common room echoed and stood empty but for the innkeeper. Yeolani could hear the crackling fire and the clink of rearranging glasses behind the enormous counter, but no one had come for news. The entire town knew about the plague and didn't want to share their grief yet. Honiea ordered two suppers from the morose barkeeper and then guided Yeolani to a dark corner far away from the fire. On a warm spring evening, they didn't need the heat, and apparently, their conversation required privacy. Yeolani's innate curiosity nearly choked him as he set the packs down and watched how Honiea deliberately sat with her face toward the door, her back to the corner. What had a healer, a magical healer, to fear from being overheard?

She didn't say anything until the cook brought them each a plate of fish baked in cream and spring vegetables. Yeolani's stomach growled at him, and he began wolfing down this fine food like a dog, barely tasting it. He also sampled his first ale and decided he didn't like it, though it was better than going thirsty with no water. Honiea watched him eat and was covering a private smile before he noticed, and he realized his manners probably spoke volumes. Self-consciously, he stopped with his fork halfway to his mouth and put it down.

"No," she insisted. "You need to eat. If you were a sailor, I don't doubt you need nourishment. You're skin and bones and a growing boy. Let me guess – sea-sick?"

Yeolani nodded wearily. "Sick as a cur dog every single day," he mumbled, swallowed, and then repeated it. "I could never hold a thing down when I was aboard. How did you know?"

"Because you're a magician. I can't go to sea either and for the same reason. Magical people cannot cross the water without...well, let's just say it's not the best state of being, and I have yet to find a cure. Believe me, I've tried."

"Magical?" Yeolani wasn't actually agreeing with the preposterous statement. He knew of magic's existence and didn't doubt Honiea's claim of magic for herself, but he had never seen demonstrations of the art unless her healing touch counted. But to apply that mystical skill to himself seemed alien. Yeolani had expected magic would involve sparks and spells, potions and puffs of smoke, not just her gentle touch. Besides, he was a failed sailor, not a magician.

"Oh, you can be both," Honiea assured him, and only then did Yeolani realize she had heard his inner thoughts, for he hadn't spoken his doubts out loud. "I'm surprised you stuck with fishing as long as you did. I would have gone inland and found another way."

"You didn't have a father who beat you to liver and expected you to take over the ship someday, a mother and sister who needed you as a buffer from...from him. I failed at both, and now I have to suffer the consequences. I'm alone, without skills other than fishing, which I cannot do, and now you say I'm a magician? I don't mean to be rude, but, lady, I highly doubt what you are telling me."

Honiea nodded her understanding as if his skepticism didn't surprise her. "I would doubt me too. I also doubted the first time I was told about my powers. Here in the Land, obvious magic is so rare as to be non-existent. The actual magic all lies underground like water in a well. In other countries, there would be a dozen magicians in a town the size of Simten, and they could have stopped the cholera outbreak before it even got started. Instead, there is just me and two others in this whole nation. That's simply not enough, and we have been Seeking for you to add to our numbers. I've been looking for you for years. Now, I find you here in the middle of an epidemic, without a single skill and with no way to help you trust me when I say, yes, you are a magician...or will be. Right now, you are too young and too inexperienced in the ways of the world to take on the power, I think."

"What's that mean? I'm a slick-eared calf then?" He bristled at the implied lack of maturity.

"Essentially, yes. It means that I shouldn't open the door to magic to you until you grow up a little, that's all. If I was to start training you now, you would be frozen as you are now: sixteen, gawky and not full grown. You admit that you have no skills and have never seen more than this town. It is not right for you to make any decision about magic until you've seen more than the sea and a tiny village beside it. Have you ever been into the Fallon Forest?" Honiea asked bluntly.

"Any idiot here has. I've been on the edge, cutting wood," he provided, a little proud of the bravery it took to go into that deep place. The rumors of what lurked in the trees sent chills down his spine.

"And have you lived on your own, defended yourself, and struggled to feed yourself?"

"Well," he equivocated, "no, but my family always has...had to struggle. It's not easy." Something in Honiea's smile set off his sarcastic side, and he chided her. "You try pulling sail line while you're losing your supper and dodging your captain's fist."

"Oh, I believe you," she admitted heartily. "There are many ways to learn how to survive. I could not do what you have done any more than you could do what I've done to make my way. The point I'm trying to make is you will need to learn and master new ways and meet new people before magic can be real for you. What have you planned to do with your life now that your family is dead?"

Reluctantly, Yeolani set down his fork completely and looked the lady in the eye. Part of him wanted to bare his soul to her, and he suspected magic subtly urged him to do this. Another part realized he could be manipulated into making decisions she would want, not what he really desired, and if he ever were free to make his own path, now it must be.

"I...I've decided to go into Fallon Forest and make my way there. I've got nothing to lose, and now there's nothing holding me back except for my own fear."

Honiea nodded understanding. "Very good. Truly, this is the time to make your own way. Explore the world and learn all you can," she advised. "Is there anything you need to make your way easier?"

Yeolani's mouth fell open in amazement. "You aren't going to try to talk me out of it? Ask me to come learn magic? Teach me some nifty trick that will make me hungry for more?"

Honiea's expression grew secretive as she shook her head. "No, that is not the way of good magic. It would be wrong to manipulate you, and as I said, you're really too young to take on magic as of yet. It's more important that you learn to live independent of the life you've led so far. The magic will be yours when you are ready, when you need it, and you will come to it willingly. For right now, you need a pack."

Her clever eyes must have caught sight of his impromptu bag. Without explanation, she leaned over to open her own sizable pack and pulled from it a sturdy leather knapsack capable of carrying everything he had lugged from home in a coat. Along with it, she also brought forth a thick candle and a hunting knife with a sheath he could wear on his belt. Yeolani knew his eyes probably bugged out, but he managed to shut his mouth when she placed these fine and valuable items on the table.

"You need a knife if I'm not mistaken, as well as something better than a jacket to carry all your things in."

With effort, Yeolani nodded, for now he had proof she

indeed had been wandering through his mind and had conjured the things he wanted most, probably created with a magical thought from her own bag. No one who happened to be watching them from across the deserted room would ever realize those things were not there a minute before.

"Yeolani, magic here in the Land is subtle. Most people who meet me don't know I am a magician unless they witness an act of healing, and it's best to keep it that way. This life is not easy. There are some things you must understand, even if you choose not to ever pursue magic. For one thing, there are powers out in the world that will notice you. You noticed me when you saw me at the bonfire. That... that recognition will work against you in some ways. Other magical creatures, maybe even sorcerers and demons who manipulate magic for evil, will sense you and seek you out."

Yeolani's voice cracked dramatically. "I thought you said magicians in the Land were as rare as hen's teeth." He didn't want to even think about the demons he'd heard tales of, not when he was about to go into Fallon on his own.

Honiea nodded. "True magicians, born to it natively, are incredibly rare, yes. There are only three at this time, not counting you. Here in the Land, there will eventually only be sixteen of us, the Wise Ones, according to prophesy. But this Land is...or *was* sealed from magic for many years, so it developed differently. Of course, anyone who wanted to make a deal with demons could be gifted with sorcery, but here in the Land, the magic is far stronger but also more subtle. I don't have to say a spell or make a potion to use my power. I only have to possess this."

Yeolani's eyes blurred a little like he was observing her from underwater, but then he realized she'd put a kind of invisible shield around them, further protecting them from prying eyes. If he turned his head to look at the innkeeper across the room, he saw only a blurry shape, almost indistinguishable from the bar itself, but when he focused on Honiea alone, she seemed perfectly normal. She then held a small blue-white globe in her hand to show him. It pulsed with a gentle beat, white and bright as a summer sun.

"This is a Heart Stone. All you have to do is touch it, and the magic within you will be sparked. This one is mine, but I carry yours as well. God gave it to me when he gave me your name so I would know who I was Seeking. This leads me to another important thing: your name. You must leave it behind."

"My name? Why, by a dragon's back tooth, do I need to change my name?" he asked. It surprised him almost as much as the unmistakable urge to reach out and touch the Heart Stone she held.

As if she understood the temptation, the little orb disappeared back into Honiea's pocket and the shield against anyone observing them now faded with it. "Because of those other type of magicians out there. Remember, the ones that purchased their power from demons? There's an evil in that power. That kind of magic demands blood sacrifice and spells, and the user loses his or her soul to it. Their magic craves the native, natural power you and I possess, and it will do anything to control it. If they know your name, they can control you. You must not give them your name."

"Control me? How?"

Honiea's eyes flashed with a hidden challenge and what he hoped was a hint of compassion as she commanded him, "Yeolani, bark like a dog."

Before he could react, Yeolani let out a yelp that drew the quizzical eye of the barkeeper who polished glasses across the room. Appalled, the boy tried to cover the second bark behind his hand. Then Honiea ordered him to stop before he made another animal sound. Instead, Yeolani let out a more human gasp and pushed away from the healer across the table from him, "Hell's bells!" he swore in fear.

"Do you see?" she whispered, obviously pained by the fear she had caused Yeolani. "I cannot harm you. It would be against the ethics of the Wise Ones, and the Heart Stone would block me. However, the sorcerers and demons have no such inhibitions. If they knew your name and that you are magical, they would use you terribly. They could even order you to die and .... and you would have to obey them. It almost happened to me."

Yeolani waited for the story that must have been attached to a statement like that; but Honiea's expression clouded, and she shook her head, refusing to elaborate. "That is a story for another age," she whispered.

Abruptly, a thousand thoughts rolled through Yeolani's mind: fear foremost, curiosity, and revulsion. How would slavery to another impact him? He had often felt like a slave aboard his father's ship, with orders barked at him and no escape from the lash. Could he have endured more of it? No, but he was free now, free to think for himself.

Yeolani thought about his mother and his love for her. He wanted to honor her and the name she had given him. Yeolani wanted something of that mother's love to remain in the world as vengeance for the abuse she had withstood. Something in Lani's son dripped with anger, and to this emotion, he reacted. He rebelled. Why would he bother with this magical claptrap if it was so manipulative? He had no desire for power. He wanted peace, quiet, and some security that he could build for himself, not relying on an unstable sea-faring life or an even less stable father. Honiea's Wise One magic sounded like more work and restriction than anything.

Rattled and now feeling severely abused, Yeolani stood up and reached for his pack, not realizing that somehow, magically,

Honiea had replaced his makeshift bag with the one she had given him. "I thank you for the meal, my Lady, but I'll be going now. I've no interest in magic," he announced with a shaky voice, and he left the inn, his life and all thought of magic behind in one swift move.

3

A TREE FALLS

*T*hree months later he wanted to reconsider. Oh, at first, he had been fine with his decision and had walked the woods, sleeping under the stars and having little interaction with humans in the forest. It only took him a few days to recognize that many of the horror tales about Fallon were fiction. No demons stalked him. No dragons hunted here. Instead, he faced far more real issues than those fairy tales threatened. Yeolani wandered between the trees eating anything he could find before he realized he would soon starve if he didn't find some reliable means of hunting or trading for food. Winter was coming, and he couldn't afford to wait to find that security. He grew tired of struggling to net fish from the rivers or raiding squirrels for their hoards, and despite his desire to find his own way, he knew he wouldn't survive without help from other humans.

As fall descended, he finally made up his mind. He couldn't continue eating hand-to-mouth and washing only when he came across a creek. He dreaded sleeping out in the open when the rains began. And worst of all, the haunting of the fairy lights would drive him insane if he didn't get under some shelter. He had heard stories of the fairies, far less frightening than demons, but at least these were real. The little sprites filled the Fallon Forest like mosquitoes on a pond. Their constant cloud of lights overhead kept him awake, and their fluttering wings invaded his dreams. He yearned for a shelter to help keep them at bay, and Yeolani deeply regretted not asking Honiea for a tent, but it was too late now.

So, one miserably rainy evening, he finally approached one of the logging crews that supplied fuel for Simten and Savone on the forest's edge and asked for work. At first, the leader of the crew, Bowdry, looked at his scrawny frame and mocked him. "You'll not last a week."

Again, Yeolani's temper drove his tongue. "I'll wager you I can chop as much wood as the best man on your team," he boasted, knowing he was a fool for doing so, but he was desperate, and the smell of the stew on the evening fire captivated him. "Just give me some food, and tomorrow I'll prove I can be an asset to your crew."

Fully half-a-dozen woodsmen in the group laughed, as if it were a joke, and encouraged Captain Bowdry to at least not back down from the challenge. Meanwhile, Yeolani stood by the fire in the center of the makeshift camp, stubbornly looking the leader in the eye, unashamed of his worn clothing or shoddy appearance. Of course, Yeolani looked needy; he was. He hadn't been able to eat or wash much over the last few days, and the constant harassment of the fairies kept him awake half the night.

"And what happens if you don't bring in more wood than me? What am I to get in return for this meal?" Bowdry demanded cheerfully.

"I've got...I've got a ...a very good knife. It's small, great for gutting fish. You can have it if I don't perform." In fact, it was the magically crafted one Honiea had put in his newly created pack along with a candle which she also, for some unknown reason, had given him. Yeolani really didn't want to part with the knife, but he figured that would be the only thing he owned that would tempt the crew into taking a risk on him.

"Here, let's see what else you've got," chuckled another crew member who snatched Yeolani's pack off his shoulder. He wanted to protest but resisted, realizing these men, all rough and most probably at least his father's age, would not steal from him. He had nothing they would want. Yeolani watched impassively as the lumberjacks dumped his belongings out on the ground. Once they found the jug filled with water, not ale, they began muttering in discontent.

Then to his surprise, one of the men lifted the candle, and everyone stopped speaking. They all turned to peer at Yeolani, a look on their faces that he couldn't interpret.

"Where did you get the candle?" Bowdry asked in a careful voice.

Yeolani didn't know how to answer. A candle? He had used it a few times to light his way when he had to find a place to sleep and found nothing magical about it, but obviously, these men knew something about it that he didn't. Yeolani dare not reveal his ignorance. So instead he remained silent. Stoically, he stood in the firelight waiting for an explanation, pretending he understood but had nothing to say.

Finally, when he realized Yeolani wouldn't speak, Bowdry capitulated. "Very well, if you want work, there's a place to be had. We only have two requirements: work hard and, when there's a need, let us use the candle."

Yeolani felt his jaw drop open in wonder, but he recovered quickly. "Candle it is. Now, where's my bowl?" He would think about what he didn't know later. Right now, he was more interested in the stew.

And that is how Yeolani managed to survive his first winter in Fallon Forest. Moving with a whole crew of woodsmen taught him much: how to chop and fell trees, but also how to interact with a variety of men and make deals with them as he listened to the crew chief Bowdry selling loads of wood at the hamlets deep in the forest or at towns closer to the edge. Yeolani managed to hold his own and bulked up with the benefit of reliable meals and hefty work. This did nothing to teach him the self-reliance he craved. While his companions weren't great hunters, they could bring down a deer with a well-placed ax throw. Quarry rarely came within range, for cutting timber drove off most of the game, but the men were always ready, nonetheless.

The crew slept in tents which thankfully kept the fairies away at night, much to Yeolani's relief. However, that did not stop these pesky creatures from buzzing over him when they worked during the day. Their bright lights hovered just beyond reach over his head. He alone seemed to be irritated with them, although they swooped throughout the camp. One evening, early in spring, one of the other men caught him trying to swat at one and chided him.

"If you've got the attention of the fae, you shouldn't try to sweep them away," Arvid, his friend, said frankly. "Most of us can't see them, so you should be grateful that you interest them."

"I'd rather have a lady's interest," Yeolani replied in amazement. He had not realized no one else noticed the fairies that flew in flocks around Arvid's head.

Arvid chuckled at that. "Almost as good as a lady. No, the fairies are a sign of good luck. My sister Rashel, supposedly she's got them hovering about her head all the time. And a good thing. They kept her from falling in the well once, and our ma, she claims they're protecting her from evil."

"But...but if you can't see them, isn't that...well, odd? They're more of a nuisance than a sliver in your toe. They keep me up at night if I'm outside the tents."

Arvid, the only other younger man in the wood crew, simply shrugged. "Maybe they're the reason why you've not been injured in your time here," and he suggestively pointed at his boot.

Arvid had already told him the tale of how he had accidentally planted his ax blade between his toes after he'd been at the work only a few weeks and then added that it was a minor miracle that Yeolani hadn't hurt himself already in the dangerous work of a lumberjack. "Most of the men don't believe in the fairies, but I've seen my sister with that look...bedazzled by the fairy lights. And the others say you're freakishly lucky so far. You've got some kind of protection for sure."

At that comment, Yeolani remembered, for the first time in ages, his conversation with Honiea. He didn't think the two things, magic and fairies, could be related, but maybe being plagued by fairies was a magical signal like his seasickness had been. He would not ever be completely free of Honiea's world, he reasoned. And if that meant the fairies were concerned for him, he could deal with that far better than seasickness. Generally, these creatures didn't interfere with his work by day, and now, sleeping in a tent, they didn't keep him awake either. Yeolani didn't pursue more about the fairies. He could ignore them just as easily as he could his curiosity of magic, and he did well at that until the summer. Then everything changed again.

The crew planned that morning to cut down a massive tree. Ten men could not complete a ring about it, and its top was lost in the sun's glare. Yeolani noted that fairies covered it more than other trees he'd seen. It was thick with them, so Yeolani could not even see the lower branches where he had cast his guideline. He wasn't on the cutting crew at the moment, so he wasn't exactly watching the first swing of the ax. The blow simply sounded wrong. That one swing made every fairy's light go out. Abruptly, the tree began to fall. It shattered, revealing its rotten, unstable core. It twisted as it fell. Yeolani saw it all from his place on the guide rope. It swung as if some invisible giant rolled the falling timber toward them. The massive tree snapped with a bang, bounced off its jagged stump and swept in an arc toward the other side's guide ropes. They didn't stand a chance. Four men were struck and bowled over and one remained pinned under the log when it finally came to a rest.

Everyone dropped their lines or axes and scrambled toward the fallen men. Luckily, two had fallen in the soft loamy earth and had been pressed into the ground rather than crushed, but two were not so well off. One had broken ribs, and his breathing came labored. And then there was Arvid, still pinned under the massive tree. He was still conscious but raving in pain. Someone went running for shovels to start digging out around him, but the camp was half-a-mile away.

"Yeolani, where's your pack?" barked Bowdry, who shoved Yeolani off toward the camp, assuming he'd left it with the tents. Quite often the young man brought it with him since it was amazingly light, and he liked to have access to his jug of water. Yeolani staggered the mere yards to where they had started the morning at the edge of the clearing and snatched up his pack, bringing it back as fast as he could run.

Captain Bowdry looked gratified that Yeolani didn't have to run as far as the camp. "Get out the candle. We need her help," he ordered.

Obediently Yeolani did as he was instructed. He dumped out his pack and lifted the candle from the pile, confused as to what to do next.

"Well, light it, boy," barked the captain.

Still not sure what good a candle would do for his friend or the men who now knelt around Arvid's body, using their hands to scoop the ground underneath his pinned legs, Yeolani did as he was ordered. His hands shook as he gathered a pile of dry pine needles and then found his flint and steel from his belongings. It seemed to take forever to get a smoke to start, and then he fished around on the ground for a stick that would light. His hands barely held the tiny flame steady as he set the stick to the candle's wick. Once he knew it was lit, he looked over at Bowdry and felt a well of fear. Everyone in the crew knew that this candle was magic and so was he.

Without quite knowing why, Yeolani lifted the light high and began wishing that Honiea and her magical healing hands would come to this signal. No wonder these men were willing to let him join them; he had been given a magic candle that could call for help. Honiea hadn't given him the explanation, but somehow this must have been known among many others that worked amidst the dangers of the forest.

It didn't take long. One moment she wasn't there, and the next, she was. Yeolani saw the honey hair and a bright flash of lavender before his eyes normalized and Honiea, appearing exactly like she had come from a surgery, with bloody smudges on her apron and carrying her pack.

"You didn't give me a chance to explain," she said in a low murmur and then took the candle from him, blew it out, and then handed it back without another comment. Then she purposefully walked around Yeolani like he was a tree in the forest and stepped up to Arvid's side. Bowdry simply nodded a greeting but didn't question Honiea's magical arrival.

Wordlessly, she assessed the situation and knelt to see under to Arvid's crushed legs. Then she rose and motioned to everyone. "Step away from him, from the tree," she ordered. "I don't want anyone else to get hurt. You too," and she waved at Yeolani who was too stunned to react. Hastily, he finally moved aside and joined the remainder of the men, away from the fallen tree and their pathetic excavation efforts. Like a statue, she stood over Arvid and pushed up her sleeves as if she were about to do some hard labor.

Honiea lifted her arms high, and the tree rose magically at this signal without even her touch. She brought the massive trunk up a few feet, hovering effortlessly as if it were light as a feather. Then Honiea bent her wrists, and the log swung on its lighter end. Finally, Honiea lowered her arms, and the timber came to rest just beyond Arvid's legs.

Now, everyone stood there with his mouth open in awe.

"Boy, bring me my pack," she ordered, and Yeolani jumped at the command. He lugged her pack as she knelt at Arvid's side and began moving her hands over his crushed body. Mercifully, he'd finally passed out, but Yeolani could see his legs and feet looked all wrong, and now blood from his crushed limbs began seeping through his pants. "Take his boots off carefully," Honiea ordered. "And what name are you using with these men?" she added silently.

Yeolani almost answered aloud before he realized her mouth hadn't moved with that final question. Honiea was speaking directly into his mind.

"Yeolani," he replied carefully, under his breath and didn't look up but addressed his careful effort to not harm his friend as he pulled the boots free from his feet. What he saw, with bone and blood coming directly out from punctured skin, would normally have made most men sick, but Yeolani forced himself to look at Arvid's pale leg like it was simply a dead fish and moved to his friend's other boot.

"That wasn't wise," came Honiea's silent reply.

Rather than open himself up to discovery or argument, Yeolani ignored her comment and continued working as directed and changed the subject. "The fairies, they were thick over this particular tree. Did they make it fall that way on purpose?"

Honiea ignored him as her hands hovered over Arvid's legs and they squirmed as if there were some alien creatures in a sack rather than fractured bones and ruptured muscles moving into place.

"There's wine in my pack. If he wakes while I'm doing this, give him some," she ordered aloud, and obediently, Yeolani rose to go rummage in her bag.

To his surprise, there was nothing in the bag except a flask which he pulled out and then returned to Arvid's side. Next, she sent the other men to make splints for braces and poles for stretchers while Yeolani returned once again to the huge pack for bandages to tie the braces. Again, he found nothing but a long spool of linen gauze. When the men came with the splints, he helped lift Arvid's legs as she carefully set a brace on either side of his leg and wound the gauze around him until his leg had completely disappeared under the white wrapping. Then, without actually touching her work, she made it harden into a plaster cast, stiff and protective.

Then, without comment, Honiea turned to address the other lumberjack with broken ribs and a punctured lung. Yeolani watched her gentle hands move over this man's pained body, and immediately the patient began breathing easier. The other uninjured men gathered around their comrades and began to fashion the stretchers to carry them back to camp. Yeolani stood by Arvid's side with the wine and didn't move to help, as if Honiea's magic included him and held him frozen.

He watched his work companions make their ways back towards the camp while he felt completely rooted to the ground. They had left him there with Honiea, and she turned toward him, wiping her hands on a rag that hadn't been there before. Her movement finally shifted his mind back into gear, and he could ask questions, though too many percolated to the surface.

Where had she been? How did the candle figure into her work? Was this all she could do, rescue fallen men and battle plagues? Where did she go when there was no candle calling her? How did that work, anyway? Was she the only one who could do this? Why had she given him the candle? Would any old candle work? Why here and not somewhere else in the Land, for surely there must be other emergencies to call her?

Not one question came out of his mouth.

Honiea, without his asking, began answering quite matter-of-factly. "I am called the Queen of Healing. It is what I do as a Wise One, though I can do just about anything I have the imagination to do. For example, lift a tree, make a knife, or listen to your thoughts. You too will one day have those abilities, though you won't have the healing instincts as I do. You will be the King of...of something else. We do not know yet where your gifts will reside."

"My husband, Vamilion, for example, is the King of Mountains. He works with earthquakes and avalanches, volcanoes, stone, gems and erosion, building with stone. He knows how to help the people who live in the mountains, miners and goatherds and the like. He is drawn to them. You too will be drawn to some kind of magic in the Land," she promised and then continued with her explanation.

"The candle is my Talisman. The people who make a living in dangerous ways...like lumberjacks, they know they can light a candle and it will call me. Also, I have a candle that allows me to travel instantly from wherever I am to where I am needed, and the healers know this as well. I gave you a candle so you could call me anytime you needed my help. My husband, on the other hand, can travel from mountain to mountain without such a device. However, this limits him. He must often walk where he needs to go if it's on the coast or plains. Most often those that need his magic come to him at his home in the southern mountains. I spend most of my time flitting from crisis to crisis somewhere around the Land. It's a good life, but I travel a lot."

"Also, you should know about Talismans. When a Wise One first goes Seeking they are searching for certain tools like my candle that they will use to help the Land. These, my candle and my pack, were specifically crafted to help me. You too will have Talismans that you will be drawn to and must Seek. Once you have found them, as well as the means to break the seal around your home, you will no longer be a Seeking King but a Seated King. Now, does that answer all your questions?"

Yeolani rolled his eyes in alarm and sighed. "Hardly! For every question you answer, up pops two more like weeds I must pull in a garden. Why didn't you show you were this powerful? You could have stopped that Simten plague with a thought, but instead, you only helped us plug up the well and burn bodies. Why didn't you stop the tree from snapping like that? You could do anything. You could ...you could be worshipped."

Honiea shook her head sadly and began walking slowly toward the camp, and Yeolani was obliged to follow if he were to hear her reply.

"I don't... I can't be everywhere. I came to Simten when I heard about the plague and by that time there were too many sick for me to stop what had started. I have no foreknowledge of accidents or epidemics. Life happens, and even God does not stop such bad things from occurring. It's life, and we learn and grow from the experiences we undergo. A Wise One would not be wise to prevent every mishap or bad thing from happening. Look at you: would you have grown and come into the forest, leaving your home and venturing out into the world if that plague had not taken your family? Or if your father had not beaten you? Perhaps if you were never seasick? Those bad things formed the nudge for you to launch yourself into the world, and you've become more than a peasant fisherman. And you will become even more someday. You will become a King, armed with magic, and will serve the people of the Land in miraculous ways. But you will not stop loss and pain, no matter how powerful you become. It is not the way of the wise."

Yeolani could not think of what to say in response for the longest time. Finally, he took a swig of the wine he still held and then stopped in the path, suddenly exhausted by this conversation. "First, it was rules and danger. Now it's 'not wise.' You have a poor way of making ultimate magical power seem like a good lifestyle. I thought you wanted me to be a magician. You're not convincing me very well."

Honiea walked back to him and reached for the wine, sharing a sip with him and giving it back. Then she sighed and looked up into the sky where their clearing had opened to the summer, not a fairy in sight. "I'm not good at this," she admitted finally. "We're human if you haven't noticed, and hardly worth worshipping. Wise Ones simply have talents that we're encouraged to use. I cannot and should not force you into magic. I'm just here to inform you of your options. You'll decide for yourself, and it's best to know all the good as well as the bad sides of a decision. But let me put it this way; would you still have come into the forest to become a woodsman if you knew how hard that work would be?"

"Yes," he admitted frankly. "I was as hungry as a bear in spring, but I'm free to make up my mind. I knew it would be hard...but...but life is hard."

Honiea smiled, nodding. "And so is being a magician. It's a bit like being a woodsman. It's just different work. We aren't worshipped for holding power over men, though the terms king or queen might suggest otherwise. I am the Queen of Healing because I control that aspect of the world, not the world itself. You too will find your gifts and then simply decide to pursue them or not. No one should force you."

Something about her tone and her steady gaze into the sky again made Yeolani look at her quizzically. "What?" he asked.

"Oh, I'm just reminding the fairies of that fact. They've been encouraging you, trying to convince you of your magical abilities, that's all."

Yeolani looked down at his hands, suddenly embarrassed at his behavior toward the little sprites. "Encouraging, is that what they call it?"

Yeolani then peered up into the sky too, but either they had fled, or the sun had grown too bright. "What am I supposed to tell my friends back at the camp? They'll want to know...they'll be curious as a dog poking at an empty supper bowl."

Before she answered, Honiea deliberately took the bottle of wine from Yeolani's hand and made it disappear. "That's up to you, but you've shared your real name with them. It was unwise, and now your name and my magic will be connected in their thoughts. If you remain, your innate magic will only grow, and they'll suspect something. You should move on and find another place. You still have the candle and know how to use it now. Call me if you need help...and when you're ready to learn more."

Then in a shimmering light, not unlike the fairies, she disappeared into the sky. Yeolani stood there in the clearing for quite a while, but eventually, with a sigh, he returned to the fallen tree, gathered up his scattered things and marched off toward camp with his mind full of many thoughts flitting like fairies.

4

GIL

*B*y mid-winter Yeolani was alone and starving again, approaching the base of the mountains. He had left the wood crew soon after he saw that Arvid recovered fully. It wasn't that he didn't like the companionship or having reliable meals, but Yeolani agreed deep down that staying behind would only bring magic to mind, and that couldn't be good.

As he walked through the snow, Yeolani thought again about why he was so reluctant to give up his name. He clung like a barnacle to the memory of his parents, and he wanted to retain his name for their sake. Somehow giving up his name also meant embracing the magic and all the manipulation it would do to his life. On the other hand, how stubborn could he be if he deliberately did not remain anywhere for long? Perhaps Honiea had hexed him and made it impossible to stay where he'd settled. Maybe he just didn't want to give up his past. Either way, he found himself again on his own, scrounging for food and hoping for shelter.

Not that there wasn't something to learn and experience. He had never seen mountains before, and as the trees thinned before him, he felt a sense of awe and a latent fear. How could anything so big exist? He strained to comprehend the vastness of the Land he had never explored. He thought of Honiea's husband and wondered again at the magic encased in a mountain. Avalanches he could now somewhat comprehend, and perhaps earthquakes. But what about volcanoes? How terrifying must that be? The sheer size of the closest peak and those that grew up like weeds beyond it, they humbled him. What kind of magician would Vamilion be if he 'controlled' mountains?

At the base of the nearest peak, the forest thinned and, so too, the opportunities for chopping wood in exchange for a night in someone's barn or on a warm hearth. He dearly wanted to learn to hunt so he wouldn't have to beg and hope he was within a day's walk of the next cabin in the forest. Yeolani wanted to learn more than just a night's lessons would afford him, and he needed someone to teach him. Where could he find someone willing to teach him how to survive?

Yeolani had not seen a cabin in three days when the forest abruptly ended there at the foot of a sheer face of a mountain and he had to stop. He felt only the bitter cold of deep winter, even through his father's coat into which he had finally grown. His hand-made boots needed patching, and he had no more food. He knew the next human he came across had better be a kindly soul, or Yeolani was going to die out here. Somewhere deep inside, he suspected that Honiea would never let him freeze and he could always call her by candle, but he was stubborn there too. He would need to be dead before he would humble himself that far.

Yeolani walked the timberline for more than an hour, and just when the sun began to sink, he saw the telltale smoke of a cabin just under the forest rim. He struggled through the knee-deep snow, trying to beat the sun behind the trees, but didn't make it and had to grope in the dark until he reached a small, humble home in the shadows. He could smell bread and some kind of meat roasting even from outside as he pounded on the door. Thankfully, the cook, an old man, came to the door with an ax and a suspicious look on his wrinkled face but eased his grip on the hatchet as soon as he saw Yeolani's weathered and weak figure.

"Please, sir, I'm looking for a place to sleep tonight. I can work in exchange."

The old man peered past his guest on the stoop as if he expected other, less savory visitors might take this opportunity to rush the door, but seeing none, the old man waved Yeolani inside.

"Yer a sad wisp of a lad," the old man grumbled. "What brings you out on a night like this? It's bitter cold."

"Yes, sir, I know. I've been walking for months. I need someplace to winter over and find work," Yeolani replied, leaning toward a warm hearth and the wonderful smells emanating from there.

"What's your name, boy," growled the man in a voice that must have once been powerful but now sounded more like gravel at the bottom of a creek.

"Yeolani, sir," he replied and then bit his lip. He hadn't meant to give away his name like that, intending to do as Honiea had admonished him, but it was too late now.

"You can call me Gil," the gentleman announced. "And you can serve that bread up, and by the time you're done, that soup should be ready, though I've not made much. Enough for me." With that, the ancient man settled himself at his table, easing painfully into the seat as if his arthritis might not let him rise again.

Obediently, Yeolani jumped to the duties the old man had given him. He found an entire loaf that would surely make up for the lack of soup for two and cut it up, finding a pad of butter up near the one window in the cabin where it would be cooler. Next, he found a bowl and then fished out his own dishes to supplement the oldster's humble crockery and set the table. He then used a piece of wood to hook the pot off the embers on the fire and was pleased to see that there would be more than enough for both of them. He dished them both up, and by that time, the old man was smiling, creating deeper valleys in the weathered grin.

"It's been a long time since I've seen someone move that fast. You must be hungry if you'll work that quick for your supper. What other work have you been doing, Yeolani?"

Over a wonderful supper of venison stew and hard bread, Yeolani told Gil about his work on the ship and how he had left because of the seasickness and then his time in the wood cutting crew, skipping over his interludes with Honiea. "When my friend was nearly crushed by that log, I decided that there must be safer ways to make a living in the forest," he added to explain why he now found himself with no vocation in the forest in the middle of winter. "That's when I decided I need to learn some more skills, and I've been looking for a teacher ever since.

"And what kind of skills would you find useful?" Gil asked frankly.

Yeolani looked around the bare cabin, his eyes watchful for clues as to how a man alone in the woods could survive to be Gil's age, and he saw plenty to inform him. The bed in the corner boasted a bearskin blanket and snowshoes hung by the door. A bow and quiver of arrows, as well as a hooked staff Yeolani couldn't name, rested beside the hearth. Finally, on the floor by the single chair, a mound of wood shavings hinted at many a winter evening carving dishes, tools, and whatnots.

"Can you teach me to hunt, sir? I could live on my own

then, instead of leaning on the kindness of others," Yeolani blurted out, hoping he'd read the setting correctly.

"What?" the old man half gasped, half chuckled. "You hardly know me, and I certainly don't know you. Hunting is a long-term prospect. I don't know if you are capable of learning, boy, and you don't know if I can teach."

"But you can hunt, can't you, sir?" Yeolani protested.

Gil's gnarled hands rested on the tabletop, and he tried to hide the tremor in them. "I used to hunt. Now I can barely tie a snare. Both skills I know from my childhood, but I've never taught anyone to do them. And what of you, boy? You've not learned much in your few years. How do I know you'll be able to learn?"

"You could try me," insisted Yeolani. "I learned how to fish and sail, but there's no water here to demonstrate. I learned how to cut timber, and no one complained about my ability to work hard. I will learn to hunt if you can teach me, but I have to find a teacher. And...and...and frankly, sir, you look like you could use someone to do the chores around this place. I will do whatever you ask me to do, cut and haul, cook and clean if you will teach me to hunt."

Gil straightened up out of his perpetual hunch and gave Yeolani a piercing glare with his watery gray eyes. "Boy, will you stick with the training? How long did you last with the wood crew? Months? How about with the fishing? Did you master it, or did you give up because you were sea-sick? Something else might just pop up and make you think you cannot do this either. What if you faint at the sight of blood or get squeamish at the thought of killing? Am I to do all this training and have you give up halfway? If I want to teach this, I won't just have you into the woods and let you take a stab at it. You must learn how to make your bow, your arrows. Your eyesight, your hearing, your sense of smell might not be up to the task of tracking your prey. You must master how to clean a carcass and tan the hides and preserve the meat. You need to learn the rope tricks and how to tie the knots. It will take years. Are you willing to commit for that long?"

Yeolani hadn't anticipated that much of a challenge, but again he couldn't survive without these skills, and the old man obviously knew the details needed. So, Yeolani had to ask himself those very questions. Would he stick it out? Could he endure the training and discipline? Would the old man survive long enough to finish the job seemed like a more apt question. Gil looked to be on his last legs, and if he could barely tie a snare, how did he expect to teach Yeolani what he wanted to know?

But Gil seemed his only option, and Yeolani acknowledged it. "Sir, I promise, I will work as hard as I can, and you'll find no fault in my effort. I might not get it at first, but I will keep at it until you are satisfied," Yeolani swore. "But I have no way to assure you but with time. What can I do but give you my word?"

Gil's eyes disappeared into the wrinkles around them as his serious glare changed into a chuckle. "You can wash up the dishes then. The creek is frozen, so I've been using snow for water. The bucket's beside the door."

And that's how Yeolani came to reach his adulthood in the shadow of the mountains. He did as he promised: worked hard, obeyed instructions, and learned as quickly as his bright mind could master. Gil, for his part, worked Yeolani with dedicated precision. During the remaining winter months, he guided his young protégé in knapping his own arrowheads and stripping the straightest shafts for his arrows. They gathered feathers for fletching only after a long trek to a little lake hidden between two mountains where they collected cast feathers from the summer before.

On the way, Yeolani worried that Gil wasn't up to such a trip, but the old man insisted and wouldn't allow the process to be taught out of order. "As I learned, so shall you," was all he spoke of the matter.

Curiosity piqued, Yeolani asked about who had taught Gil his hunting skill, but the old man avoided the question or muttered something about his father. It seemed strange that such an old man once might have been a boy like him. He didn't seem to have any stories from his past or family to speak of and again resisted conversation on the matter. For his own part, Yeolani knew not to suggest it as a topic; he had his own reasons for not speaking of family.

It was on the trip to the lake while trying to sleep under the stars that Yeolani remembered his former issues with the fairies and carefully schooled himself not to go looking at them as they camped out in the night. He didn't want Gil knowing how the fairies hovered, but it surprised him that the creatures also hovered over the old man's head like a crown of light, though the gentleman never seemed to notice. What had Gil done with his life that the fairies would be interested in him?

After their week-long trip to the lake and back, with Gil instructing him on how to look for animal trails and other signs along the way, Yeolani next undertook the effort to make a bow, a far more tedious task. The bow had to be made to the person, crafted specifically for their precise size and strength, and since both those things were still changing on him, Yeolani's work inevitably failed. Gil insisted that this first bow would only be for practice, and that once he stopped growing, Yeolani could reliably make a more permanent weapon.

When spring finally arrived, Gil had him outside in the sun practicing with the old forester's weapon which took tremendous strength to draw, let alone strike with any accuracy. It might not fit him, but this bow would teach Yeolani the technique and strengthen the needed muscles until he could utilize his own weapon on which they worked in the evenings. Twice during the spring, Yeolani had spied deer wandering near the cabin, but Gil would not let him try to shoot at them.

"You'll only scare them away. They don't feel in danger here and later that will make your job easier," was his explanation. Yeolani grumbled about it but let it go. He trusted Gil despite the restrictions.

Finally, as summer came into full swing, Yeolani finished his bow and hoped that now he would be allowed to go hunting. He practiced against a target set against a tree and pulled his own arrows back and fired, marveling at how much easier it was to deal with his own equipment compared to that of the old man. He practiced direct and lofted shots, went to the forest edge where the wind swept off the mountain and learned how to compensate for breezes. Then he even tried his hand at shooting at fish in the creek. When he brought back a trout for dinner instead of the dried venison they had eaten all year, Yeolani foolishly expected some appreciation.

"Don't like fish," grumbled the old man and insisted that venison would do well enough for their meal. Rebelliously, Yeolani cooked the fish he had caught for himself and served his mentor his venison too. When Gil groused at the waste of cooking two meals, Yeolani insisted that now he wanted to go hunting.

"I've done everything you asked, but now our stores of venison are getting old, and I'm tired of it. Can't we go hunting and eat something fresh?"

"Something fresh...yes, berries. We'll find them on the way to the best hunting site I've found. Bring the bucket."

It took hours of walking and a full bucket of berries before they got to the spot where Gil insisted they could hunt. And then Gil required him to rub the berries on his clothes, apparently masking some of the scents of man. Finally, the old man's definition of hunting meant climbing up a tree to a convenient branch and watching from the heights. While Yeolani had no inherent fear of heights, having been up in the rigging of his father's ship for years, hunting prey from a height seemed somewhat wrong. He didn't complain about the requirement, but he didn't enjoy the buzzing fairies that seemed to relish the berries, and he almost fell out the tree twice trying to swat them away.

Finally, at dusk, with the sun putting the world below in silhouette, Yeolani saw movement between the golden towers of trees. The nearly bare ground left little to rustle, but the delicate thread of a buck pacing through the woods made Yeolani's heart beat faster. Gil's constant drilling chanted through his mind. Sight just above the shoulder mark, hold your breath, stop to sense the wind, point toward your mark, and draw only when you are ready to shoot. Yeolani's eyes followed the tawny shape, watching the play of muscle under its thin fur. The buck had not yet come into full view of his place in the trees, but any closer and Yeolani's shot would have to come down on its back rather than down its neck, striking the heart. Still not breathing, Yeolani drew until the string brushed his cheek and released.

True to all the training, the arrow sank into the very spot he had aimed, right at the neck and down into the heart. The animal bucked, startled to its haunches, and Yeolani lost sight of it behind the tree, but Gil came from his place three trees over, walking as if nothing was amiss, and so Yeolani slithered off his perch. Two trees beyond, the buck lay on its side, only its eyes moving now in alarm. Without remorse, Yeolani drew Honiea's magical knife and slit the throat to put the animal out of its terror and pain.

And so Yeolani had accomplished his goal. He could now feed himself in the forest. He felt little sense of accomplishment. He still had some hard work to do, and they would be spending the night in the forest, for he would not want to drag the carcass all the way to the cabin in the dark. Also, he needed to get Gil settled before it grew too late. They set up camp and strung up the animal to drain it and keep the other creatures from reaching the meat. They would bring it home in the morning. It was quite late by the time Yeolani settled into his bedroll under the stars.

Only then did he realize that the fairies had disappeared, at least for that night.

5

LESSON OF THE COIN

And so Yeolani came to make his way in Fallon. He mastered hunting on the forest floor, tracking his prey. He learned how to strip and dry, preserving a variety of game. Gil encouraged him to purchase and train a dog, which he did, trading skins for a pup that together the two named Marit. The adaptable, long-haired hound followed Yeolani faithfully and learned to flush birds so that Yeolani could put his shooting skills to the prime test. When they were truly desperate for food, Yeolani even went shooting salmon in the creek. And everywhere they walked, they gathered other foods to supplement their heavily meat diet. During the winter, Yeolani learned to work leather more skillfully than he ever bothered in the wood crew, and he also crafted snowshoes so that he could trek the mountain and forest in deep winter. Marit went with him everywhere, regardless of the game they sought, and that companionship was all Yeolani needed.

Then, at the first snowfall of winter in the second year with Gil, after Yeolani had brought in enough wood for a week, Gil motioned him over to the hearth and sat close to the fire, poking a stick in the flames. "Do you know how to read," the old man began.

Yeolani had never heard the term, let alone recognize the scratches that the old man began tracing in char across the hearthstones. At first, Gil simply drew, and the younger man followed his movements, gouging the marks in the packed earth of the cabin floor. Then Gil applied sounds to each shape.

"Where did you learn this kind of silent message?" Yeolani asked curiously as he washed the char away and they began again with a clean slate. "It seems very efficient. I can leave you a message, and you can see it and know what I'm doing far later."

"It's called writing. I write and you read, or vice versa. It is efficient. I was born in a land far to the south and east of here, far older than the culture of the Land. We had this writing for ages, but very few of the people who emigrated here could do this art, so it hasn't been established here. The Land has only had people settling here for about a hundred years. It was almost empty before then."

"What a waste. Why was it empty?" asked Yeolani, again following his curiosity.

In reply, Gil scratched out a message on the hearth and Yeolani laboriously read out the sounds. "It...w..a..s, was...se...al..e..e...d. It was sealed?"

Gil nodded and continued to write as he explained. "The Land was sealed. No one could come here. Boats found themselves pushed away from the shore. Travelers overland could simply go no farther. The high mountains blocked some borders, and an invisible force stopped all other travel. Then one day, it wasn't Sealed. I was a trader and often traveled along the Seal, so I knew when it broke and got curious. I loved being able to travel to places I'd never entered before. I've been moving ever since, exploring this Land."

"That's amazing. How old were you back then, Old Man?"

"Oh, a bit older than you are now. I had a family, but they're gone now."

Yeolani knew better than pursue that kind of topic and instead went with other curiosities. "What kind of power would seal a land and then suddenly let people in for no reason?"

"Oh, there's a reason," Gil disagreed. "We just don't know it yet. Perhaps we never will understand, but know this, there are great powers here in the Land, more than either you or I can comprehend."

Yeolani bit his lip in sudden fear: Honiea. She was part of this. Yeolani remembered the pure will she had displayed lifting a huge tree off his friend Arvid and then mending his crushed legs. That kind of power, that could seal off the Land from anyone entering. That magic could do anything. Where did it spring from? Yeolani hadn't thought about Honiea in over a year, but now he realized his curiosity would drag him back to her, for he wanted to know. Someday he would meet her and ask for more lessons on becoming a Wise One.

"Magic," he whispered, and Gil began scratching the word in ash on the stones. Yeolani read it and recognized there lay his future. He might hunt and help Gil, but the fairies and Honiea would still be hovering, reminding him that he had a magical fate.

Over that winter and on into the following years, Yeolani studied reading. At a suggestion from Gil, Yeolani crafted a map on one of the many skins he had from hunting. He would walk through the forest, counting his paces and noting the landmarks he crossed in little marks across the paper, always keeping the mountains in one direction, the creeks and hills in mind. He had a fair map of Fallon and seriously considered going to Simten and Savone to add them to his map. But then everything changed.

In the summer when Yeolani turned twenty-two, he came tramping back to the cabin near dusk with his map as well as his hunting prizes, Marit at his side. The cabin had not come into view, but Yeolani smelled smoke and a lot of it. He noticed the haze filled the trees with a ghostly mist like masts in a fog bank. Yeolani's abrupt fear drove him, and he dropped his burdens and ran toward the cabin, almost losing his way in the strange, altered scenery. And his fears were founded.

The cabin glowed, fully in flames. He couldn't approach without choking on the fumes, but he went in any way, covering his mouth and nose with his sleeve. The fire around the door licked at his arms, and Marit cowered away, more intelligent than he. Yeolani could barely see for the smoke, but the beams and rafters already fully engaged in flames lit the way. He staggered to where he knew Gil would be at this hour, in the chair whittling or carving. Yeolani groped his way to the spot before the hearth, but the roar of cracking beams and rushing fire warned him away. Gil's chair stood empty. If the old man were inside here, he was dead already, Yeolani knew, but he kept looking. Then, to his horror, he found something charred and still on the bed.

The roof might be seconds away from collapsing. The heat might kill Yeolani at any moment. If he tried much longer to breathe in this inferno, he would asphyxiate, so Yeolani gave up and staggered toward the door. He made it just as the wall and roof came down, shoving him down the stoop, and he landed on the ground gasping and coughing with Marit trying to lick his face. It took Yeolani a few moments to catch his breath before his mind kicked in and he leaped up and ran for his pack. The candle. Honiea could help.

His hands trembled so that he could barely hold the taper,

but at least he didn't have to start his own spark. He reached for the nearest ember from the cabin and lit the candle, holding it high in the smoke, but he didn't remember much after that. He fainted, the candle still clutched in his hand.

Sometime later, he woke with Marit again licking his face and the smoke even thicker than before, but he could not hear the fire and he sat up, dazed, and looked around. The cabin looked like the plague pyre, just a smoking heap of glowing cinders. Beside it, almost blending in with the smoke, stood Honiea, but not as Yeolani had ever seen her.

She wore a purple silk gown embroidered with lilies stitched in silver until the hem stood out stiff with the sparkling threads. At her back she carried a quiver crafted of crystal, filled with arrows fletched with swan feathers. Over the top half of her body, she boasted a bodice of silver etched with more of the lily motif. Her hair, usually in a messy bun or a braid to stay out of her face when she worked, now flowed up in a spectacular setting of silver braid, lilies, and diamonds. Her skin glowed, and it could not be a trick of the smoke and fading light that she seemed to shake the very air around her.

"Yeolani," she said regally, and he obediently scrambled to his feet, afraid to face this new phenomenon.

"Lady?" he gasped, unsure of what to say. "You...you came too late. I'm sorry. I...I, couldn't get him out before..."

"What are you apologizing for, Yeolani? You've done nothing wrong. You stayed with him and served him – an exchange of services. Gil was grateful for the company and your work. And for your part, you learned many things from him. But now that phase is over. It is time to move on."

"You know about Gil?" Yeolani asked in wonder. Perhaps his mind hadn't quite caught up again with the new situation. Of course, she knew. She probably had spied on them daily.

Honiea's smile held no such secret. "Yes, I know, for he is

my husband," she replied frankly. Her silver clad hand lifted, gestured out in the smoke, and a shadowy figure came toward them, moving slowly, bent and old.

Yeolani recognized the familiar shape of Gil approaching them. Marit's tail wagging witnessed this was indeed Gil, but then as he came up to Honiea's side, his face began to change. The old man's wrinkles faded, and the thin white hair thickened up. This new Gil wore a tidy beard, and his hair, stone gray or black, gave him the look of a man strong, tall and sturdy. He seemed only in his mid-thirties but more physically strong than Yeolani himself in his early twenties. This man's eyes still twinkled with the stony gray Gil's had, but instead of watery, struggling sight, Honiea's husband could see a thousand miles.

His clothing also changed with his physical transformation. Instead of hand-crafted leathers, this man wore polished leather breeches the color of the mountain beyond the burned-out cabin and a fitted tunic of wine-colored velvet. Into the fabric had been stitched in silver and gold a run of mountains topped with snow crafted of diamond dust, and along a finely tooled strap, he carried carving and climbing implements fitting the King of the Mountains. Yeolani had no problem recognizing another Wise One like Honiea.

"May I present my husband, Vamilion, King of the Mountains," she said.

The two magicians stood side by side, very different from each other but amazingly the same, matched in power and purpose, though obviously their talents and gifts would be used in far different ways. They had come to him not to display their power but simply to introduce themselves, and Yeolani's mind still could not grasp the reasoning. His legs trembled a little, and he decided he'd better sit down before he fell. He reached for Marit's head to caress her, something real that had not changed in the last few minutes.

"That's some trick. You deceived me," Yeolani finally managed to say, unsure if he felt hurt by the ruse or not.

Honiea shook her head, but it was Vamilion who spoke. "You were not ready for more. It was important that Honiea have you protected while you learned about the world, but she didn't feel like she could watch over you the way that Gil did. I taught you only the things you needed to know, and I never lied to you."

Mocking laughter burst out of Yeolani. "Really? How can you claim that? I've lived under your roof for years and not once did you tell me the truth."

"When I introduced myself, I said 'you may call me Gil,' not that it was my name. And other than that and my appearance, everything was true. I did come from another land far away and I did travel here, exploring. The writing and hunting, those are skills I could give you without using magic. You found me when you were ready, not because you were forced to. You wanted a way to learn to survive, and I was willing to teach you. There was no deception there."

"You even noticed how the fairies followed him as much as you. They're drawn to magic, and he didn't hide that fact," Honiea pointed out.

Yeolani wanted to be angry at their interference, but the more sensible part of his mind could understand a little. "And when I was in the wood crew, when the tree fell after only one blow, were you part of that as well?"

"No," Honiea answered with a sigh. "But when the tree snapped, I did wonder if darker powers might be testing you. So, when you called and I realized the woodsmen knew about the candle and that you'd given them your real name, I felt it better to keep a closer eye on your actions in any case."

"In case? I made a fool of myself there. Then was there some evil magic in the tree falling?" asked Yeolani.

Honiea's brows drew down and a look of frustration crossed her delicate face. "I'm still unsure. It seems terribly convenient that your best friend in the crew was the one harmed and that tree's fall was anything but natural. The fairies were always adamant that you should take up magic immediately. However, I was unable to prove they had any hand in it. Let's put it this way, I was grateful that you decided to move on."

"Did you encourage that with some of your witchery?" Yeolani suspiciously suggested.

The queen shook her head. "No, that would have happened in any case. It's in the Wise One's nature to be about in the Land, exploring. We are the guardians here, and we cannot long stay where we are not needed."

Yeolani knew deep down this was true. He had sensed the urge to leave the forest now for a few months but had resisted because of a perceived responsibility to Gil, an old man who needed his help.

"Which is why we severed that tie, to let you move on," Gil-turned-Vamilion replied to the thoughts Yeolani hadn't expressed. That realization made the younger man cringe.

"Rolling around in my head, are you?" Yeolani almost growled, resentful of them listening in on his thoughts.

Honiea glared at him, and she reminded him perfectly, painfully of his mother. "You can be angry at us, but we are your parents after a fashion, your parents in magic, and this is what good parents do. We watched over you, let you learn from your mistakes, and made sure you didn't hurt yourself too badly. Now we're cutting off that support, and we will see if you've grown strong enough to move to the next level."

Am I a broken bone to be mended, Yeolani wondered, *or a*

future magician? "Very well," he sighed. "I can appreciate that. Next level...magic, I expect."

Honiea nodded, but before she brought out the Heart Stone, she qualified it. "Only if you are ready and take it willingly. There are obligations and restrictions that you must acknowledge, and you must know that before you take the burden. There are two sides to this coin."

"Two sides? A burden?" Yeolani didn't like the sound of that, but he still felt little option. If he didn't learn the consequences now, he would always wonder, and he didn't want to live without at least knowing what might have been.

"There are always two sides to every coin," Honiea began in her best tutoring voice. "When you see the power we have, the ability to do anything we really wish to do, there is also a cost to go with it. We will live forever, without aging, but that means we also will lose everyone we have or will love...unless it is another Wise One."

She turned toward Vamilion briefly, and Yeolani saw a strange look pass between them, something he had never witnessed before. Love? He doubted his own parents had ever looked at each other that way.

"Also, you will be driven," Vamilion continued, "enticed by the magic, to use it in service to the people of the Land, so in a way the magic manipulates you. Essentially, you're a good person and your own nature will drive you to this service. It will be part of your make-up, and while you will be content, you will never be free of it. The Heart Stone will prevent you from using magic for selfish purposes, though you still might do harm."

"But that can be a good thing as well," his wife qualified. "I often have to cause pain in order to heal someone. Unfortunately, that is life in itself."

"And then there are the dangers," Vamilion added. "You

will be battling many things that you cannot anticipate. You are still human and, until fully Seated, can still be physically harmed. Sickness and spells will dog you as you go out Seeking. Those are the terms we use: Seated and Seeking. Until you have found all the pieces to your magic, you are Seeking. There are Talismans you must Seek, as Honiea once explained. And Seeking is a dangerous proposition."

"So I've heard. But nothing you've told me seems so dangerous. What can be so bad about adventure and limitless power?" Yeolani tried to reason.

"That's just it," Honiea replied carefully. "Your power makes you think you can do anything, but you will soon discover you cannot. I could not save Simten from the plague. The tree would still have snapped and your dog there will still die. Another thing is that much of your eternal life you will be alone until you find the next Wise One. Sometimes even then. And no matter how much you help others, you will always question what more you could have done. The what-might-have-been is a burden that will always be yours, though you will eventually find someone with whom to share it. But that could be ages from now. Vamilion found me relatively easily but...but..."

"But," Vamilion rescued her in her difficulty, "it has taken her your entire life to find you, and if you don't accept the Heart Stone, she will continue to go Seeking."

Yeolani got a distinct impression that Vamilion's explanation wasn't exactly what Honiea had wanted to say. Still, it was something.

"So, I will not be as all-powerful as it seems and will have to live forever with the guilt of not being able to do everything. Is there more?"

"Yes, but we cannot possibly warn you of all the circumstances you might face or pain you will feel.

Responsibility," the queen sighed, "is a burden you'll want to set aside, and you will find it difficult to do so for very long." The unspoken words echoed between them. The Wise Ones would never be able to set aside their covenants.

Yeolani looked down at Marit's dark, loving eyes and thought for a while before he came up with another question. "Will I be trained?"

"If you'll have me, I will walk with you a while," Vamilion replied. "But eventually you'll go your own path. That too is the Wise One way."

Yeolani sighed in relief. He really had no idea what he'd do with magic in his life, but he was fairly certain he would mess it up somehow and would need help.

"We all fail sometimes. We're human," Honiea commented.

"And that's the first thing I want to learn – how to listen to someone's thoughts."

Honiea smiled in understanding and then pulled from her pocket the glowing little orb she had shown him years before. It pulsed with a beat like a heart – like his heart, he realized as he watched the flashing grow quicker with his inner nerves and anticipation. Detached, he watched his hand move across the space between them as if it were not even part of him. He could not even make the tremor of fear leave his fingers as he touched the cool stone.

Nothing miraculous happened as he half expected. Part of him looked up into the sky above his head, expecting the fairies to at least dance a bit. Instead, their latent light dimmed, making it hard to see in the night-filled forest. He had expected something more.

"It's only a key to magic, not the magic itself," Vamilion replied to his unspoken thoughts. "You must walk through the door yourself, actively using the magic, and then you will find the power."

"What should I do first?" Yeolani asked frankly. He could think of half-a-dozen things he wanted to try at that moment, but still had no idea of how to go about it.

"How about supper?" Honiea suggested since it was well past dusk and the three of them stood in the forest without even a fire remaining in the ruins of the cabin.

FAIRIES

The three of them stayed at the side of the burned-out cabin that night, and Yeolani learned how to create something out of nothing.

"No, not nothing," Vamilion corrected that thought. "We draw on the substance of the earth. You are going to turn a bit of soil into a loaf of bread. Use your imagination, think of the ground beneath your feet and how you want it to be bread. Good, now hold out your hand and wish for the bread."

It worked, much to Yeolani's surprise. He thought perhaps he would be unable to use the magic, given his past sins. Wasn't there some terrible price to pay for being a murderer? He didn't vocalize his doubts, but Honiea chuckled. "It might be sourdough bread, but that's about it. You defended your mother and yourself. If we had to be perfect, none of us would be Wise Ones."

"I was thinking of wheat bread," Yeolani replied, pleased with the warm crusty loaf that appeared in his open hand. He gave it a sniff and realized Honiea was simply teasing him. She wasn't nearly as intimidating now, for both she and Vamilion had changed appearance, back into more typical clothing, though the old man Gil did not reappear.

"Can you make a knife to cut it? Or a plate to set it on?"

And so Yeolani began exercising his newly minted conjuring skills by creating everything they needed for a simple supper. It took effort and concentration, leaving Yeolani almost too tired to eat. Watching all this, Marit grew skittish and stood outside the firelight, unwilling to approach the strangers, though technically Gil was still there. He must have smelled different to the dog. Directly after supper, Honiea announced that she had another calling, someone needing her help, and so she left, shimmering away in the night, and this did little to reassure the poor dog.

"Do you often get called away?" Yeolani asked Vamilion as he watched the spot where the Queen had left. "It seems very demanding, having to go deal with every injury or illness in the Land."

"For her, yes. She is going about constantly, but she's also training other, non-magical healers. It's the nature of her gift. Me, not so much. I deal with earthquakes, volcanoes, and avalanches as emergencies, but for the most part, my dealings are with the people in the mountains. I teach them the way I taught you. I teach them to mill grain, harness water, and forge steel, all the skills that they need to pass down through the ages. That's one reason why we live so long: to teach these skills and be sure they're not lost. I was about to start bringing writing to the Land, but then Honiea found you, which changed the plan."

"Well," Yeolani sighed. "Thank you for teaching me. I don't think I could stumble on this...this ...barrel of fish without it."

"You probably can't," Vamilion admitted with a chuckle. "I kind of had to do that. Owailion isn't very patient with teaching, and he was the only magician at the time."

"Owailion?"

"He is the first Wise One. He awoke here in the Land with no memory of where he was born. He had these powers and learned how to use them from the dragons but with the Land sealed. God Himself gave him his Seeking tasks to make our Talismans and our palaces. It's one of his..."

"Wait," Yeolani interrupted. "Palaces? Like big stone walls and ramparts and such? Honiea didn't mention palaces."

Vamilion nodded. "She didn't want that to tempt you, for they are glorious. There are sixteen grand homes scattered throughout the Land. One of your tasks, when you are Seeking, is to find the one that belongs to you. Mine is in the south in the Vamilion Mountains, which is where I get my common name. It's one way we can claim the title 'King.' With emigrants from so many lands, they have trouble respecting our magic because we don't use it like magicians in other lands. We have these places to garner the people's respect. The fancy clothing also does that. But we rarely sit in our palaces or travel about wearing such finery."

"I was going to ask about that," Yeolani added. "What's with all the gold and silk in the middle of a burned-out forest? It seems a bit silly."

Vamilion chuckled, admitting to that. "It probably is. However, the change in our clothing is a little out of our control much of the time. Whenever we do high magic or take an oath, we change into that finery as a witness of who we are. It shows I'm Vamilion, the King of the Mountains."

"And what will I be the King of?" Yeolani asked eagerly. "King of Forests and Hunting? Please, not King of the Sea."

Vamilion shrugged. "That's for the future to reveal. I knew when I first saw the mountains. My homeland is mostly forest, and I had only seen the mountains from afar. Then when I changed into my finery the first time, I was curious. Finally, when I saw the Vamilion Mountains, I felt such a sense of awe..." his voice trailed off lost in wonder, and Yeolani had to tease him.

"Like you'd seen the most beautiful woman in the world?" Yeolani teased.

Vamilion blushed and looked down. "Precisely. The mountains suddenly made so much sense to me. I could feel the different types of rock and understand their thoughts and motives."

"Whoa, wait...their thoughts? Rocks have thoughts?"

"I don't know what else to call it. They give me promptings. I can sense when they are under pressure and are about to slip, causing an earthquake. I perceive it as anger or unrest. Are they sentient; no, but they are aware of me as I am aware of them. They don't really react to mankind in general unless it's the miners, but the stone reacts to me and does as I ask."

Yeolani sat back under the late-night sky and considered what Vamilion said. He could have asked a thousand more questions, but something in him wanted to stop and think as well, testing his new perceptions, looking for clues.

"That's probably a wise thing to do," Vamilion commented to Yeolani's unspoken musings.

"Which reminds me. How do you do that listening to my thoughts?"

"Aren't you tired? You've learned much tonight. You should stop and think about what you've been taught. And sleep. You'll dream, and dreams for a Wise One are windows to where your Seeking should guide you."

Yeolani was about to argue the point, but overhead the fairies began dancing and blended in with the stars, and he drifted off to sleep wondering if Vamilion had put a hex on him.

In the night the fairies began speaking to him, buzzing

about his head and even touching his face with their delicate wings. He heard their voices, shrill and insistent, but speaking a tongue he could not quite understand. The wind seemed to blow them away from him, and they struggled to remain above him, lighting his way. In his dream, he dashed through the trees, running faster than humanly possible toward the edge of the forest. He had to get out, and the fairies kept blocking his line of sight. If they didn't get out of his way, he'd plow right into one of the trees that stood thick around him like soldiers, enemy sentinels. He ran without panic, but he definitely felt an urgency. He must get out of the forest, out of the closed in, suffocating closeness of the trees.

Then he burst free from the branches to an opening so vast it might as well have been the ocean. Off to his left, he noted the mountains, so he must have run south out of Fallon, but he couldn't care less. The blue sky overhead seemed to burn with summer brightness. And fresh spring grasses, knee high and blowing gently, stirred in him a longing to roll in the green. He froze in awe, and the fairies caught up, hovering, clouding his vision of the open plains. Angrily he waved them away...and woke up with a start.

"Damn the fairies!" he growled as he sat up in the dawning light.

It was too dark to see, but he heard the gentle thumps as fairies fell, lightless, all around him like pinecones shaken from the trees above. Every one of them was dead. In horror, he picked one up off his blanket and saw the creature for the first time without their flitting and glow interfering. Like a tiny woman, dressed in finest gauze, with the wings of a dragonfly, she could have been human in form except for the extreme size. She was no more than the length of his little finger.

"Vamilion!" he shouted, horrified by what he'd done. "I killed them."

Vamilion, who lay wrapped in blankets on the other side of the cold fire, sat up blearily and tried to focus. He must have gleaned enough just from the scene, as well as Yeolani's thoughts, for he bolted from his bed and came to Yeolani's side. Then, without a thought, the King of the Mountains stuck his hand into the air, conjured a lit candle, and held it high.

Honiea came immediately, stepping out of the dawning sun. She too was wordless, letting her eyes make her conclusions. She began gathering dead fairies into her apron with an alien look on her face: half fear, half revulsion. Yeolani could barely keep himself from crying, not only at the dead fairies but the piercing disappointment his mentors must have in him. To his horror, he realized that he had done this with magic.

"How?" Honiea asked, still gathering bodies.

"I...I...I was dreaming. They were blocking my view. I was so irritated that I...I cursed them, and it woke me, and they all came raining down like this. Can you heal them?"

Honiea sat on the ground with her lap full of dead, lightless fairies and shook her head regretfully. "I can't cure dead...but fairies don't die. They're magical, like us. I've never seen anything like this. I don't know."

"You have to try," Yeolani begged. "They can't die. It will be my fault, my magic, and it will be so wrong. I'll never use magic again if..."

"Make no oaths, boy," growled Vamilion. "Let's let Honiea work."

Vamilion bodily lifted Yeolani off the ground from where he knelt grieving and marshaled him away from their camp, toward the mountains in the east. For his part, Yeolani couldn't think. His mind seemed to bog down in a tar pit of guilt, and he could barely move.

"Sit," Vamilion ordered, and Yeolani obeyed, perching on a

boulder that had fallen down the face of the mountain and onto the bank of the creek that lined the forest. In the slightly more open air, Yeolani almost managed to breathe again.

"Now, you wanted to learn to listen in on thoughts? Listen to Honiea's. Hear her work to save those fairies. She is performing enough magic right now that you should have no problem getting through her shields. Close your eyes and hear her mind's voice. She's just through the trees there. You can sense her. Stretch out and touch Honiea's mind."

Yeolani didn't want to try. He felt afraid of what he might hear, that he might harm her somehow with a stray thought or distract her from her desperate efforts. He also couldn't resist listening in. He imagined his way back into the woods, past the burned-out cabin and into the cool shadows. In his mind's eye, he saw Honiea's golden head bent in concentration over the remains lying in her apron. He imagined she was speaking aloud to the fairies so he could hear... and to his surprise, he could.

"Where do you go when you have no body then? A place like Limbo is not safe with all those demons. Is that where are you now? Where can you go instead?" Yeolani heard Honiea's questioning.

"Who is she speaking to?" Yeolani wondered aloud.

"The souls of the dead fairies," answered Vamilion. "They might be in Limbo, and she's trying to encourage them to come back to their bodies. But Limbo is where human souls go, passing through on their way to heaven. It's also where demons lurk. It's their natural home. Honiea fears for them and wants them to come back here. If she can persuade them..."

"I can help you," Honiea insisted. "It's safe. He didn't mean to harm you. He's new to magic and did not realize. You followed a dream. Your bodies are not damaged, just empty."

Some form of reply must have been given but Yeolani

wasn't hearing the fairy souls. He could only comprehend one side of the conversation. With an effort, he expanded his listening and realized that he was hearing the fairies' reply, but the language still eluded him. Were they even capable of spoken words? Impressions only came to him. He sensed grief, confusion, a rallying around each other to struggle in their comprehension of what had happened to them.

"Well, can I give you another body? Can I somehow give you another purpose too? It is not safe to follow the magicians anymore," Honiea insisted.

The fairy spirits replied something incomprehensible, but the tone sounded bitterly angry or frustrated. The squeaky little minds began coalescing, coming to a consensus.

"But you cannot pass over," Honiea tried again. "That is not your right. You are meant to be here in the Land. You can find another purpose. I will speak for you."

"Yeolani, break it off," Vamilion ordered suddenly.

Obedient to the abrupt command, the younger man pulled back into his own mind, bewildered. "Why? Did I do something wrong again?"

"This is Honiea's private magic. If I'm not mistaken, she is going to approach God and ask for help. You are not ready for that kind of conversation. Neither am I. It's part of Honiea being a healer."

Yeolani sighed, relieved that he didn't have to listen to such a difficult interview. His head was pounding, and he wanted to melt into the ground with sorrow. So, this is what they had meant; guilt over what magic made you do. Well, he had that regret and would carry it for an eternity. What more would he have to endure if already, in less than a day, he had cursed a group of sentient beings into oblivion? Couldn't he undo what was done by accident?

Vamilion obviously knew the answers to all these

questions, but something in the Wise One's stony face looked like Gil, refusing to go in that direction. Instead, Vamilion redirected him. "Why don't you eat something, and then I'll teach you how to block others from reading your thoughts?" Vamilion might have made it a question, but he didn't allow it to be less than a command. He conjured two bowls of hot cereal, and they ate in the quiet beyond the creek in the morning's summer sun. Yeolani slowly began to relax, calming and looking at what had happened with some perspective.

"Good," Vamilion began. "You've got to have a clear mind in order to defend your thoughts from invasion."

"Invasion? Maybe that's what my instincts felt when I was dreaming about the fairies? Could they have been invading my dreams?" Yeolani asked eagerly.

"Well, why don't you tell me about your dream," ordered Vamilion.

In a way sharing about the dream unburdened Yeolani. The tension eased from his neck, and he began to feel less frantic. He bared his soul, trying to recall every nuance of the simple dream of rushing through the forest to the southern edge and encountering the open grassland. When he came to the part where the fairies clouded over him, blocking his view, he had to admit that he had been irritated with them at the time.

"Can you show me? Remember the dream in your mind and then pass it to me like a handful of memory." Vamilion demonstrated by passing to Yeolani a memory of the first day they'd met. Gil of the past stood at the front door with an ax and the boy, gaunt and haggard, standing in the cold. Yeolani rocked back at the clarity of the memory. His mind tried to savor it. Those days of innocence in the cabin seemed like ages ago. Was it only a day before that he had left to go hunting with Marit?

"Focus," Vamilion reminded him. "Remember your dream for me."

Well, thought Yeolani as he gathered his scattered memories, recalled the remarkably well-preserved dream, and then magically passed it to his mentor. The younger man watched Vamilion's face as he processed what he saw and couldn't judge his opinion of the vision. Daring boldly, Yeolani tried his hand at listening into the King of Mountains' thoughts, and unlike when he listened in to Honiea, he met a thick wall of resistance. Rather than getting himself caught invading private thoughts, Yeolani backed off and waited for the results of the dream interpretation.

Vamilion's eyes opened thoughtfully, and he nodded. "The fairies did invade your dream and got overly excited because it is a message of where your magic is going. You need to get out of this forest and away from its fairies. They tend to be...how would you say this...over-enthusiastic about magic. With you being so new, they blocked the whole message of the dream in their eagerness."

"That's still no reason to kill them," Yeolani muttered. "I just didn't know to swear at them would kill them," he reasoned.

"Neither did they. The fairies simply lack the good sense to leave you alone. You didn't kill every fairy in the forest, just the ones that invaded your dream."

"How many?" Yeolani sighed. First his parents and now fairies. He probably should feel somewhat responsible for what had happened to his friend Arvid too.

"You can't do that," Vamilion advised. "You'll have plenty of legitimate guilt without piling on for being in the wrong place at the wrong time. It doesn't matter how many fairies are now in Limbo. They were in the wrong place and you weren't. Now, let's focus on your dream. I want you to try to get through my shield to find out what I think of what you showed me."

"Through that wall?" Yeolani was less than trusting of his ability – or even the safety of trying – to get through Vamilion's shields.

The King of the Mountains chuckled. "Walls are my specialty. Yes, you can do it. And you cannot hurt me, so I'm the perfect person on which to try. Now, if you haven't noticed, the use of the imagination is the strongest skill a Wise One can invoke to tap into their magic."

The sun passed overhead, and they barely moved away from their spot on the edge of the forest as Yeolani battered his mind at the wall around Vamilion's thoughts. At first, neither noticed the passage of time. Sometimes the younger man had to climb the wall or throw a mental hook at the shield, but Vamilion's barrier only grew higher, more slippery, and even formed so it enclosed Yeolani in a prison where he couldn't work any magic without devising some way out of the magical traps. Then he had to do all this while constructing and forming his own walls. They took magical stabs at each other until Yeolani sat on his rock trembling with exhaustion.

"Can we call a break before I pass out," he grumbled sometime after the sun had already set. "I'm about to vomit...if I had anything in my stomach," and he conjured a haunch of venison for something he could eat without having to think of anything else.

Vamilion didn't object. Instead, he sat down beside his student and conjured his own supper. "So, that's why you never bother hiding your name," he commented as he surveyed his full meal plate to show you didn't have to do one magic thing at a time. He had crafted a three-course meal, broke through Yeolani's lax mental guard, and continued the conversation, all at once.

"No fair. I wasn't ready," Yeolani mumbled with his mouth full and continued eating, not really caring that Vamilion was once again traipsing through his mind and right over the curb-sized shield he hadn't reinforced.

"Ready or not, your shields should be up and strong constantly, especially when you are Seeking. There is evil magic out there, and you won't even know it's there before it attacks...in your sleep even. And I say again, that is still a silly reason not to protect your name."

"It's personal, old man. If you'd murdered your parents..."

"I didn't, and neither did you. Listen," Vamilion tried to reason with him, "your mother is dead at the hand of an abusive husband and your father is dead because he was a murderer. I'm sure she appreciates the effort to honor her, but I'm also sure she would want her magical son to survive. That means you drop your birth name. And why would you want to honor a wreck like your father..."

"Yeon, so I don't forget how he was a wreck, and Lani, so I don't forget her love. It's that simple. If I'm going to live forever, I'll be the only one to remember, and everyone should be remembered by someone."

"Then you had better think of a way to keep it a secret that you're magical. If you must keep it, at least just share it with a trusted Wise One."

Yeolani sighed with frustration. "No one knew I was magic until I made the mistake of swatting at fairies," he muttered. "And that's another thing, why are they so fascinated with me? I'm about as interesting as an old stump."

Vamilion was about to reply when Honiea came out of the forest looking haggard as if she'd been doing hard labor for weeks and hadn't stopped to rest. Both men rose, Vamilion to comfort her, and Yeolani suspected he might have to catch her before she fell. She looked twice as exhausted as he felt.

"They love you," she replied to his forgotten question,

"because you are like them, young, new, and magical. You're their new toy."

Yeolani didn't comment on that but began conjuring a chair and then a more respectable effort at a supper and a fire. He and Vamilion had not bothered. Obviously, Honiea had been working far harder than they had and needed to refresh herself or she would be worthless. What had Vamilion called it: private magic? Well, it had left her as weak as a wet rag, and Vamilion had to practically carry her to the seat and hold the fork for her once she sat. She ate slowly at first as if she felt too tired and wanted to just lay her head down amid the dishes and fall asleep there, but she was too much of a healer to let herself do that. She needed to replenish. Once she got going, she ate with single-mindedness, and the two men let her eat in peace, content to wait for her explanation.

Finally, after she'd eaten twice as much as they had, Honiea leaned back in the dark and explained what she'd done with the fairies that Yeolani had cursed.

"Fairy magic is meant to be a harbinger," she clarified. "Owailion used to be coated with them whenever he came deep enough into the Fallon. They aren't like demons, living in Limbo until they get an opportunity to come to the physical world. They are native here in the Land and have a mandate from God to 'welcome' new magic, but their reputation for being troublemakers sometimes gets in the way of their decorum. So, I've found a new job for these particular fairies."

She must have hidden the bag magically, but now she pulled into existence a sack that writhed oddly. The leftover dishes disappeared as Honiea put her burden on the table and she poured it out. Dozens of furry little creatures, eyeless, limbless, and without mouths or tails rolled out and began exploring the edges of the table. Each gave off a soft burping sort of purr.

"What, on God's green earth, are they?" Yeolani asked, reaching out a hand to pet one, perhaps to pick it up, but the little furball scurried away with an offended yip.

"Life Givers," Honiea explained. "Remade fairies. They have a new task. They will be helpers to the Seeking. They will be in service to magic and far less bothersome in these new bodies. If they do their duty, they will return to their old form someday."

"Not all fairies," Yeolani wanted to be sure, "just the ones I cursed? What is this new service?"

"They will escort someone's human soul back from Limbo if they have died. The human body will still need to be repaired, but they'll come back, and the fairy soul will get a new body capable of flitting between the two worlds."

"That sounds as complicated as...as...as a snowstorm on a fishing boat," Yeolani murmured.

"That sounds amazing," countered Vamilion. "I've never seen magic on that scale unless it's something Owailion...and his lady, did as he established the Wise Ones." Vamilion was obviously proud of his wife and said as much.

When Yeolani tried once again to reach for one of the little Life Givers, they still did not trust him and scurried for the edge of the table nearest Honiea. With a concerned look, she gathered them up and began putting them back in her sack.

"I'm afraid that they don't trust you much right now," she apologized. "It will take a while, but as you're the only Seeking Wise One right now, they'll be drawn to you eventually."

"Very well," Yeolani replied frankly. "I don't much trust them either...about as much as I trust myself."

7

EAST AND WEST

A month later, Yeolani walked out from under the southern edge of the forest and onto the open plains. There he finally saw the same image from his aborted dream, but this time, without the fairy interference, he could truly appreciate it. In fact, the only fairy nearby was the single fluffy little Life Giver that had followed him, rolling and bumping along the forest floor in Marit's wake on the day they had left. It had looked pathetic by the end of that first day, covered in dirt and pine needles. Eventually, Yeolani had taken pity, snatched up the creature against its protests, and picked it free of debris. After that, the Life Giver allowed itself to be carried in Yeolani's pack, almost forgotten.

Certainly forgotten as Yeolani finally saw what he had come to find: the plains. He had never seen anything so fascinating. In the late summer, with the grass all bronzed gold, with the wind whipping late summer clouds into a flurry, he felt the majesty of the sea without its terrible memories. It even moved in waves, interrupted only by the slow bend of the western branch of the Lara River that Yeolani had followed out of the forest. He also forgot Vamilion who had come with him, still training him in the mental exercises needed to utilize his magic. Yeolani still couldn't get through to Vamilion's thoughts without permission, but neither could the King of Mountains get into the younger man's shields now that he had strengthened his endurance and lost some of his inhibitions.

Looking out over the open plains, Vamilion paused too but peered knowingly at his young protégé, caring little for the scenery himself. When Yeolani didn't move, Vamilion smiled. "Like you've just seen the most beautiful woman in the world."

"What?" Yeolani started, distracted from admiring of the landscape and had forgotten he even had a companion.

"You are the King of the Plains," Vamilion announced frankly. "You dreamed of them, and now that you've seen them, they've put you in a spell...like the most beautiful woman in the world."

"Hell's Bells," Yeolani acknowledged it. "I need to...to be here."

He'd almost gotten accustomed to the strange things magic had done to him: making him think more deeply about the nature around him, recognizing the life in every speck of the world, and the relationship between each facet, but he had not expected to be so overcome with awe and the feeling that he had come home. Indeed, it was as if he'd seen something so glorious that he doubted he would be able to move from this spot. He wanted to run as fast as he had in his dream and embrace this wondrous grassland like a lover. Dancing under the thunderclouds seemed like a fine pastime. He could lie down in the deep grasses and disappear forever and be content.

"And then there's your appearance," Vamilion commented, directing Yeolani's attention away from the scenery and closer to home.

Yeolani looked down at his clothing and felt his jaw drop

further. Now, under this magical influence, he wore sage green leather breeches with gold thread depicting wheat growing up to his knees and boots the color of rich earth, polished to a high shine. His shirt, a stunning white to match the color of the rising summer clouds, billowed in the wind. Over that he wore a vest of brushed gold velvet that stood stiffly against his body with stitching depicting horses running across the plains and on his back, a gold and storm gray cloak of velvet fell down to his ankles.

"But...but I didn't do any high magic. How did this... I can't go about... Make it go."

"It's almost an oath. Whenever we make a magical connection this profound, you will shift into the regalia of a King. It also affirms that you are indeed the King of the Plains."

Yeolani brushed at the ornate embroidery in alarm. "I can't go walking the world, looking like some...some dandy. How do I make it disappear?" But before he could get the words out, the magic faded as if almost on his request, and he watched as the fine clothing shifted back into the traveling leathers he had magically crafted for himself when he was experimenting with conjuring supplies for this trip south.

"Well, a lot of good that did. Now that I know where my connection is, what am I supposed to do with that knowledge? What are the powers of a King of the Plains?" Yeolani asked simply.

"Where does your instinct want you to go? Something out there must be calling to you, demanding your attention," replied Vamilion.

"How would I...know...I know there's something...south of here. Along the river. How did I know that?"

Vamilion laughed back at him. "You are a Seeking King. Follow those instincts. And at this point, I leave you. You'll learn what you're capable of just by experimenting and following the Wise One instincts you've been given. You're able to communicate with me from afar if you need to," he added when he saw the panicked look on his protégé's face.

"But...but I've still got so much to learn. I only just found out I'm the King of the Plains, and I have no idea what that means."

Vamilion chuckled. "Neither do I. This is like when you were learning to hunt. I've given you the tools. Now you must go hunting." Then without further comment, Vamilion disappeared, not unlike how his wife often just shimmered out of existence.

"Like how do you do that disappearing act?" Yeolani shouted out at the sky to no one. When he got no reply, he had to relent. With no other ideas, he then took a steadying breath, holding it as he would before firing an arrow, and indeed he did feel like the free wind was pushing him south toward the river. Yeolani swallowed his fear and began walking, followed by Marit, who frolicked in the long grass.

Yeolani walked for a week before he began seeing signs of civilization: a footpath along the bank of the river that began to widen into a cart path. Then he saw a cabin up under the bank's trees, a cultivated field with wheat, and cows out grazing. Yeolani paused every evening to work on his map that he was crafting. Vamilion's maps only focused on the geological markings of sea, river, mountains, and plains. Yeolani knew there were people out there, and he wanted to mark villages and towns like the one he expected soon to show up on this river.

At dusk of his sixth day on the plains, he wasn't disappointed. A sizeable town, larger than Simten, appeared on the eastern shore of the river, and with the torch lights visible for over a mile, Yeolani couldn't wait to sleep in a real bed again. Unfortunately, he was coming down the western shore of this branch of the Lara River, and he feared he might not find a village on his side.

He looked down at Marit, whose tail wagged patiently, hoping for supper. "Should I toss you in and swim over, or is there a bridge?" Yeolani asked, but the dog remained silent.

This too must be part of Yeolani's training; wait and see for yourself. So, Yeolani didn't bother hoping for a river crossing at dusk, but decided if he kept walking, he would get an idea of how to do what he was feeling prompted to try, whatever that was. So, the magician and his dog would keep walking.

An hour later, in the solid shadows of night, Yeolani saw that there was indeed a village on the west side of the river opposite the much larger eastern side town. He had lost it in the lights and glare off the river. Good, he would still be able to find his warm bed after all and not bother crossing the water. From what little he could see, this much smaller town seemed dedicated to shipping grain down the river. It boasted several docks and roads spread out into the prairie with little direction, off to unseen farms. He passed a huge pen meant for cattle, but it stood empty, and no one seemed to be on the paths. On the other side, however, the streets echoed with the sounds of busy shops and inns with conversation and music drifting across the water.

Yeolani walked into the empty streets of West looking for an inn and found one with little trouble. As he surveyed the shabby buildings and stretched out his mind, he got a sense of the people who were living here. They seemed tired and depressed. There were few of them too, as if everyone had gone over to the eastern shore to join the party, leaving just those whose work required them to stay on the western side. Yeolani wondered about the differences as he stepped into the only inn this side of the river boasted.

"Oy, the dog can't come in," called someone with a gruff

voice from within the dark common room. Only a single fire, burning low, lit the room, and no one else seemed to frequent this pitiful inn. Yeolani ordered Marit to stay on the stoop, and then he stepped deeper into the murk and up to the barkeeper who stood uselessly polishing already clean glasses at the bar.

"Where is everyone? Is your cooking so bad that you've made this a tomb?" Yeolani commented to the wary barkeeper. Yeolani's magical senses told him he was the only human in the whole establishment. "Or are they all on the other side celebrating something I'm missing?"

The barkeeper didn't answer but went to his hearth and served up a meat pie he had made and then placed before him. "My food's fine. What are you drinking, sir?" He wasn't too pleased when Yeolani asked for water, but he ladled that up and then went back to washing his glasses, ignoring the question.

"Come, sir," Yeolani insisted, feeling the need to engage in a conversation at least. "If I'm going to spend the night or be of some help, can't you at least tell me what's happened?" And greatly daring, he put a little magical prompting into the innkeeper's mind and brought up the fire with a thought to lighten the gloomy atmosphere.

With that encouragement, the innkeeper came over and sat at the table with Yeolani and began bearing his burdens to his client. "It's been a year since the new lord came to East," began the poor business owner. "At first, he was all talk about combining the towns, building a bridge across the river to this side and making this a great city like over the sea. He wanted to trade on ships coming this far north and then bring goods back off the plains and out of the forest. But in order to do that, the West needed to pay into East's coffers, its half for a bridge and the dock improvements. West's mayor, Dinek, he paid the taxes, up until it got to be too much, and with little to show for it.

Tribute, more like. The money went to troops, outlander troops that came up the river to do the building but ended up just staying to bully more money out of us. Dinek's dead now, and we're still paying to have these troops here on our shore, and meanwhile East has gotten bigger and richer. There's no business here, and we're paying the same tribute."

Yeolani's heart sank. What good would magic be in this situation? Of course, the prompting had been to come down the Westside, to the people who were suffering the abuses of the East. And it sounded truly like East thrived under these tactics, but it left West desolate and deserted. How was a novice magician supposed to cure this problem?

"Why don't you move your inn to the other side?" Yeolani replied inanely, not really thinking about what that entailed.

"You, sir, are a fool," the bartender grumbled, looking hurt. "I serve the farmers and ranchers on this side of the river because they need me. My family has owned this place for three generations. I'm not about to walk away from it because it gets difficult. I'd rather fight the East than give into it. A man would, and you're a coward."

Yeolani rocked back in surprise and put down his fork, feeling foolish. Of course, his host was right. He hadn't been using his head. Here he had offered his help to this man, and now he wasn't even listening. Something of the Wise One instincts finally kicked in, and he carefully considered his next words before he spoke this time.

"I'm sorry. You're right, I am a fool. Please, tell me more about this Lord in the East. How many soldiers has he brought?"

The innkeeper dropped his rag on the table in disgust, his hands trembling with ire. "What's a young whelp like you going to do about city politics?" In fact, his anger got the better of him, and he started to throw down the mug he also held, ready to smash it to make his point, but Yeolani acted quicker.

The expected shattering of crockery never came. Yeolani stopped the mug before it hit the slate floor and lifted it slowly so the barkeeper could see it hovering and set it lightly on the counter. For good measure, Yeolani filled it with ale magically and then passed it toward the man, all without breaking eye contact with the bewildered innkeeper.

"That's no way to treat your own crockery, let alone a fine ale. I've come to help because I was sent. Now, as I was asking, please tell me about this Lord and all you can about the men he's brought into East. You and I need to make a plan."

Yeolani walked through the crowded streets of East, observing, counting and hoping he didn't stand out. He held his magic at low levels, and except for his personal shields, no one would have any reason to think he was not a native of the town. He had even left Marit with Sethan, the innkeeper who finally admitted the dog would cause no issues and probably would protect the inn from the ramifications of what they were plotting. It took a week of spying and plotting with Sethan, the innkeeper, and his few farmer friends, but they had a plan that should work, or so Yeolani hoped.

He felt fairly confident of his estimations gathered over the previous week. He knew who was magical among the newcomers to East and who was simply under orders. The Lord of East had plenty of minions, but only a few were magical, and he himself was only a spokesman for the outlanders. That realization gave Yeolani an idea, and while it took some heavy convincing, he had talked Sethan into becoming the spokesman for the West. Yeolani kept in mind that, when this was done, the two towns must be able to function with the new arrangement without further magical intervention. That required someone with Sethan's willingness to stay and work for his people. Yeolani's magic could only be in the background. The actual uniting work would have to be performed by the townsfolk, not him.

And the perfect time to launch their plan had arrived. Harvest was imminent, and the ships on the river came and went loaded with the bounty of the year like at no other time. Soon East would be celebrating with a yearly harvest festival, and this would provide the best opportunity to make their point. So, West had been promised a bridge, a better port, and that they would become a great city like those across the sea. In that case, Yeolani would give them some of what they were promised and get rid of the outlander magicians at the same time. He just had to be sure he had covered all the possible reactions of the East and that he had the full support of the people of West.

That afternoon, Yeolani walked through the market of East as the citizens prepared for the festival that would begin as the harvest moon rose in a few hours. Yeolani wanted his face recognized by the shopkeepers so they would not think he was a stranger. He also wanted to keep his ear open for the general mood when West made its move. Yeolani checked again his mental notes of everyone he needed to neutralize. He felt that everything was ready as long as his friends in West did not change their minds.

At sundown, he bought fried bread and some chilled juice and headed toward the port to watch the ships and to do his magic. First, he sat down on the dock, and one of the Western men helped him move a few barrels into a more protective location so he could go unobserved. With the amount of magic he was about to invoke, his appearance would change, and he would have to be shielded and concentrating on other things, not dodging those who would be trying to find him. From his hide on the docks, he could see everything he needed to do and yet be out of sight.

As the music began at the fair behind him, Yeolani saw movement on the West's bank, with Sethan at the fore. Yeolani watched as all of the few stubborn residents of West gathered on their side of the bank. They climbed to the roof of the most prominent warehouse on their side of the river and stood over the water, solemnly witnessing the celebrations on the far side. Yeolani held his breath in anticipation when Sethan stepped forward and began. With a small surge of magic, Yeolani amplified the innkeeper's voice so that it boomed over the water, echoing among the festival goers.

"People of the East, hear me," Sethan shouted, and Yeolani, from his hide, cast his magic out, bringing the lights on the Eastern shore down so that the only illumination was the moon and the torches on the West. Their stage was set.

"Listen to me. We have paid your tribute. We were promised a bridge. We were told that this port would be developed. And we have paid for this. We've worked and sacrificed for your tribute. And all we've been given in return is outlander mockery."

That was Yeolani's cue. He surged again magically and began lifting from the riverbed the stone pilings of a bridge. It would span from the warehouse district near where Sethan and his supporters stood to the main port road east and west. Solid stone monoliths rose up at least one story high above the river's surface. He anticipated a bridge tall enough to allow boat traffic of significant size and sturdy enough to endure hundreds of years of water passing around them. The river roiled and boiled as it parted for the pilings. The sound of the flow stirring almost muted the startled gasps of onlookers and partiers on the East side. The festival music faded as the musicians joined the audience to these strange phenomena happening in the river beside the fairgrounds. Even the citizens of West sounded startled as they saw this magic, though Yeolani had forewarned them this would happen.

Sethan got hold of himself as the pilings finished formation and continued his speech. "Citizens of East, you have allowed your elected leader to do this, but he is not one of you. He is an outlander who uses magic and our gold to line his own pockets instead of keeping his promises to us. What will happen when there is no longer a West to bleed dry? His soldiers will come for you as well."

As if on cue, the soldiers Sethan spoke of began pushing through the stunned crowd on the East bank, drawing swords and marching toward the river as Yeolani began his second building step, still unobserved behind a stack of barrels on a dock. He began crafting wooden shafts secured to his pilings, lifting twelve trunks soaked in tar to grow out of the stones, bringing the bridge farther out of the water. The gasps of the crowd changed to protests as the soldiers began forcing the citizens of East away from the shore, away from the spectacle they wanted to follow.

"Please, citizens of East," called Sethan. "Send the outlanders away. They will only occupy your homes as they have ours, cut off your livelihood, and tax your goods until you have none left. You are losing your freedom. They will take away your rights as well unless you do not stand for it, until you force them away."

Spanning beams began to stretch across the pillars of the bridge, and the thunder of planking and railing going up overwhelmed the shouted orders of the soldiers. The outlander troops that had been assigned to West only now became aware of what was happening on their side of the river, and they moved toward the warehouse, intent on attacking. However, a block away from their goal, they found they could move no farther. Yeolani had already set a shield around Sethan and his friends exactly like the seal around a Wise One's palace. Even with their swords beating on it, the soldiers could not approach the warehouse to bring an end to Sethan's revolutionary speech.

"We wish to remain friends, so we will have what we paid for. West will have a bridge between us. Our trade will be as equals. The port is open to all who come in peace, but we will no longer allow these outlanders to cut us off from you. See how they react when good magic builds a link between us that they cannot control."

The outlander soldiers on both sides began lighting arrows and firing in either direction, trying to stop the bridge that now began attaching railings for foot and wagon traffic. When the barrage of arrows did not succeed in lighting the bridge afire, the arrows changed directions, at the heart of West's business district. Yeolani snuffed them out as they flew, and they fell harmlessly, for all the citizens of West that remained had hidden in their homes or were with Sethan on the warehouse roof.

Someone, an officer on the East side perhaps, might have been a magician, for he miraculously managed to get his men to form up. They decided to strengthen their brethren on the West side and began marching across the nearly completed bridge to do so. Yeolani didn't allow this but began pitching them over the side as soon as they made it halfway. Their screams as they fell over the edge brought cheers from the citizens on both sides.

"People of East, we are your brothers. Please be our brothers again. Do not allow us to be cut off from you. Banish your Lord and become your own leaders. A boat is here to take them back to where they have come from. Fill it with your outlanders and send them home. In East, in West, in all the Land, there will be no magicians who rise up to control us. That is the mandate of the Land. Magic is meant to draw us together, not cut us apart."

And with that, a barge tied just at Yeolani's feet came free of its moorings and drifted down to the newly crafted bridge to wait for the passengers. He held it there against the pull of the river's current and watched over Sethan as he ended his speech and then came down off the warehouse roof.

Now it was up to the citizens of East.

Yeolani strengthened the shields around the members of the West's contingent and then confirmed that all his magic had eased, putting him back into his regular clothing. Then Yeolani peeked around the barrels that made up his hide. He felt a shiver of excitement to see the people of East getting into verbal arguments with soldiers who reluctantly pushed back, though no swords were in evidence. The citizens pointed to the barge and the bridge, arguing and simply outnumbering the soldiers, shoving them back toward the bridge.

Another group of people at the center of the party grounds had surrounded someone in a purple robe. While Yeolani couldn't make out the individual words, the sorcerer's angry tone echoed down to him as he came out of his hide. So, this was the magical power behind all the outlander invasions. Yeolani couldn't decide which group to join: the people on the bridge or those moving against the sorcerer at the center of town. In the end, he decided his best choice lay in joining the protests on the bridge or he might end up in a pitched magical battle with a sorcerer.

He ran off the dock and up his newly minted bridge with the swell of people crossing over from East to West, pushing soldiers before them and almost physically forcing them over the railing of the bridge and onto the barge that floated below, waiting for them. The enthusiasm of the crowd thrilled him, and Yeolani joined in, cheering, shouting slogans of freedom. Yeolani was about to turn back to see how it faired with the sorcerer in the square when something hit his personal shield so hard he lost his footing. He saw a flash of fire and felt his whole body lifted up and off the bridge.

Darkness hit him before the water took him away.

8

GRASS AND GROUNDHOGS

*Y*eolani woke face up and noted it was daylight. He felt wretched, but if that was because of the explosion or the slowly spinning world, he couldn't tell. He looked up at the sky, wondering at the blue above him, the few clouds, and the fact that he still lived. He could not wrap his head around the recognition that he was well on his way to floating down the river toward the sea, and he had better swim to shore.

His limbs ached and felt sluggish, but he managed to roll over and slogged his way toward the bank; east or west, he didn't care. When his knees finally scraped on the sandy bottom, he crawled up the beach and collapsed with his feet still in the water while the rest of him baked in the sun. Yeolani didn't feel so ill once he was out of the water, and he rested there for the remainder of the day until he finally felt capable of doing more: conjuring a supper for himself and making a camp for the night. He would survey his situation once dawn came and hopefully with his strength returned.

The next day Yeolani began walking north, back towards

West to see what had happened in his absence. How far had he floated unconscious? He couldn't guess, but he kept an eye on the river for other debris as he went upstream. To his surprise, he found nothing else one wouldn't expect in a summer run of a river. He saw a few boats pass, and he tried to hail them to ask from where they sailed, but if he didn't want to use magic, the crews wouldn't hear him. He tried to judge by the width from shore to shore how far he'd come, but he had nothing with which to compare it. Obviously, he had floated south, but how far? Had anyone else been blown free by the blast as well? Was his personal shield all that protected him? Had everyone else been killed?

Then at noon, he saw something on the northern horizon that surprised him. At first, he thought it might be a mountain on the edge of the prairie, but it looked too uniform and pristine. And the closer he got the more it looked manmade to Yeolani. He also noted how the river, green and languid up till now, seemed to grow brown with silt and grow louder as if cataracts nearby roiled up the water. Finally, Yeolani put these clues together and recognized the white spires of a Wise One palace at the forks of the Lara River.

Yeolani paused in his trek north to appreciate the graceful towering spires and splendid carving even on the outer protective walls. It sparkled in the sun like the icebergs he used to see during spring fishing voyages. A black banner with a silver star as an emblem flew out over the silvery gray steeples, rippling with the prairie breeze. Was the building even occupied? It didn't seem so, for the rich grass grew up against the walls without being trampled. Yeolani appreciated his chance to see the grand palace of Lara, but was it his? He very much doubted it. Nothing about the very pretty place attracted him other than its placement on the plains. He couldn't approach it, for it occupied the V between the river branches and he walked the western shore, but at least he got a good look before the sun went down and he had to camp again.

Overall, it took him two full days walking to reach the towns he had connected with his bridge. Even then, he saw the glow of fires just before the stars came out on the second day. Yeolani's stomach sank with guilt to see that the fires must be the city burning, and although he wanted to hurry, he hadn't yet found a magical way to travel. Running in after having gone missing for days would hardly be conducive to stealth. He had to consider what he would do when he got closer. Coming into West was safest, he figured, for the East was where the magicians most likely waited unless the people had driven them out. He had passed no barges full of ousted outlanders, but then he had also spent half this trip unconscious.

By mid-morning he had a good idea of what had happened, though he couldn't understand what had caused what he was seeing. Magic from the eastern shore still flared up everywhere in strange explosive ways. Fires burned in the oddest spots: tops of trees, in the middle of streets, and even one on the side of an otherwise intact building. It flared in strange colors, giving off noxious green smoke. He passed one woman who was beating at a sickly purple blaze on top of her chicken coop, but the water she threw at the blaze only spread it and she could not douse it with rugs or anything else she had at hand. Yeolani helpfully smothered the flames in a magical load of salt and that did the trick. How he knew salt would work, he could not tell her. Besides, her chickens were dead, and he could do nothing for that. He simply moved on to the next crisis, putting out another fire, lifting fallen obstacles, and helping where he could.

All through that day, Yeolani felt so guilty he could barely move. His eyes brimmed with unshed tears at the ashes and smoking heaps in the city of East as well as West. Mist choked both sides and a sickly blue and green glow witnessed of magic still afoot, especially on the eastern shore. His bridge remained intact, so while East still burned, the people had all shifted to West if they could. The streets of West teamed with bewildered citizens scavenging for food and shelter. Bedraggled as he was, Yeolani, grieving and ash-smeared, fit in perfectly. He kept his head down looking for Marit in the press of people. The poor dog would be traumatized too.

The horrible pressure of minds on his brain also stripped Yeolani of any semblance of peace. He tried to shield out the freely shared grief and only concentrate on helping snuff out fires but found it difficult to even move. He did not even realize he had limits in his capacity to work magic until he recognized he simply could not conjure another bucket of water. He stood like a statue in the street that ran with mud and could not think. In a daze, he decided he needed an island in the storm.

Yeolani staggered down to Sethan's inn on the wharf. The building had survived the fires thanks to the shields that Yeolani originally set on them, but the magical blows from East had done their damage here as well. One wall was caved in on the top floor, and men were diligently trying to do the repairs. The flow of people in and out of the common room hadn't suffered for all of that. Thankfully, Marit still guarded the porch and sat out of the way. Her tail wagged at his approach. Yeolani motioned his little friend to stay where she was as he went into the inn to see what kind of greeting he would get here with so many people coming in and out.

The inn looked like a refugee camp. Cots had taken the place of the tables which were pressed over to the side to form a buffet for those that needed to eat. Sethan's cook stood behind the table barricade ladling out soup to all comers, and Sethan himself worked in the back of the room handing out blankets. Refugees from East huddled in little family groups or worked to hand out supplies and news to others about the room. Sethan made eye contact with Yeolani from across the space but didn't react one way or the other, just nodded and went about his tasks.

Where were Honiea and Vamilion, Yeolani wondered? Without thinking about it, he slipped behind the bar and conjured a candle, lit it and held it low, wishing Honiea's help to come. She arrived, crouched low like he was behind the bar, and smiled at him, the only smile he'd seen in days. She must have already known about the situation, for her face showed evidence of ash and hard work.

"We're here," she assured him and then stood up, found a child near the door who had a burn on his arm, and left to go tend him. Vamilion took a little longer to arrive, for he walked down the inn's steps with the building crew to get them supper when Yeolani saw him.

Hours later, after the refugees had settled in the shelters prepared for them and after the fires of East had turned to eerie glows in the dark, Yeolani found Sethan so they could chat. The innkeeper approached Yeolani feeding Marit who waited patiently for her master's attention.

"Sir," Sethan began since he didn't know Yeolani's name and they had agreed to keep it that way. "I saw you blown off the bridge. I thought you were dead."

"No, just thrown into the water like the rotten fish I am. I washed downstream so it took me a day to come back. What happened here after I went over the side? East has been burning like a torch at mid-winter, I see. What happened to the soldiers and magicians? The Lord of East?"

"Little is known for sure," the innkeeper shrugged, looking utterly exhausted. He sat down on the other side of the dog to rub her ears but more just to keep from collapsing himself. Subtly, Yeolani reached over and put his hand on his friend's shoulder, funneling some magical energy into the man who must have been working constantly since the night of the rebellion.

"The people who came across the bridge at first were pushing soldiers onto your barge. You must have seen them. Then there was the explosion...that...that I saw you...well, you're the only one we know who was on the bridge to survive that blast. Frankly, I'm surprised the bridge is still intact. It was a magic-driven explosion, so we know it was the outlanders that did it. It frightened everyone, and the people rushed the bridge, trying to come over, and left the outlanders on the other side. When you went under, the barge broke free and the soldiers on board floated down the river. That must have left just a few, mostly outlander magicians, on the East side."

"What of the outlanders on West's side?"

"We gave them two options: depart and go overland to the coast where they must depart the Land or use their weapons to defend the bridge. They may not go over to the East side to join their kin. I'd say about half of them will stay here and help defend West rather than fighting us. Refugees have been escaping from East for the last three days, swimming for their lives or sneaking across on boats, but no one dares take the bridge any longer. Anyone who tries to cross that way gets the same treatment you did, explosions on the bridge."

Yeolani shuddered with grief at what he'd crafted. However, he couldn't let that stop his finishing this battle. "And the fires?"

Sethan nodded dejectedly. "We've heard tales from the refugees. It's their Lord Kreftor, who is ordering the city razed. He would rather leave char and cinders than anything worth keeping. After they strip a building of anything of worth, Kreftor's men set it afire."

Yeolani peered toward East, although he could not really

see through the walls, not until he rested up a bit. "What's happening to the people who remain or cannot get over from the East side?"

"No one knows," Sethan sighed with regret. "I never thought our little demonstration would become such a...such..." He couldn't come up with a word to fit the situation and neither could Yeolani.

"You cannot predict what evil will do, only what is good and right," Yeolani said gently, wondering at the words that he, as a simple young man with little experience, could craft. These were the words of the Wise Ones.

Sethan crumbled a little. "Nearly a third of East's population is dead, injured, or unaccounted for because of us. I keep asking myself if it was all really necessary."

"How many of them would have wanted to die in a rebellion? None, but how many wanted some way to have freedom from the outlander magic?" asked Yeolani, again tapping into the Wise One instinct.

Sethan dropped his head further. "It was my selfish desire, my pride. I wanted to push them into getting rid of Lord Kreftor. Wouldn't they have done it eventually for themselves? They might have rebelled in a more peaceful fashion."

Yeolani shook his head before he realized that the innkeeper couldn't see the gesture. "No, you must fight evil whenever you see it. If it had gone on any longer, it would have been all that more set, like barnacles on a hull. None of us want to start the fight, but we have a duty to resist evil when we see it. If anyone should feel guilty, it is me."

And his own words haunted him. Was that why he had confronted his father? He would never have rebelled if his father had not taken the abuse to his mother. He would have endured neglect and abuse forever if not for her.

When Sethan didn't reply, Yeolani realized his friend had

fallen asleep. It was a warm enough night and getting him into his own bed seemed a waste of time. Yeolani conjured a pillow to tuck under his friend's head and a blanket he then draped over the sleeping innkeeper. Yeolani left Marit to watch over Sethan through the night. Then, instinctively, Yeolani went back into the quiet of the common room, for he knew that Honiea and Vamilion would be waiting for him there.

They sat at a table tucked back in the kitchen, with Honiea's candle as their only source of light, waiting for him patiently. The three Wise Ones needed to talk out a plan, and Yeolani was grateful he wasn't alone anymore in this magic. In fact, his first words were thanks. But then he surrounded them with a shield of invisibility and silence to mute their conversation.

"Quite an adventure for your first magical foray," Vamilion commented.

Yeolani only shrugged. "You said to follow my instincts, and the wretched promptings led me here like a flock of fairies. The people of West needed my help. If Lord Kreftor on the East side had continued, he would have been completely entrenched here and it would have been that much more difficult to break him free. He's a barnacle, sucking the life out of these towns."

"We aren't questioning that it needed to be done," Honiea reassured him as she sensed how he felt they were critical of his choice. "We just are a bit concerned about your methods. You've put these people in great danger. They don't know how to fight magic. Many of them died without even knowing why they were fighting."

The guilt and the latent depression Yeolani carried woke from its slumber. He felt he could do nothing without worsening the circumstances. He might be able to reassure Sethan but not himself that he had done the right thing.

"What would you have done in this situation?" he asked, not in anger or frustration. He sincerely wanted to learn better how to avoid a pitched battle with non-magical folk in the line of fire next time. The old Yeolani would have been angry or defensive, but the Wise One instincts blocked that.

"I'm not sure there was something better to do," Vamilion reassured him, "but it is always wisest to do anything as naturally as possible. Building a bridge is not a natural act. It was impressive and flashy. Could you have found a subtle way to show the people of East that they needed to support their friends in West? They only needed to acknowledge it."

A hundred possible scenarios rippled through Yeolani's mind like wind through grasses, but none of them stayed, short of confronting the sorcerer Kreftor himself. Yeolani would still have to do that, no doubt. The outlanders had not left the East yet and would probably have to be encouraged to do so. Rather than admit that his plan had not turned out the way he had hoped, Yeolani nodded his agreement. He could see their point. Just because he had the power did not mean it was always the wisest to use it. He had tried to be subtle for himself, hiding behind barrels and not using his magic openly, but that was just to protect himself, not the people. Using magic sparingly, without being so blatant, would have been a better step.

"I'll have to confront Lord Kreftor still, or he won't leave the Land," Yeolani warned his companions. "Do you have any suggestions?"

Vamilion and Honiea looked at each other, and again it struck Yeolani like a knife how much they loved and relied on each other. How wonderful would it be to have someone that matched you, supported you, allowed you to consider ideas as equals? He wanted that for himself. Having a partner would have prevented much of the foolishness he'd done here.

However, Honiea shook her head before he could go down the road of self-pity.

"We'll support anything you decide to do as long as you wait until tomorrow. Right now, we all need to rest."

The next day, after he had slept himself out, Yeolani knew what he had to do. He said goodbye to his friends in West, packed his things, being sure he included the furry Life Giver, his Heart Stone, Honiea's candle, and newly created maps in his pack, and then walked over to the bridge. Marit hung back as Yeolani surged magically, anchoring himself to the plains before he stepped onto the bridge. He wouldn't be thrown off this time. But using that shielding magic put him into his royal clothing which now also included a breastplate of gold and a sword at his side. It seemed ridiculous to Yeolani, for he had never touched a sword and would have preferred a bow and arrows. However, he reminded himself this costume was for show, to convince these outlanders that there was magic in the Land and they were outmatched.

The bridge, which had become a symbol of the rebellion, erupted in explosions as Yeolani crossed over to the East side, but he wasn't thrown over this time. The prairie on either side of the river held him steady, and he felt its peace and serenity as a counterbalance to the panicked magic of the outlander sorcerers that attacked him...and from his own anger at the destruction. How could they have done this? The senseless burning and ruin numbed him.

From the safety of the West, the refugees and citizens watched as he made his trek safely and then began weaving his way through the burned-out buildings toward Lord Kreftor's mansion on the far eastern edge of the city. Only once she had lost sight of him did Marit follow behind, unharmed as she trotted over the bridge, seeking her master. His passage had broken the bridge's spell, making it safe for all.

The Lord's house seemed a poor imitation of the grand palace that Yeolani had seen on his walk back up the river, but if he hadn't seen Lara, he would have been very impressed. Of white stone, with a steep slate roof spire and many glazed windows, with gold and purple banners flying in the autumn sun, it seemed cheery, as if the festival continued here despite the smoke and ruins all around it. The high walls protecting the building reminded Yeolani faintly of his mind invasion exercises against Vamilion, and he felt pride that he had no problem reading the minds beyond these walls. He knew exactly how many and what powers he faced.

He walked up to the gate, an ornately gilded affair. Behind it, he faced non-magical soldiers like the ones he had encountered in West who had come over and sworn their allegiance to the Land rather than being forced to leave. These men looked at him in barely controlled terror.

"I am the King of the Plains," Yeolani announced needlessly. "I demand to speak with the filthy worm, lord of this misbegotten house."

The guards said nothing but stepped back as a minor sorcerer wearing a purple and gold robe crossed over the courtyard to address him. "So, you are King of the Plains? What type of sad little powers does the prairie give you?" the sorcerer commented in a thick accent. "You can make grass grow and groundhogs scurry? I'm not impressed."

At the mocking words, Yeolani abruptly remembered his father chiding him for being sea-sick. That memory brought thunderstorms building behind his eyes, and Yeolani encouraged it. He hadn't yet explored the capabilities that being the King of the Plains would give him. However, he could imagine there might be something more than grass and groundhogs. Over to the east, he saw thunderheads rising despite the earliness of the day and smiled to himself.

"I haven't come to mince words with an underling who couldn't catch a fish without a pole," he growled while the wind picked up around him. "Your Lord is the one who must meet with me if he dares. You and all your ...your compatriots must leave. And Lord Kreftor will order it, now."

"Compatriots? Where did a boy like you learn a word like that?" scoffed the sorcerer.

Yeolani had much the same question, for he had never heard it used before, though it must have meant something to the outlander magician. As the cynical comment came at him, so too did an invisible wave of pure magic, rippling from one of the towers beyond the gate. Yeolani endured the wave, feeling rooted to the earth like the pilings of the bridge he had crafted. Up there, in that tower, there hid the true power behind the throne, and Yeolani wasn't going to wait to confront that. He pushed back.

With a wave of his hand, Yeolani made the gilded gate disappear and threw the guards as well as the arrogant underling back across the courtyard where they landed, sprawled on their backs. Yeolani walked through the opening, pushing against the magic that shoved against him like a stiff wind. He could do it with a little determination. His cloak billowed out behind him in the magical bluster, and the roar of it in Yeolani's ears made him deaf to the shouts and alarms his entry now brought to the courtyard. Their outlander weapons couldn't penetrate his shields. Even though twenty more soldiers thundered down at him out of the house itself, he gave them little heed.

He pushed his way through the outlander troops with a mind-wind and marched up a winding set of stairs. He could see illusions as he moved up the spiral steps. When he didn't look closely, he saw an impenetrable jungle, vines gripping at his arms and legs as he progressed, but he used magic to alter the false imagery to that of a wind-funnel, and he felt it lift him physically through space, sucked up into the top of the stairway. At the apex of the spire, he found a simple wooden door on the landing, and he distrusted it as an illusion. He put his hand on the face of the passageway, and it even gave him the feel of wood grain under his hands, but he knew it for an apparition.

Yeolani took a careful breath, walked through the false door, and stepped into an elegant chamber. Its insides reflected what one would expect from the outside: rich mahogany desks, matching chairs, and a finely carved bed. However, the stench of magic and the simplicity of the light and reflections on the furniture spoke louder of spells and illusions. Moreover, Yeolani sensed a hidden mind holding tight to the imagery and at the same time trying unsuccessfully to hold their magic low to avoid detection. Perhaps the sorcerer hoped Yeolani wouldn't notice the odor of blood magic and would leave, thinking the room stood empty.

"I know you're here, hiding like a snail in its shell, so don't bother resisting with your enchantments and spells. You'll only wear yourself out trying. Can't have that," Yeolani said in his most bored tone. Since no one answered and there was no place to sit unless he wanted to risk sitting on an illusion, Yeolani conjured himself a seat, causing ripples in the imagery. The foreign sorcerer could not absorb something real, like a conjured chair, moving into the spell-work, so it all wavered like flowing water.

Then, as if he had all the time to carry on the one-sided conversation, Yeolani sat back and crossed one elegantly booted leg over his knee. "So, I understand the soldiers below are your puppets. Haven't you sent them away yet? That is sad, for I am going to have to pack you all back in the same boat. They won't be sea-sick, but you will, won't you?"

At that implied threat, the illusion finally eased, and Yeolani heard a gasp of exhaustion. The room took basically the same form but without the furniture. Bloody markings emerged on the white stone walls. Finally, shimmering out of the darkest corner, an ancient looking sorcerer materialized, old enough to look like Gil but with far more wrinkles and weakened by his fruitless efforts. Kreftor also dressed in a purple robe like his minion below, but this one boasted the arcane markings that Yeolani assumed blood magic required.

"Much better," Yeolani commented and conjured a second seat for Kreftor as if they would have a comfortable conversation. "Now we can talk."

The sorcerer looked annoyed and reluctant to sit but instead played with a worry stick in his hand, leaking nervous energy. He began to pace like his lair had become a prison.

Yeolani let him suffer. "You've come to the Land, and we do not allow blood magic to remain here. It stinks up the place worse than a barrel of rotten fish," he insisted.

"You cannot make us all leave. There are more like me." Kreftor's thick accent made him almost unintelligible, but he didn't react to the insult. Instead, he sat down, at last, looking down at the stones at his feet. "The Land's magic is attractive and so...so underused."

"Too bad you cannot possess it, no matter how much you stumble around trying to sink in your claws," Yeolani flatly pointed out. "We will drive you out like the roaches you are, wherever we find you."

"And how would you make sure I leave?" Kreftor asked, daring to look up.

Yeolani smirked. "Have you ever seen fish caught in a net?

That's you now, and then I will put you in a barrel, seal it, and put it in the hold of the first boat I can conjure. I'll send it down the river and off to your own hovels. And this very convenient river goes all the way through the plains to the coast. As you know, I am the King of the Plains. I'll sense it if the ship so much as starts to take on water. Is that how you want to go?"

The sorcerer already looked ill at the thought. "The demons and sorcerers will continue to come to the Land, you know that," Kreftor pointed out logically. "You cannot drive us all out."

That truth broke some of the passion Yeolani had been mastering over the last few days. Add to that the frustration at still not knowing how to travel more quickly and something slipped into place, quashing some of his naturally playful nature. The gloom of yesterday met head-on with the frustration at knowing that Kreftor was right; the Land would have to be sealed again before outlanders stopped sending sorcerers who coveted the Land's magic. These things swirled in Yeolani's mind and formed something alien and powerful.

"Yes," Yeolani sighed, "and I will fight you forever. Now, are you going peacefully, or shall I stomp on you roaches here and now? If so, I've got something outside to show you. I sweep up after myself."

Unwillingly, Kreftor hobbled to the eastern window, and Yeolani watched his shoulders slump in defeat. Just beyond the gates of the mansion spun a trio of tornadoes waiting for Yeolani's signal. They roared and snarled, gouging the ground and whipping the air wickedly like waiting attack dogs. "I'll send you home in a quicker fashion, but you'll not survive that kind of transport. Neither will your less-than-magical brethren. Which shall it be, Roach?"

A demon lurking inside the sorcerer suddenly cackled, no longer accented like Kreftor. Yeolani saw two images, one of the old man and the other of an upright centipede-like creature twisted around Kreftor. Its bulging eyes glowed a toxic green, glaring back at Yeolani even as its human host remained looking out the window. It boasted antennas that snaked all the way to the ground, creeping out toward Yeolani's feet. Yeolani carefully pulled back a bit, just for the comfort of not being quite so near the monster within the man.

"You're Roach."

"We are a nest of roaches. You cannot kill us all. Roach will just find other bodies willing to take us inside, and we will come to the Land again."

The multi-toned voice sent shivers down Yeolani's back, but he stood firm, keeping his oath as a Wise One. "And we will fight you every time you come. Now, you will leave this town in peace. You will leave the Land and find somewhere else to dwell. Your only decision is how," Yeolani reiterated, feeling the straining of the tornadoes like chained animals.

Kreftor moved back from the window, and Yeolani saw the demon in his eyes wanting to lunge. With his tension ready to react at any moment, the King of the Plains found it almost impossible to remain in his relaxed pose, waiting for the reaction he expected. He knew it the moment the decision was made and the demon-filled sorcerer leaped at him. Yeolani felt the tornadoes sweep in, shattering glass and sucking the roof off the tower before the grasping hands or the whipping antennas could come near Yeolani's neck. A deafening roar swept them both into the air, but Yeolani felt safe, cradled in the wind's embrace as his pet tornadoes cleaned East of its invaders and swept away the ash heaps. He watched from the eye of the storm as his own body phased away from him to be one with the wind.

When he was sure all three tornadoes had accounted for every one of the outlanders, Yeolani guided them down the river, across the plains, and toward the sea. He feared that most of the non-magical men would die in the buffeting, and perhaps even the sorcerers if their demons abandoned them, but he could not afford to be merciful. Lances of blue and green lightning attempted to quell his storms, but nothing would stop his anger and power. He kept them fueled by the very plains beneath them. The cyclones ran the prairie and launched off the cliffs and onto the ocean, gathering the power that Yeolani now funneled into them with the summer heat burning off the Land, combining with the cool of autumn winds coming from the north coast. Perfect weather for storms, he realized.

When he estimated no one would be able to swim back to shore, Yeolani released the magic of the tornadoes, and the men fell out of the sky and into the water far below. Few had survived the vicious winds, and none would last the impact with the surface, but Yeolani did not stay to be sure. He spun his personal tornado back into the sky and returned to the Land.

Dusk had settled over East by the time he came to the ground finally, trembling with exhaustion. He staggered into his human body at the foot of the now empty tower, the only building to survive even partially intact in East. No fires burned, and only the West's lights reflected on the river. Yeolani couldn't bear to return to the chaos and celebrations that occupied the villagers on the other side of the river this night. Instead, he sank his mind into the ground at his feet and felt the patient strength of the prairie that restored him a little. At least he had found a way to travel magically, even if he left a wide path of destruction wherever he went.

With a grieving sigh, Yeolani whistled for Marit. She came running through the empty, blackened streets and together they walked off toward the north and into the night.

9

CHANGELING

*W*inter bore down on Yeolani before he made it to
the mountains, but for some reason, he felt
reluctant to use magic to speed up the trek he had decided to
make. He wouldn't return to the Fallon Forest, but his
northeastern path skimmed along its edge and up against the
mountains where hundreds of little creeks fell out onto the
plains. He avoided starving by hunting and selling his catch in
the villages he passed, but the game became scarce with
winter's arrival.

And then there was Marit. She had gotten herself pregnant
while she was at West, and now she suffered along with him. It
must have been her first time encountering another dog, so it
was bound to happen. Catering to her needs put pressure on
Yeolani to make some changes. He must find someplace to
winter over for her sake rather than continuing his stubborn
refusal to perform magic or do something useful with his gifts.

Finally, Yeolani settled on a cave tucked in behind a frozen
waterfall just outside Fallon, on a creek that came out of the
mountains, a few hours walk from a town where he could trade

for the things he wouldn't conjure. He gathered wood and as much food as he could before the first storms came thundering down over his head. He went hunting for Marit but not for himself and instead sat in the dark and cold wondering why he felt so reluctant to use his magic.

It came down to guilt, he decided. He had been wrong to engage in the problem at East. When he had gotten involved, he managed to get people killed as well. Too flashy, he agreed with Vamilion, but also too cocky. He could have found a better way to persuade Kreftor to move off and never involved the townsfolk. Worst of all, using tornadoes instead of simply binding the magicians and sending them down the river in fish barrels like he threatened, that was overkill. If he always overused his magic, he would continue to harm innocents. And so, he punished himself by using no magic at all, living on the edge of starvation or freezing. He was miserable and felt he deserved such a fate. He justified it by telling himself that he wasn't going to harm anyone with magic if he didn't use any.

Marit's patient companionship kept him alive. He would conjure wood and make a fire to heat the cavern for her. He gave her the furs from the few animals he was able to hunt to make herself a bed, and she ate like a queen, but her solemn brown eyes accused him. They kept him from drifting deeper into his depression.

Then the night that Marit dragged her bed furs farther into the back of the cave and wouldn't let him come after her, he knew he was about to have puppies on his hands. She wanted to be alone, and so he stoked up the fire and sat looking at the frozen waterfall, drifting off in his melancholy into a dream.

Yeolani dreamt that he stood knee-deep in summer grasses on the prairie. The blue sky rolled uninterrupted overhead. He was about to sit down and luxuriate in the deep grasses when he found himself sinking right through them into the rich soil.

He didn't panic; how could he when this was the one place where he belonged. He passed through the earth, past gopher holes and earthworms, and wondered again at what power the prairie could provide. Then he passed effortlessly through the stone floor of the earth and felt no distress. Perhaps the prairie thought he had died and now was burying him.

Then abruptly, the stone gave way to a low shallow cavern, and he dropped to the bare rock floor of the space, staggering a bit, and then straightened up to see where he had arrived. He could see in the space, for the fairies had followed him down into the gullet of the earth. Their glow lit it well enough, and he looked out and saw the cavern ceiling loomed low, dripping with muddy crystals stabbing toward him. As far as his light would stretch, the low arch covered a body of water just smaller than a sea. It didn't move like the ocean, but he stood on the shoreline of a cistern that stretched to prairie-sized proportions. The drip from above and the resulting ripples made little splashes that echoed in the monstrous space. Was there truly an aquifer like this beneath every acre of the plains?

Curiously he reached up and touched the roof, drawing his hand over the frosting of crystals just above his head. The smaller shards that dusted the cavern ceiling crumbled at his touch, but one larger chunk, about the size of his thumb, fell at his feet. He bent to pick it up and caressed the silky sides of the hexagonal shaft. In the blue-white light of the fairies, it looked almost brown and muddy, but the refraction of light might change in bright sunlight; certainly not clear like a diamond, but opaquer, like quartz.

As he stood in his dream wondering at the faceted piece in his hand, the fairies came low around him and hovered at a respectful height, leery of his curse. He would not have cursed them again, but they still didn't trust him; another reason to feel guilty. They began dancing above him, and he let their movements hypnotize him. He thought he heard their tinny little voices like he had when Honiea was speaking with them, trying to mitigate his curse on them, but this time he could understand them.

"Why can I understand you now? You decided to make sense?" Yeolani asked in wonder, and his mind-voice echoed in the cavern even though he didn't speak aloud.

"You never tried to understand us after you touched the Heart Stone. You have to try in order to receive the message."

"What message?" he asked out of duty, not for any interest.

"You cannot give up. You will only feel more guilt if you stop your Seeking. The world needs you."

"No, the world is far safer without me bumbling about in it."

"No," replied the fairies in their compounded voices. "We love you. We need you. Your Talismans, your Lady, your future all need you. You need to Seek them, or they will be lost."

"Lady?" Yeolani asked in surprise, maybe even aloud in his sleep. He had forgotten that finding a mate was a possibility. He wasn't interested in the power of a Wise One, and the duties only meant more ways to mess up and feel guiltier. But a lady was waiting for him? That piqued his interest more than some mysterious cavern far away. It wasn't as if he weren't interested in finding a mate, but...but what would that mean? He had been alone for so long that the thought of even courting a girl seemed more alien than swallowing a tornado, which was completely within his abilities.

No, he wasn't going to go off like an idiot and try to find his future wife. That would only be inviting trouble. Besides, Marit would not be able to travel for months now, and he must concentrate on the things he could handle here – raising puppies and feeding Marit. That he could do without using magic foolishly.

"Foolish?" the fairies seemed to say. "You are foolish to not try. Very well, we'll give you something to make you realize how foolish you have truly become."

Yeolani woke to the first mewling of a pup, but he didn't move, just staring at the low ceiling of the cavern behind the waterfall, comparing it to the one from his dream. He knew it would take hours for Marit to finish her birthing process, so he didn't rise to go see how she fared. He could lie here and consider all the imagery from his dream. Besides, he had other things to think about. Was there actually an aquifer someplace beneath the Land? What would he find there? Perhaps his Lady? How would he know this woman? She would probably be magical. He couldn't imagine a Wise One marrying anyone who wasn't also powerful, but how did you tell if someone were magical if there wasn't a flock of fairies following them around? Or was there something more? Well, he wasn't interested in exploring it right now, but the idea of a lady in his life might be enough to draw him out of these mountains and prevent him from turning completely to stone and ice.

Another sound from the back of the cavern made Yeolani lift his head. This did not sound the same as before. He really wanted to see how Marit was doing, but he also didn't want to frighten her. Maybe if he crawled in on his belly. Moving carefully, he made his way toward where he assumed his dog had made her nest, but in the flickering light of fairies and a fire, he couldn't be sure.

Then the entire cave echoed with the angry howl of a baby... a human baby. Yeolani froze right where he was. He recognized the sound from the uncomfortable time when his mother gave birth to his sister when he was just a six-year-old boy. That sound was unmistakable, and Yeolani couldn't move with the sudden demands that cry threw down on him like the entire mountain had collapsed. He stood up and looked around frantically. Every instinct in him demanded that he find the source of the wail. What alien magic was this?

He ran about the cavern, terrified as the screaming child made his head ring with its demands. Groping in the flickering dark Yeolani found a baby in the shadows up above where he'd most recently dropped his pack. He pulled the bundled child off the rock and brought it to the firelight with trembling hands.

The newborn glared at him from scrunched up eyes. Swaddled in tightly wrapped blankets, Yeolani couldn't guess how he had appeared here. What had the fairies done? He had heard of changelings – children taken from their cradles and replaced with something magical that would fade, but he never knew what became of the human child that was taken. Did fairies always do this, leaving them in a cavern for a reluctant magical hermit?

The baby's cries did not still as Yeolani began gingerly unwrapping the child. The infant was a boy, new enough to still have the umbilical cord attached. Frightened beyond thinking, Yeolani rewrapped the child and with unpracticed hands tried to rock the child as he'd seen his mother do, hoping to still his squawking. How could the fairies have done this to him?

Foolish? Was that the word? There could not be a single person on the planet less prepared to take care of a child than Yeolani. What must this baby's mother think? How was he going to do this? Magic, a must in this situation, wouldn't be enough. Magic wouldn't teach him how to dress and feed an infant. It wouldn't prevent him from dropping the baby or letting him get a rash. How do you keep a baby clean? Yeolani was no wet nurse. What was he to do?

"What's your name, little one?" Yeolani whispered, frightened by the sound of his own voice.

Nothing answered him but another whine from Marit's

side of the cavern and a squeak from the baby. Yeolani looked up at the ceiling, but all signs of the fairies had left him. Well, he would have to do magic until he figured out what to do with the changeling. This much was obvious. Greatly daring, he conjured a milk skin, warmed it in his hand, and then presented it to the baby who turned away from it and resumed crying.

Well, that wasn't going to work. Yeolani rocked the baby, but he kept up his protests until Yeolani was about to go crazy with stress. Then, with a suspicious peek, he checked the swaddling and found the real reason for the complaint. So, this is where the great Wise One magic would take him, cleaning up messes for an incontinent child. Yeolani held the child away from himself and wished the mess away, washed the offending bottom, and wrapped the babe up again without actually thinking about what he was doing but just hanging the child up in the air by his arms. When he was done, the child stopped crying and Yeolani set him back in his lap and tried his improvised milk skin again. This time it worked, and the child drank greedily.

Yeolani was the first one asleep, even before the baby, Marit, or any of her pups that night.

And the next morning, after a miserable time punctuated with similar struggles to get the child to drink, the problem had not gone away. Eventually, Yeolani gave the child a name: Nevai, named after his dead sister Nevia. At least with a name, he could use name magic to command the child to stop crying, go to sleep, or to eat when he didn't really want to. Marit's four pups were equally obedient but less bother for their mother. She at least had the instincts to deal with her brood and Yeolani didn't. Human babies woke every two hours demanding something, and Yeolani's patience wasn't nearly as well developed as Marit's. He wanted to go hunting but didn't dare leave the child alone for fear Nevai would wake while Yeolani was gone. If Yeolani magically required the infant to sleep, he fretted that he would addle Nevai's mind with too alien a schedule. He couldn't seem to remember how often his baby sister had cried for food, a change, or even how long she had slept. It was all too much of a mystery.

Finally, Yeolani realized magic wasn't going to solve his problem; he needed a human to ask for help. And the best human for that job would have to be Honiea. He held up Honiea's candle and waited patiently with Nevai fussing in his lap. The Queen of Healing came almost immediately and took one look at the cranky baby and a flustered, exhausted Yeolani and began to laugh uncontrollably.

"This isn't funny," Yeolani protested. "I'm about as prepared for this as a groundhog."

"Obviously," Honiea agreed, sitting down beside Yeolani on the cold rock floor, but she didn't even reach for the baby. "So, how did you come to be possessed of a child?"

With a grumpy sigh, Yeolani told her of the dream, leaving out the cistern and the talk of a Lady, but he admitted to his reluctance to use magic and the threat to make him truly feel foolish, which now he did. The fairies had their revenge, gave him the baby and abandoned him. Finally, Yeolani confessed his confusion and hope that she would be able to help him with his problem.

"And what on God's green earth makes you think I know anything about babies? If they aren't sick, I can't fix them. I was an only child, and Wise Ones can't have children," she admitted.

"What? You never said that when you were trying to convince me of both sides of the coin," Yeolani protested.

"It slipped my mind," Honiea replied sheepishly. "And it

wasn't as if you would notice. You being a father seemed far down the list of your ambitions. Does this offend you?"

Yeolani's snort must have been mixed with disgust as well as pure hilarity, and it startled the baby. "I'm the last person in the Land who should be a parent. So, why on God's green earth did the fairies make me into one? Can I give him back? Can I pass him onto someone else who wants him? Is there some desperate mother somewhere cursing fairies for me, wanting her child back?"

Honiea shook her head sagely, ignoring his ire. "I think the fairies did something wonderful for you. You were being foolish for ignoring your magic, and this baby will force you to see that. You won't be able to pawn this responsibility off on anyone else because it is now a part of your Seeking. It will drive you back into the world, and for the child's sake, not your own. You will learn discretion with magic and love for those you serve. I will not take it from you. The most I will tell you is the baby is cranky because you're not burping him. He'll tell you that if you listen to his mind."

Then, without even saying goodbye, Honiea disappeared.

Yeolani let his head drop in frustration and realized that everyone in his life probably had the right of it. He picked up the baby and held him out at arm's length, undergoing the serious stare of the barely focusing eyes and listening to the mind behind them. He felt the uncomfortable tightness in Nevai's gut, the stress that must be a reflection of Yeolani's own distress and an ethereal thought that he loved this man who was holding him up like some strange animal. Nevai loved Yeolani? The thoughts weren't verbalized; Nevai was too young for words, but like Marit, his thoughts were emotional and loving.

"I'm sorry, baby. I wasn't listening. How can I help you?" Yeolani thought back to the baby. There was no impression of words, but mostly longing. Carefully Yeolani put Nevai against his shoulder and began patting gently like he'd seen his mother do long ago. It worked, and Yeolani got a smelly mess down his shoulder but also a wave of relief from Nevai's mind. Yeolani magically disappeared the mess and patted Nevai's back until they both fell asleep.

The next morning Yeolani made a decision and told Marit, just in case. "I need to go to town to learn more about how to care for babies. Or find Nevai's mother. It's five hours walk one way so I can't take the baby unless I go faster, which means I go by magic. Will you be fine with your babies while I'm gone?"

Marit gave him a placid look and a single thump of her tail.

"Yes, I know. Leave plenty of food, and you'll do the rest," he interpreted it. "Do you think I could conjure a horse? It would go faster, but I've never been a rider. I'd get more respect in town if I had a horse, and perhaps it's a skill I need to learn. Yes, I'll try that. And what about Nevai? I'll take him with me, but how? Invisible? No, I don't want to be flashy, and how would I explain if he was to wake up and let out one of his famous howls and people hear that? No, I'll carry him the way any normal person does. I'll make a pack and make do."

Having met Marit's approval, Yeolani began to do his conjuring. He made a woven basket for his back where he could perch Nevai, cover him up, and include all the things a normal parent would carry for a trip with a baby, things he had been conjuring at the need. With Nevai at ease asleep inside, he packed in around the baby and magically added a bit of warmth in case the weather grew too bitter, and then put his own arms through the straps and stepped outside the cave for the next step.

A horse. Growing up in Simten, he had always envied the few people rich enough to own a horse. Horses meant travel, adventure, and freedom. The mayor had one and often traveled to neighboring towns, and Yeolani had watched with jealousy. Now, faced with giving himself that opportunity, he realized he wasn't actually prepared. A real horse would buck him off as an inexperienced rider, and he didn't want to risk hurting Nevai with this experiment. Carefully, Yeolani removed the pack and left the baby against the door of the cave and then thought of what kind of steed would fit him. The King of the Plains probably would have a grand golden stallion, but Yeolani the sailor turned hunter and erstwhile father needed something safer like an old placid gelding accustomed to carts more than riders.

Yeolani put thought into action and conjured a simple horse, brown and not too tall, but sturdy with a winter coat in need of a brush. He added a saddle that he would have been made of hides he had hunted. He practiced the actual skill of putting the equipment on the magically stilled horse. Then greatly daring, Yeolani hoisted himself into his saddle. The horse didn't stir so Yeolani slid back out of the seat, back and forth a few more times before he felt safe enough to include the baby. Nevai didn't give a single peep as Yeolani pulled himself into the saddle and kicked the steed into a careful walk west toward town.

10

AUCTIONED

*I*t might have been innate instinct or part of being the King of the Plains, but Yeolani felt very comfortable in the saddle. Part of him recognized this sensation from his first dream as a Wise One, racing through the forest at a pace that only a rider could achieve. He experimented with kicking the horse into a canter and then a trot. The snowy landscape blew past him, and he reveled in it. If he wanted, he could probably change the horse into a grander creature and encouraged a flat-out gallop, but why bother. It might wake the baby, and he didn't need that kind of attention.

He had to stop once to feed Nevai, who woke naturally and squalled at the jostling, but once fed, he fell back into his nap and the gentle motion of the horse's gait probably lulled him more quickly than otherwise. By noon, Yeolani began to recognize the indications of the town with a sign labeling it Edgewood. The cobbled streets brimmed with warehouses full of wood from the forest and goods from the storage houses for the townsfolk. It wasn't a large town, probably about the size of

Simten, and boasted a few sizable farms about the area, but most of its livelihood came from the forest.

He rode through the main part of town, looking for an inn or a market open where women might gather, but didn't find much. Where was everyone? Of course, with the cold, he didn't wonder that most townsfolk wanted to be inside, but literally, no one was walking the streets. Finally, he had to dismount, stiff and sore from his novice ride, and went into the inn seeking someone with whom to speak.

"They's all at the auction," said a drudge who tended the fire in the otherwise empty common room.

"Where is this auction?" Yeolani asked and got a wave in the general direction of the north end of town.

Yeolani returned to his horse and walked him down to the great hay barn at the end of the road. The snow at the edge of the street had been trampled as if every citizen of the town had decided to come to this barn all at the same time, so Yeolani left his horse outside and approached the closed doors hoping no one thought he was breaking and entering. His mind moving ahead of him told him this was where most everyone had gathered.

However, he couldn't have predicted what he saw there. All the men of the town and quite a few women as well, all in their best dress, had gathered. Lanterns hung from the hayloft, and everyone sat or stood beyond the hay bales arranged in a large circle. In the center, a gentleman, dressed as the mayor of Simten would have done, stood with his arms up, speaking to the gathered townsfolk. Just beyond him, a pretty young woman with chestnut hair and pale skin also stood in what was probably her best dress, a clean apron and a leather bodice with a carefully stitched pattern on it. She had a humble look to her, with her hands neatly folded before her and head down to look at her farm hardened boots. She seemed almost ashamed to be here at this point. They must be auctioning off her farm.

"...Comes with nineteen milk cows and a hundred acres cleared, as well as twelve more in the forest. You've seen the home: a good solid cabin with room to expand as the children come. The fencing needs repair, but the land's flat and dry. The well's adequate. Three generations have lived there and more as likely to come," called the gentleman conducting the meeting.

Yeolani had guessed right; they were auctioning a farm off. But why did the girl look so distressed? Yeolani wished she would look up, for she was pretty, and he wanted to see her eyes. Was she the heir to the farm and found it too big a job without a man in the house? Had her father died and she had no brothers? No husband? She might be a bit young for a man in her house, but she certainly was attractive enough to have suitors lining up, and if a farm might come as a dowry with the marriage, she would be a fine catch.

The auctioneer continued. "And with the farm comes the daughter. She'll work hard and be a healthy mother," he barked out, and Yeolani felt his heart sinking. She wasn't being courted, she was being sold as a slave, right along with her cows and cabin.

As if she heard his thoughts of horror, the girl lifted her head and looked directly at Yeolani across the open ring. He felt like he had been struck by lightning. Her eyes flashed green and blue, one of each, and it pierced his heart. What had the fairies said about a lady? Well, this was a woman that would put him in awe. Just with her glance, he felt his knees grow weak. Part of him was horrified at what was happening to her and the other part of him wished suddenly that he was rich enough to buy her, farm and all. It wasn't the place of a Wise One, he reminded himself, for this was not a magical lady.

"She's a hard worker, a comely catch, and a maid as well," the gentleman babbled, making Yeolani's ears red with embarrassment at this description. "She'll do as she's told, milk the cows, bear your children, and never give you a moment's grief, won't you, Rashel?"

Rashel? Had Yeolani heard the name before? He couldn't recall where. That name meant something to him, but he didn't get the chance to remember, for Nevai decided just then to let out his customary howl to announce his presence. Yeolani started, and the audience all turned toward him, laughing as he scrambled to get out of the straps of the bag to attend to the baby. By the time he'd got Nevai out of the contraption, the girl had looked away and the auction continued. Her spell over him was broken.

Yeolani fed Nevai while the auction began bidding, and he watched grimly as old, hardened men and younger drunk and bawdy men threw offers out to be considered. Some asked to come inspect Rashel, who endured their ogling her a bit, but her glare gave many of them pause.

One man asked a bold question, "So what happened to your father and your brother? Did you drive them off?"

Rashel looked back down at her feet, the humble part back in control. "My father drove Arvid off, and I've not heard from him since. My father simply died in the forest, so I'm... I'm the last. I didn't drive anyone off," she explained in a voice that put shivers down Yeolani's back. So that's where he had heard her name. His old friend, Arvid, the one almost crushed by the tree, he must have mentioned his little sister.

"Shall we let the bidding begin again?" the auctioneer called. "Only serious offers this time, please; and if you've already got a wife, see that you get her approval first." That comment brought chuckles. Rashel's strange eyes flashed with irritation, but Yeolani wanted to vomit at the jokes at her expense.

This warning brought reasonable bids this time, and only two men really came to the fore, one a huge, hard-looking man with a beard past his shoulders and a heavy hand. Rashel bravely looked at him as he offered to buy the farm since his own sat right next to hers. He offered to pay for it with the proceeds of a mine in the mountains that brought out iron and tin. The other man, an oldster, obviously not interested in the girl for sexual reasons, seemed more interested in Rashel as a housekeeper or nurse. He offered to sell water rights to the town as well as several head of fine horses and his shop in the town. His son would take over the farm to work it. There was little in the way of cash to buy such a large farm and the woman who went with it. If she hadn't been part of the deal, more men would have participated and just absorbed the land into their own, but because she was tied to it, they had to consider her as part of the assets even if she weren't sellable like the cattle. Or maybe she was?

Then the younger, rough man offered to sell off his own farm and take over the new one against the debts Rashel's farm owed. "You know I need a woman for my kids, and she's healthy," he reasoned, and Yeolani cringed at that fate. Wife to a man with half a dozen kids already, worked to the bone to service a man and run a farm that should be hers. Rashel didn't look happy with this arrangement, but it might be better than becoming the nursemaid for a feeble old shopkeeper. The oldster looked like he would argue against that as well.

"I've got gold," Yeolani heard himself calling out, and it started Nevai into squawking again. "And a baby that needs a mother. I'll pay straight mined gold."

Now, how foolish was he being?

The crowd all turned back to him, and Yeolani felt like he

could melt with embarrassment into the earth at his feet. What was he doing bidding in this awful auction? He couldn't marry this girl, let alone 'own' her as a nursemaid, and while Nevai needed a mother, this was ridiculous. He could conjure himself the gold, but these people wouldn't know what to do with it. What was he thinking?

"Where's the child's mother?" the auctioneer called.

Yeolani couldn't think of what to say to that. He felt compelled to speak the truth, but to do the whole truth would just frighten everyone. He opened his mouth to lie, but abruptly found he couldn't. He struggled a bit with the strange loss of words before he came out with one word.

"Gone," he replied. Apparently, being a Wise One, flat out lying seemed impossible for him. "He's only days old, and I cannot raise him myself. I know nothing about children, but I... I'll pay for someone to help me."

"And what's your name, stranger, and from where do you hail?" asked the younger bidder who didn't like this new competition.

"Simten," Yeolani replied, completely ignoring the requested name. "I used to be a fisherman, but now...now I've got this child and I came looking for someone to help me."

"We don't trust you or your gold," grumbled the elder of the bidders.

Yeolani could not fathom how he had got himself in this situation, but he caught the eye of the girl through the protesting and suspicious crowd, and suddenly he wanted to slow down time. He wanted the baby to still, the townsfolk to disappear, and to take the time to actually get Rashel's thoughts on the matter. She was a victim in this travesty of an auction and deserved to be heard. Something magical and mercurial - fairies maybe - had driven Yeolani to this impasse, and he needed to think it through. He did not feel right invading Rashel's private thoughts, but he needed time to consider and actually do something carefully planned and not driven by impulse.

So, he did what he wanted. Yeolani froze time. Nevai grew quiet, as well as the squabbling townsfolk. Everyone stood like statues, mouths open in silent protest, unaware of their change of state. It almost frightened Yeolani at the power he had just invoked, but he would take advantage of it. Still carrying the baby against his shoulder, he wove his way through the bales of hay toward Rashel who watched him. Deliberately, he had left her out of his freezing spell, though her fear held her in place more than his magic.

Rashel's two-toned eyes fascinated Yeolani, and he felt distracted a little too much, but he shook his head and tried to focus while his spell lasted. There was only so much time, and he had much to say and learn. He stepped past the auctioneer and faced her with trepidation. He had never revealed himself as a magician this much before, not even in his confrontations at East.

"Rashel, I know your brother, Arvid. I used to work with him in the forest. He once told me the fairies protected you. I'm magic, as you can see, and I think they wanted me to help you, but I want to know what you want in this situation."

"Arvid? You know where he is? He left so many years ago..." she whispered, revealing her concern for her brother, not for her own predicament.

"Yes," Yeolani admitted. "Seven years ago. I haven't seen him since I left. I don't know if he's alive. Would you like me to find him for you?"

Rashel's polished chestnut hair shifted in the lanterns as she shook her head. "No, he wanted his freedom. He left when our father disowned him. He shouldn't come back here and be bound to a farm he didn't want. I thank you for the offer, but Arvid has his freedom."

"Then, what can I do for you?" Yeolani insisted. "You obviously don't want to be owned...or to marry these men."

Rashel's eyes grew huge with horror, realizing this magical stranger might know how upset she felt at her problem. Did she think he was reading her mind? Yeolani would never do so without her permission, but he could not reassure her of that without making the situation worse.

"Norton," she nodded toward the younger of the serious bidders, the huge burly man with children who needed a mother, "he...he's got a reputation for being violent. He probably killed his first wife, and the second has left him. He'll beat me. And he owns most of the debts against the farm. He might still get the farm by simply foreclosing, but then there would be nothing for me. The townsfolk don't want that to happen. That's why they tied me to the property, hoping to make a place for me. They'd probably like to see me taken care of, and they think that by marrying me off to him, it will solve both problems. The farm is simply too big and too indebted to buy. I cannot run it alone."

"And what of the old man?" Yeolani asked. "You don't want to run his shop and have the farm leave you completely, do you?"

"It is the better of my options, but I doubt he can do it. His son doesn't want to take over my farm. His son would rather keep the shop and tend to his father himself. I think the old gentleman, Hodge – he is doing it out of pity for me and to thwart Norton. You see, Norton's first wife was Hodge's daughter, and he can't get over her death, so he is trying to buy my farm to spite Norton."

"And what do you want, Rashel? The fairies were

concerned enough to send me to you," Yeolani pointed out with all sincerity.

The girl looked around the crowded barn as if afraid that all these villagers would suddenly reanimate and catch her in confessing her thoughts. She took a great steadying breath and a hundred heartbeats before she could verbalize her secret desires.

"I...I would be content if I could run the farm myself, but I can't. I've tried for the last year. I could leave it to the town and walk away into the forest. I would let the fairies follow me and die content. I...I..." Her eyes filled with tears, blending the blue and green into a silvery haze that put its spell on Yeolani completely.

"May I give you another option?" he whispered, suddenly gentler than he'd ever been, even with Marit or Nevai. "As I said, I have gold. I can pay off the debts against the farm. I can do the repairs and help you run the farm. Magic can do all of this. The one thing magic cannot do is raise a baby. I'm completely out of my depth. If you will raise Nevai, I will see that the farm is worked and maintained. If the townsfolk will allow you to be the landowner, having a voice in this auction, would you be willing to do this?"

Her stunned silence made him wonder if she had joined the townsfolk with his freezing spell. Rashel trembled there for a bit and then unexpectedly looked over at the baby he still held asleep against his shoulder. Without asking, she drew Nevai away from him and cradled him with far more natural instinct than Yeolani possessed, rocking and cooing at the baby in his sleep. "A boy?" she asked with delight, the tears still on the verge of falling but from a different cause. "What's his name again?"

"Nevai. The fairies gave him to me. He's not mine," he reassured her. For some reason, it seemed important that she should know. "I think they gave him to me so I could give him to you. Not that you need more responsibilities."

At the word responsibilities, Rashel looked up with alarm, realizing there could be more implied in Yeolani's offer. "I would raise the boy, you would pay off the debts and run the farm, and I would...I would..."

"No, I will not even live there. My magic makes many demands on me, and I will often be away. You will not be my wife, though the townsfolk might feel free to think that. Magic will do most of the work on the farm, but I assure you that it will be well within your abilities to raise this child and run the farm yourself, without having me underfoot."

Rashel blushed with the awkwardness of the conversation, and Yeolani heard in her public thoughts that she thought she owed him something for the option. "Oh, but sir, surely there is more I can do. It's such a generous offer that..."

Yeolani interrupted her. "No, my lady, you must not do more than that. It is not right what they are doing to you, and it would not be right for me to do the same as them, treating you as part of..of...spoils I've won. You deserve to fall in love and find someone you want to spend your life with, not a magician. I feel you will be a perfect mother, and if we can get the townsfolk to agree, we can shake hands on it."

Rashel looked again over the audience still suspended in time, and she hastily gave Nevai back to him. "They won't agree if they suspect there is magic here. They cannot know that the farm is run with magic. They're so suspicious. Can you do it without them knowing it's magic?"

Yeolani nodded reassuringly and then smiled. "I'll do what it takes to be seen about the farm. It shouldn't be a problem. Rashel, I will try to do anything if it helps you."

And he meant it. A bit of him, bitterly frustrated with magic at that moment, wanted to fall in love with Rashel and be as other men, but he would only be playing at having a wife, a child, a farm. Now he began to see how Honiea had warned him, and she hadn't even mentioned love when she introduced the two sides of the coin. He knew instinctively that it would be wrong to court Rashel. She wasn't a Wise One, and somewhere out there in the world was a Lady like the fairies had insisted.

Without actually planning what he would do next, Yeolani carried Nevai back across the auction boards, back to where he stood when he froze time. He turned back so he faced Rashel once again. Across the room, she carefully schooled her features and nodded her preparation as well.

Then Yeolani relaxed his grip on the magic. Since they had no clue they had been frozen in time, the auction house began where it had started, into the interrupted protests and demands for him to show his gold if he were going to make a credible offer. Yeolani couldn't answer all the calls, and Nevai was crying in the abrupt bedlam. As if she existed in her own serene bubble, Rashel reached out for the arm of the auctioneer and whispered a few words in his ear while Yeolani endured the tide of townsfolk questions and curiosity.

Cooperatively, the auctioneer shouted down the crowd and got control back of his audience. "Gentlemen, come now. We've three offers on the table," he summarized. "All of them seem viable, except the stranger, until the gold has been witnessed. Best offer wins. We know Norton and Hodge's offer, but we do not know you, sir. We will only hear you after you clear your offering."

Yeolani sighed in relief that they would at least listen to his proposition, that superstition and distrust of the unknown would not force them to reject him out of hand. "How much is the cost of the debts against the farm?" he asked.

The auctioneer looked over at a few of the men who had not participated in the bidding, got their approving nod, and then replied, "Three weight of gold to Norton for what he's done to keep the farm going and another six for the purchase of the farm itself, to be held in trust if you abandon the girl."

"In coined or raw ore?" Yeolani asked as he tried to convert their measures into barrels of fish like he had learned as a boy.

"Either," the auctioneer replied. "But we'll have to melt down raw ore for purity before. However, I'd pay off Norton in coin if you will." He gave the irritable bidder a sideways glance to be sure that the man would appreciate that effort."

"Don't bother," Norton growled. "This young whelp doesn't have a sliver of silver, let alone gold. Why bother with the bid?"

The auctioneer brushed aside the protest. "He's as much right as anyone else. Now, young man, where's your gold?"

Yeolani smiled and then, greatly daring, walked over to Rashel and handed the baby to her. Then he reached into Nevai's pack and conjured a fistful of coins into a leather pouch at the bottom of the bag even as he put it down to 'search' inside. "This isn't all I've access to, but I didn't come to town today planning to buy a farm. The rest, I can get within a day," he explained as he brought out the pouch with enough heft to impress without seeming suspicious as stolen gold. No one carried around that kind of coin, but he wanted to appear like a legitimate merchant.

The auctioneer and the town elders all gathered around as Yeolani set the purse down on a bale of hay, allowing them to open it up and test the quality of the coins he had conjured. Yeolani had seen coins at the various taverns and inns he encountered but never had coin himself, having always traded fish, furs, or other goods for what he needed. Now, he'd conjured flat, faceless gold, some thick and almost slabs, and then a few thin wafers of the stuff. He knew that deep under the ground, not far up the creek in which he spent the winter, pure, not conjured, gold waited to be discovered. If need be, he could bring someone up the valley to see his 'source'.

"Does this satisfy the debt against the farm?" asked the auctioneer, looking toward Norton, and he plopped twelve fat coins in Norton's hand.

The sour look on the bidder's face deepened, but he obediently inspected the coins, testing each one carefully in his teeth to be sure they weren't lead inside. He looked jealously over at Rashel who couldn't care less about the negotiations. Instead, she was making delighted faces at the baby, caressing his soft head and reveling in every gurgle Nevai might give her. Norton would never be content with this upstart owning the farm and woman that he coveted.

Norton reluctantly nodded. "The gold's good, but we can still choose differently. He's a stranger. He could be a thief. I've yet to hear how he came to have so much wealth. Stranger, what have you to say for yourself?"

"Yes," agreed Hodge, the older bidder. "We've not heard of you. What's your reputation? Who will speak for you? How will we know that you won't abandon your babe and never return, leaving Rashel in the same predicament but with a child as well?"

Yeolani didn't know quite how to answer. No one knew him truly except for Honiea and Vamilion. Having two Wise Ones come to witness for him would hardly help the situation. He also doubted his peers would approve of what he was doing right now. Honiea had already insisted that the baby could not be pawned off, and she might interpret this attempt to help Rashel as exactly that. Yeolani felt sure they would reject his implied relationship with the girl as well. Yeolani was about to ask the townsfolk what kind of proof they would believe when Rashel unexpectedly spoke up.

"My brother, Arvid, he spoke very highly of him, didn't he, sir?"

Yeolani's eyes bugged for a moment, but when he couldn't actually get his mouth to agree to the lie, he was able to master himself. He did manage to nod and smile, giving everyone the impression that he was saying yes. "I knew her brother, Arvid. We worked together on a lumber crew a few years back, and that's where I heard of Rashel." That much was honest so he could say the words.

"And what's your name, sir?" one of the townsfolk finally asked.

This time Yeolani stopped himself and seriously considered. Now, he knew he would have to decide: truly abandon his given name or hide the fact that it really was his name and that he was a magician. He took a careful breath and looked Rashel in the eye. She would be just as curious and giving anything but the truth to her seemed wrong. He made up his mind looking her in the blue and green eyes.

"You may call me Yeolani."

"Well, Master Yeolani," Norton ground the title in his mouth, mashing it with sarcasm, "how are we to know you won't abandon her.

Yeolani glared at Norton before he spoke. "I would never leave my baby, and I won't leave Rashel..." but he paused as he sensed something changing on him. An oath? That's what he was doing, and if he finished the statement, he would put himself into the royal clothing of the King of the Plains. He cursed under his breath and felt the shifting stop, hopefully without anyone noticing. At least he hadn't lost the ability to cuss like a sailor along with his ability to lie. Another thing that hadn't come up in Honiea's two sides of a coin conversation.

"And you'll marry her?" The auctioneer had just assumed he had finished his earlier sentence.

In alarm at the suggestion, Yeolani stilled his mind a moment and thought through his situation. The people in the village would expect him to marry her, but Rashel already knew he had no intention of binding her that way. This was a business arrangement only, but Yeolani suspected the townsfolk would lynch him if he refused to marry her. He didn't dare tell them blatantly that he would not marry her or the deal was off. On the other hand, with this sudden inability to lie, he couldn't tell them he would marry her, for that would be either an oath or a lie. He had to somehow make them assume one thing without making an oath that would do the other.

Then an idea came to him, an enlightened one, and he realized that Wise One magic would provide him answers if he waited long enough. "Sirs," he said carefully, with a grieved look on his face. "My baby is only days old. He has no mother for a reason. I cannot think of giving him a mother so soon. Maybe one day..." and he left it at that.

Let them assume that the baby's mother, the love of his life, had died in childbirth. Of course, it would take a while for Yeolani to even consider marrying. He became the grieving widower in the villagers' eyes, and no one protested. They would be gentlemen and not make any demands on him or Rashel, allowing him to mourn for a respectable time.

"Very well," called the auctioneer. "We have three viable options on the board. Rashel, any of these three meet our requirements, so you do have a voice in this, but you must choose one of them."

No one had any doubt about Rashel's vote. She refused to look up, having eyes only for the baby, but she nodded her agreement and then said, "I choose Master Yeolani."

The converted hay barn erupted in cheers and groans, depending on which bidder they supported. Random people came up to Yeolani, shaking his hand and congratulating him with rough slaps on the back. Hodge hobbled over and awkwardly gave him his approval with a mix of relief and suspicion still lingering in his eyes. Yeolani did his best to reassure him, but he could not quite draw his attention from Rashel on the far side of the room, now surrounded by admiring women who also wanted to hold the baby. There were many types of magic, Yeolani realized, and some he just did not possess.

Norton was not at all pleased and when he got his chance to speak to Yeolani, his handshake crushed and his growling voice threatened more than his words. "I know what you did there," the man scowled. "If you so much as sneeze, get drunk, or miss a single day's milking, I'm going to know, and I'll be ready. You will not have her."

Yeolani stiffened at the awkward threat, and he didn't hesitate to investigate Norton's cryptic words. Yeolani plunged his mind into the widower's and found he had a shield over his thoughts that, while not impossible to climb, would take more magic than he dared attempt in this public place. Instead, he gave back as good as he got.

"And if you so much as sneeze, move a fence post, or lift a hand to another person, I will know, and I will act." He then retrieved his aching hand and brushed rudely past the man toward Rashel and began packing up the baby's things. He didn't want to remain here any longer, and he desperately needed to think, plan, and understand what he had just done.

11

FARM KEEPING

*I*t would take a day or two, but Yeolani felt he could fix the farm and set up a pattern of magic that would protect Rashel from suspicion. He had followed her to the farm just east of town, putting her up on the horse's saddle, and they had talked, but not about their plans. Too many people might have a chance to overhear them on the well-traveled road. Instead, he had told her all he could remember of Arvid, including the crushing tree, and he didn't hesitate to tell her of Honiea's help.

In turn, Rashel revealed to him all the struggles she had endured since her father died. The cows she could milk, for that had always been her responsibility since Arvid left, but she couldn't move the hay or repair the roof and the crumbling well. In spring, when she would have to sow seed for fodder, she knew that would be beyond her abilities and her cattle would starve. Up till now, she had survived on the excess stores from earlier years, judiciously borrowing from Norton and the help of her neighbors bringing in the harvest her father had planted just before his death the spring before.

"Do you miss him?" Yeolani asked, thinking of how he hadn't long mourned his father, just the fact that he had been the means of removing him from the world.

Rashel obviously felt reluctant to answer, and when she did, her voice was cold. "I miss the security he brought, but it's hard to forgive him for what he did to drive Arvid away."

Were all father's that difficult, Yeolani wondered? No, he could not imagine Vamilion being anything but patient and kind. And he had every intention of being a good father for Nevai even if he could not be there every step of the way. And as the farm finally came into view, with the sun setting beyond it, Yeolani recognized that he might have to be at the farm more than he should.

The fences tilted, the roof slats rotted under a thick layer of moss, and the window glazing looked like it might pop every pane with the least puff of wind. He would have to repair the chimney, the fences, and the well. This he could tell before he even made it inside the tiny, little cabin that rivaled Gil's in size but not in comfort. The barn was a little better, but its nearly empty hayloft spoke volumes, and he doubted nineteen cows could continue the winter on what was left, let alone make it until harvest.

"What do you do with your milk?" Yeolani asked carefully, hopefully changing the subject away from wayward fathers.

"If I've got the time, I sell it in town, but recently I've not been able to do that, so I make cheese and butter, which I don't have to take to town daily," Rashel explained. "With a baby, I'll probably continue that. The income is about the same, and I don't have to go into town so often. But with a horse..."

"The horse goes with the farm," he assured her, "but you probably won't want to go to town regularly anyway. The more you avoid people asking questions about me, the better."

Once they'd arrived, without even planning it, they divided

the chores; Yeolani took the horse to the barn and Rashel took the baby to the house. He made a survey of the necessary work as he fed the cows and recognized that they needed to be milked. He might as well set up a pattern of magic right now. He closed his eyes to concentrate and worked his skills to fill the waiting buckets. It took him only minutes, and then he had to consider how he could do this twice a day from a distance. He thought about the patterns of the days, and briefly, he felt the whole world spinning beneath his feet. He crafted a strand of time and tied a knot of magic in it at dusk and dawn. Rashel found him there sitting on a milking stool and didn't disturb him. He came out of his trance a moment later and looked up to smile at her.

"I've set up a milking schedule of sorts. If neither you nor I are able to be here for the milking, it will happen automatically, but you must have each cow in their pens when the sun rises or sets or it won't happen. If not, then you'll have to milk by hand. Also, the milk will be in these barrels, if that's all right."

Rashel looked around the barn, at the fed cattle, the cooling milk, and smiled. "I'd better get it ready for the morning. There's supper on the hearth; the baby's fed and asleep. Go in and make yourself comfortable."

Inside Yeolani saw the simple cabin with two beds in the darker end of the room with a cradle in between them, both freshly laid out. On the hearth, she had set a bowl of soup and a hunk of her cheese, which Yeolani gathered up and ate as he surveyed the room's common areas. A cupboard and a washboard, large table, and two benches filled up the entire area. He couldn't imagine living here as a family now. His home at Simten or Gil's had been cheerier, and his cave under the waterfall had more light. Without thinking about it he, conjured several more lamps and set one in each of the windows.

He found the trap door down into the cellar and looked at the food stored there. He realized that Rashel must have gardened for her food. Potatoes, onions, and carrots constituted all the vegetables. There was no meat in the larder, just cheese and nuts supplemented that food. She didn't even have flour to make bread. He looked through empty barrels and hoped she wouldn't protest if he filled them with flour, rye, barley, and corn. Dried peas, beans, and lentils would help too. How had she survived so long?

After he finished eating and adding to her stores, Yeolani went back out to the barn to talk with her and found her pressing the gathered milk through a cloth and then turning the thickened material left into molds. It only took him a moment to recognize how to do the process, and Yeolani joined in, pressing the liquid out, leaving the whey in the cloth that she'd lay over pots on the far side of the barn. He loved learning these kinds of things, for he never knew when some bit of knowledge would come in handy in his wanderings.

"How long does it usually take you to do the nightly milking and the pressing for each evening?" he asked as they worked.

"About two hours, but I can't always do this kind of cheese. In the morning I do butter instead, and sometimes, if the milk amounts are low because I've had to cast off some, I make a different cheese which takes longer."

"And do you have any meat?"

She looked up at him, her face sweaty, with her hair clinging to her smile. "If I could hunt, yes, but I cannot. No, I can sometimes trade cheese for a chicken or a bit of beef. But it takes longer to cook, and I don't have wood enough to cook the cheese, let alone my own food."

"Where's your woodpile? Wood, that I can do," he replied swiftly.

She pointed toward a haphazardly stacked pile of what Yeolani had assumed was broken siding and other abandoned carpentry efforts. He clucked his tongue and conjured a heaping stack of neatly split wood. Rashel's mouth dropped open, and she straightened up with her arms covered with milky residue.

"How do you do that?" she asked simply. "I've heard of magic, but the fairies are the only thing I've actually seen of it... till you."

Yeolani spent the rest of the evening trying to explain the act of conjuring, and while she understood in principle, it didn't make any sense to her until he tapped into her mind and found her interest in gardening.

"Magic is like planting a garden. I want something, like a carrot, so I ask the earth to turn the minerals in the earth into the shape, texture, and essence of a carrot. Magic speeds up that process....and it works on more than living things too. I asked the earth for gold for the auction and essentially magic grew gold for me."

"Is 'growing' things like this all you can do?" she asked with sincere curiosity.

By now they were back in the cabin, washing her milk pails and presses with water he conjured into her water barrel rather than running to the crumbling well that he would have to mend in the morning. With a finger, he traced the glazing in the window above the wash tub and the lead resealed around the glass pieces as he replied.

"No, but it is the most impressive and helpful...flashy. I'm trying to not be flashy. I could have come into town on a grand charger, dressed like a king, but I'm simpler than that. Um, what else? I've called and used tornadoes. I can read minds and freeze time. Overall, I've not been a magician for very long, which is why I've not tried many things. It takes time to get adept at this magic, and I've messed up quite a bit."

"How so?" Rashel asked simply. "You seem pretty careful, and you've not done anything wrong with your magic that I've seen."

Yeolani sighed in regret. "Magic here in the Land cannot be evil...at least when used by me and my friends. I cannot even lie to you. I've tried to cuss, but it doesn't come out very well. Yet, because of my magic, I started a pitched battle in a city south of here and hundreds of people probably died because of my foolishness. I was only trying to help, but I ruined more than I assisted. Then I made the mistake of thinking I could walk away from my magic, leaving all the people alone and then I wouldn't hurt things. That's why the fairies gave me Nevai. They knew that having magic wouldn't help me raising him, that I would have to come back to civilization in order to get help. They sent me to you. You, I can help and hopefully not harm with my magic."

"Then thank the magic that brought you here," she whispered gently.

It had been a tremendously long day, and they wordlessly agreed, now that the work was done, that they needed to go to bed. This led to an awkward silence until Yeolani offered to go back to his cavern, but Rashel rejected that. "Nevai will be up every two hours. We can take shifts. It's always easier with two. You can sleep in my father's bed...and take the first shift."

Yeolani nodded, numb with wonder at how he'd gone from a hermit in the mountains to a farmer with a family in essentially a few days. How had magic done this to him? As he moved to the bed and sat down to pull off his boots, he realized he still needed privacy, and he conjured a screen between the two beds and lowered the lamps in the windows.

On the far side of the screen, Rashel's voice was gentle. "Thank you, sir."

"Thank you, ma'am," he replied, and before he could cringe at how formal they were between each other, he'd drifted off to sleep.

At dawn, after a night punctuated with Nevai's interruptions, neither of them felt well-rested, but the day was calling. Yeolani's mind dove in immediately. He repaired the travesty of an outhouse while he used it, contacted Marit's mind in the cave far away, refreshed her food and water, and then checked to see if his milking system was working, all within minutes of waking.

Throughout the day, he made a point of being seen out in the barnyard, lugging pails and such. The road just beyond the farm seemed well-traveled, and many people walking by must have heard about his purchase at the auction and waved to him. He mended the well at the same time that he climbed up on the cabin roof to scrape off the moss by hand rather than magic. Everyone who passed by would only see a farmer hard at work on his property and not think of the magic that went on elsewhere. The ground of the hay field was frozen right now, but underneath he easily surveyed it for noxious weeds and prepared its soil content with fish parts as he'd seen in Simten. The improvements wouldn't be noticed until spring. He mended the fence by hand while he magically lined the inside of the well and dug it deeper in order to reach better water. The crumbling chimney he lined from within at the same time he physically cleaned it out from outside where everyone could see him.

He also worked with Rashel, pressing cheese, feeding cattle, cooking meals, and bringing in stores, all while keeping an eye on Nevai and tending to his needs. It was an idyllic world Yeolani could easily fall into, but he knew it was just another kind of hermit-life he was creating, albeit far more rewarding than being alone in a cave. He knew a different, grander cave, the one from his dream, awaited his investigation and that he would need to find it.

Then there was the girl. Rashel's movements fascinated him, and he found himself staring rudely sometimes. He loved the play of her eyes, the flash of light against her shiny braid, or the wispy shorter strands that clung to her sweaty face as she worked. She was the first woman he had ever considered courting, and now, as a magician, she was out of bounds, he was sure. If he had found Rashel before Honiea came with her offer of magic, he would have quite likely not even touched his Heart Stone.

Therefore, Rashel was dangerous.

By dusk of his second day with Rashel, Yeolani felt satisfied that he had finished all he really needed to do to set the farm in order. Yet, he harbored a strange discontent. He wanted to speak with Honiea and Vamilion, and at the same time, he never wanted to leave this home again. Most of the vitally urgent needs on the farm had been met. Rashel had made bread for the first time, she claimed, in over a year because she now had the time and means. While she served the fine meal she had made, he shared with her the final plans for his departure. He must leave.

"I've got to keep moving on, but I'll be back every few days. I don't want to leave you without a way to reach me. I have two things for you here." He conjured a thick white candle and a muddy brown crystal shaft like the one he found in his dream.

"The candle is to call Honiea. I've told you how she healed your brother. She is a magician of great power, but her best gifts are in healing. If either Nevai or you are hurt or sick, just light the candle and hold it up. She will come and heal you. She's seen the baby already and will come instantly."

Rashel put the candle on the mantle above the fire for safe keeping and then nodded toward the crystal. "That's not natural," she observed. "I've never seen anything like it."

"I have," he assured her. "These crystals grow like weeds in a cavern deep under the plains, of all places. I've seen them there, and they fascinate me, so I'm putting a spell on this one. It will work like the candle does for Honiea. I will come the moment you touch it."

"What if someone comes here, looking for you?" she pointed out logically. "I cannot call you and have you arriving magically here at the table."

Yeolani sighed, wondering about a solution, but before he could dredge one up, Rashel had her own suggestion. "I'll delay, saying you're in the forest cutting wood. That excuse works year-round, and if you always come in from that direction, no one can question you. Will that do?"

"That's right, you can lie. I'm jealous," he observed with a chuckle. "I would have panicked and come in a flash of light if you touched the crystal. It's a fine plan. I'll be 'cutting wood' any time anyone comes by looking for me. And Rashel, please don't hesitate to call for me. Before the flour runs out or you have to go cut wood yourself. I'll try to return as often as I can, but really, until I develop a better way to travel than a tornado, it might be irregular. And there's one more thing. Do you mind...do you mind if I listen in on your thoughts? I can speak with you from a distance that way. I will just want to check in on Nevai and if there's something you need. I won't go deep into your thoughts, private thoughts, I mean. At a set time, maybe?"

"What do you mean?" she asked, her eyes growing wide with wonder and a bit of fear. She had probably assumed he did this all the time, but the ethics of being a Wise One dictated when it was appropriate and when it was not.

"Right now, I'm speaking to your mind and you could think your reply. What is Nevai doing right now?" Yeolani answered, his mouth not moving, just his thoughts shifting through her brain.

Rashel's mind flashed a thousand different emotions and images at him until she settled and looked over at Nevai. *He's sleeping soundly,* she thought. *I hope he starts sleeping through the night soon.*

"I do too, for your sake," Yeolani said aloud, so she could recognize he had her message. "Is that too invasive?"

"No," she replied thoughtfully, "but I don't know why. Why do I trust you? Is that magic also?"

Yeolani shook his head, suddenly anxious to move on before he was tempted to stay longer. "No, I trust you too, and that's strange. I shouldn't trust someone I've only just met. It's not in my nature. If it's magic, it's not my magic. Perhaps it's the fairies at work again." And that scared him, though he would not dare to say it aloud.

12

ANSWERS AND QUESTIONS

This time he conjured a horse worthy of a king and rode as fast as he could across the winter plains, back toward the mountain cavern behind the waterfall. He wanted to get a distance from Rashel that would not bring her to mind where she might be observed in a stray thought. He wanted to shift his brain and his goals so the location for this next confrontation must be somewhere that didn't bring that precious new world onto the stage of his mind. Besides, Marit kept sending him lonely thoughts, and he needed to settle her as well.

With his faster horse, the trip to the cavern lasted only an hour, but Yeolani's irritability with this form of travel also rose with every hoofbeat. There must be a faster way for a magician, less dangerous than a tornado. That might be a worthy goal in his Seeking. He added that to his other planned topics for this conversation. He had many, and if Honiea and Vamilion wouldn't answer, he would simply have to find a way for himself. Right now, he had little patience for any of it.

Marit greeted him heartily, and her pups waddled over

with her to smell him. He cuddled the pups, getting them accustomed to human touch before their eyes opened. Marit allowed this as long as she received her share of the attention, and he told her what he had now planned.

"I'm going to send you to look after Nevai. There's a warm barn and the lady there, Rashel. She will be kind, but you cannot come with me, not with your puppies. Nevai will be there too, and I'll need you to be sure he is watched. But do me a favor; stay away from the other dogs. You need not be a mother again, and I cannot have you so burdened with these little ones. I would like to take you with me one day."

Of course, the dog probably didn't understand, but Yeolani said it anyway, wanting to verbalize his plans if only for himself. He would warn Rashel that she would be having guests of the canine variety in the morning, but for now, he would be entertaining others himself. He encouraged Marit's family back into their nest for the evening and then surveyed the cavern. Magically, he set a fire, allowing the space to warm up, and then conjured furs as a seating arrangement worthy of the locale. Then, when all was ready, he brought forth a candle, lit it, and held it high.

"And bring Vamilion with you, please!" he added, addressing the candle as well as giving it a mental shove, though he didn't know if the call would work.

This time it took a bit more time, but the two Wise Ones arrived in the same flicker of the candle, hand in hand. Vamilion looked around the cavern with a grim eye, probably distrusting the stone roof above him to remain steady, but Yeolani didn't care. He greeted his mentors and invited them to sit.

"I've got some questions, Wise One questions, and my next move will depend on what you can tell me," Yeolani began, joining his guests to sit around the fire.

"So do I. The baby?" Honiea wouldn't be redirected. "You've settled that, haven't you?" Her quick eyes probably noted that Nevai no longer resided here, and she made a curious probe at Yeolani's mind, but he remained behind his shield and ignored her.

"I need to know why I cannot lie anymore?" Yeolani bluntly asked. "I don't dare tell anyone that he's my son because he isn't, and someone is going to string me up assuming that I've kidnapped this baby. How can I do this without lying? And why didn't you tell me about this limitation before?"

Vamilion managed to look sheepish at their omission. "It's not something we come up against much anymore. Our dealings with people are usually truthful, or we can redirect questions. You, on the other hand, have been given something unique that people are going to question out of hand. Maybe it's a blessing, to learn how to do the careful answers that your circumstances will require."

"But why can't I lie? I can manage a curse, but even that was a bit of a push. What has happened to me?"

"Wise One ethics are imposed by the Heart Stone, though you wouldn't be given one if you weren't basically a good person," Honiea continued the explanation. "You can still kill, but only if it's justified in the service of magic, protecting yourself or other innocents. You can also deceive a bit, disguise yourself and such, but that's only to protect yourself or others as well. Just like giving permission for someone to call you by another name, you can certainly redirect their questioning. Not lying shouldn't be a problem."

Yeolani sighed like an old man, beleaguered. "That's basically what I've already done. I implied that the baby's mother was dead and let them think that I was his father, but it was touch and go. If they suspected I wasn't the real father, I would have to use magic to protect him and myself from a mob."

"And what were you doing that you needed to curse?" Honiea asked curiously as she nodded approval of his simple solution.

Yeolani had thought through his careful questions before he invited his mentors to the cavern, and so he had a ready answer. "I was promising to help someone, and the magic must have taken it as an oath because it started putting me into the royal get-up. I cursed just to bring it back down, convince the Heart Stone that I'm a crude man and don't deserve to be all gussied up that way. The townsfolk would have driven me out of the village if I hadn't."

Vamilion only chuckled, but Honiea approved. "It sounds like you have a good handle on what the Heart Stone will impose on you."

Yeolani grimaced at the limitations but decided to leave that and change topics. "I have a better handle on the tornadoes," Yeolani muttered. "Which leads to my next question about magical travel. I've found a way, but it's blasted dangerous, and I don't think it will meet my needs over the next few years. I've become a tornado and torn across the plains, but it's not feasible to do when people are about, and it destroys things as I go. It will only be safe in uninhabited areas. There's got to be a better way."

Vamilion nodded, considering his problem. "There is another way, but it makes me ill. Maybe it won't for you. I can travel outside the mountains by forcing a magical leap. It's easier if there's a mind to latch on to; I reach for Honiea's if she's where I want to go. It takes a great deal of energy otherwise and is often not worth the disorientation afterward. I can teach you."

Yeolani nodded his gratitude for the additional training.

"And then there are the Talismans as a possibility for travel. One of them may help you move about, like my candle does." Honiea suggested.

"Talismans? You mentioned them, but I don't know what mine are or where to look."

"They could be anywhere," Honiea warned him. "And if tornados are too dangerous, surely Owailion would have made one of your Talismans that will allow you better movement. Being the King of the Plains means you will need to interact with the people, and it will require a swift means of travel. You will find something."

"Where? I've barely been able to Seek, what with a dog and a baby and ...and then my ... my difficulty with being too flashy. I seem to either do too much magic or not enough. First, I destroy East, and then sitting in this cavern hasn't kept me out of trouble. I need a balance."

"Perhaps finding your Talismans will benefit that as well," Vamilion suggested.

"Or maybe finding my Lady would help balance me more," suggested Yeolani slyly, trying to not sound too eager. "The fairies who gave Nevai to me hinted that I needed to find her as well. I thought at first that I would be able to get her help with the baby, but ....but I don't really know how to go about looking for her. How am I to know when I've found her?"

It might have been his imagination, but Yeolani thought Honiea and Vamilion looked uncomfortable with his question. They glanced at each other trying to decide which of them was most qualified to answer him. Suddenly, Yeolani felt like he was six again and had just asked his parents where babies come from.

"Come now, it can't be that hard. You did find each other," he pointed out just to make them suffer for not explaining this in the beginning, when they first trained him.

Again, neither of them wanted to speak, and Yeolani began to suspect they were holding a private conversation, debating how, or even if, to answer him.

"Well, then can I go and find someone I want to marry? There are plenty of very nice..."

"NO!" they almost shouted in unison. "You cannot do that," Vamilion continued in a more reasonable tone, but the bitter look of regret settled into every line of his body. "You must not fall in love with someone who is not a Wise One."

Yeolani for once held his peace, waiting for the explanation, for he had suspected this.

Vamilion finally sighed and began what must be a difficult tale. "I told you that I had been a trader in my old life. Well, I also had a wife and two children before I stepped foot in the Land. Owailion found me almost immediately and insisted that I must touch the Heart Stone and become a Wise One. I presumed that it would be easy enough and magic would be nothing but a blessing. He tried to warn me that my wife would not be able to become magical with me and that I would have to leave her behind. I did not believe that magic would be so cruel to separate us."

"However, despite the warnings Owailion gave me, I remained devoted to her and used my magic to maintain our relationship, but it was awful. She aged beyond me, and my children drifted away, bitter that I was unable to remain their father. Magic told me Honiea's name, and yet I refused to Seek for her. When I met her anyway, I gave her the Heart Stone, but I would not...could not break my vows and love for my first wife. I had to hold her in my arms when she died an old woman, and I was pretending to be her son. Such memories are not...it was not fair to either of the women that I have loved."

Yeolani let that message sink in. "And how did you know whom you were Seeking? You said magic told you?"

"I dreamed of her," Vamilion replied with a strange look crossing his face, a mix of love, regret, and memory. "I never saw her face in the dream. Instead, I was dreaming about statues, and all of them began speaking to me until I was almost driven mad by it."

"It was easier for me," commented Honiea, "because I was only supposed to find you, not fall in love with you. One of my patients, with her dying breath, told me that I needed to find someone named Yeolani. I was not as driven to find you as you will be driven to find your Lady. She's your match, and you are correct; she will balance you."

"Well, I don't have any dreams whispering in my ear. Am I supposed to learn her name and then go Seek her? What if I find her before I learn her name? Can that happen?"

"You won't feel the compulsion," Vamilion commented dryly.

"Compulsion? Are we going to be whipped into doing this?"

"The attraction will be intense and immediate when you meet her, and I presume you will know her name long before that happens. You won't want anyone else by then. Everything about her will fascinate you. It will be hard to concentrate on the others that need you...like Nevai perhaps? Let's hope that the boy is part of the spell to go with her. Either that, or he will need to grow up and be on his own before you can find her."

"I hope not," Yeolani muttered, half joking as he teased Vamilion. "How long since Gil was a twenty-two-year-old man?"

Honiea blushed. "Why don't you sleep on it. I'm sure if your lady is alive, you won't have to wait for her. You'll find her sooner if you are actively Seeking. You need to get out of this cave and travel."

Yeolani nodded his agreement. "I've made arrangements

for Nevai, and I'm just about to move Marit too so I can go Seeking, which is why I wanted to speed up the process. I'll not come back here," he vowed and then cursed under his breath to prevent his words from making him a King. "I just hope I don't get sidetracked again."

13

WELL OF DARKNESS

*Y*eolani looked out over the brilliant whiteness of the plains covered with snow. It blended with the white sky that threatened another blizzard to come, blurring the point where earth and sky met. Yeolani felt dizzy trying to focus on the nonexistent horizon. So, instead, he stood in the knee-deep drifts, waiting for inspiration. He had made it here by means of the gut-wrenching method Vamilion had taught him and swore he would never do it again. Traveling by pulling himself to the mind he wanted to reach was easier on the dizziness, but still exhausting. He had tried that method when he reached for Rashel to bring Marit and her babies to the farm.

That reunion, after only a day away, had been difficult too, but for a different reason. Yeolani had not wanted to leave, but it was necessary. After learning some of the consequences of falling in love with someone who was not a Wise One, he felt torn. The farm was running well, no one suspected Rashel was alone, and everything he cared for was there: Marit, Nevai and now Rashel. He had to admit it and didn't want to. He loved her but, hopefully, in the same way he cared for the dog and baby. He didn't dare linger to let it become a stronger bond.

His next plan was to seek out the underground aquifer from his dream. He had been given that imagery for a reason. He must find that spot, and, hopefully, there he would locate one of his Talismans, one that would allow travel without exhaustion or dizziness to the point of complete incapacitation. He had been standing here in the snowfield for an hour waiting for the effects of his magical shift to wear off. Now, he felt he had turned to ice, despite all the furs, gloves, and other warm clothing he conjured for himself before he departed Rashel's. The wind here tore through him like a knife. If he remained much longer undecided about moving again, they might find him next spring still standing in the open like a rune stone warning travelers against coming this way.

Think, how are you going to go down into the ground to see if something's there? In the dream, he had simply sunk through the earth, but the soil was so frozen it might as well be stone. Could he dig through stone? No shovel he could conjure would penetrate the earth at this late stage of winter. Maybe in the spring. He could winter over with Rashel and then come back. *No, you will not let yourself get away with that,* he told himself firmly. Now, how did people dig wells out here on the prairie?

Then something finally penetrated his foggy mind; they didn't. The prairie was an untapped resource, rich soil for farming, but anywhere far from a river, no one could live and farm because of the lack of water. And he, the King of the Plains, had not opened it up. That was the purpose of the dream, he realized, to show him that there was an aquifer here. If he would tap into it, people could spread out, away from the rivers, and they could farm here rather than leaving this land open for buffalo and little else.

This thought excited him, though Yeolani had to abandon

the hope that inside that dream he would find one of his Talismans to help him travel. Drilling a well would be an act of service, and that was just as good, he firmly told himself. *Quit being so selfish and find a way to dig a hole before you freeze to death.* He slowly turned in a circle in the snow, stretching his magical senses out in every direction. He could feel the town of Meeting to his northwest about two hundred miles, and to the southeast, he sensed the echoes of a cluster of towns on the Don River. He judged he was about halfway between the two, out in trackless open, without even a tree for shelter. If anyone built here, he or she would need more than water, but first things first.

Again, how do you dig who-knew-how-deep to the aquifer that must be down there? He wasn't even sure he was above the crystal cavern, but if he could sense Meeting two hundred miles away, surely he could find that cavern two hundred feet below him. Yeolani directed his mind down into the soil and felt his way past the hibernating and dormant life and into the depth where the pressure above had hardened the soil, not the cold. Strangely, he felt how the earth there seemed warmer, almost neutral. Then he reached bedrock with his mind and sought for fissures in the shale, the cracks where water would penetrate and finally drip from a ceiling made of crystals into an aquifer filling up so long it formed a sea. His mind reached the water and tested that, finding the depth and the chill went almost farther than possible to fathom. Drop a well bucket here, and you could water a great city.

Without much of a plan, Yeolani knelt and drew a large circle around himself in the snow. This was where he would pull his conjuring from, and he would scoop out the earth and craft cement walls for the well from the material he gleaned, pressing and securing it into the sides to shore them up. He mentally chowed through to the frigid soil, heedless of the animal life he disturbed. Stones he encountered became the wall above ground. His body went down with his excavation so he would gain a true perspective of the depth he created. Magic did not measure things well for him. When he reached shale, he looked back up through the tunnel he had built and saw only a small white circle of sky and a smooth tunnel of secure cement, but still no water. It appeared to easily be two hundred feet of soil he had carved through.

Now he would have to break through stone. Oddly enough this was easier. He wasn't distracted by the little minds of hibernating burrowers or the seeds of dead grasses. He only found the stone fascinating for its riches of gems and minerals that would eventually be ground up into more soil.

Unfortunately, he didn't pay as much attention, and so when he finally broke through into the cavern, he fell through with a startled cry and splashed into the bitterly cold underground lake. He used Vamilion's reaching method to whisk himself to the shore of the aquifer, but the chill almost killed him more than the disorientation. He lay under the crystal roof and, with teeth chattering, used magic to warm himself and dry his furs, but he felt he would never be warm again.

"That was stupid."

His words echoed eerily. He could see nothing of the cavern. The fairies, preferring their forest, had not followed him out onto the plains. All the light, what little there was, came from the pinprick his well created far out from the shore. It cast a single shaft of light down onto the lake's surface. The chill down here, out of the wind, might be less than above, but the stark black with a single ray of light made the cold all the bleaker. In his imagination, he saw a single bucket plunge down the hole on a line and realized this wouldn't work. It would only float and bob uselessly on the surface. How would a bucket make that long trek? Whatever came down must be tremendously heavy to pull down a simple bucket from that depth. It was something he'd have to think about.

Rather than freeze to death on the surface, Yeolani decided to camp here underground and conjured a fire in the eerie cavern. Next, he dumped out his belongings and found the wet and miserable Life Giver along with his soaked food. These he dried magically, but his map, the one he'd carefully crafted since before he had touched his Heart Stone, was ruined and all his drawings were blurred. He added the map as fuel for his fire.

The flames flickered and flashed against the brown crystals of the ceiling, and he found himself mesmerized by the play of light. Such a scene, with its magical movement, should be a sight anyone in the world above would pay to see just once. Here he sat in a makeshift camp, most likely the only human to witness such a display. And what did he do with that time? He thought about how to weigh down a bucket.

With no solutions, he went to sleep before the light from his well shaft had faded, indicating night had fallen above. In his conjured tent, meant for the comfort rather than fear of the weather that wouldn't touch him here on the rocky shoreline, he went to sleep, hoping to dream solutions to his well problem. Instead, he found his dreams invaded by the fairies.

Fairies again, hounding him in the cavern. Yeolani had not seen a single one of the creatures outside of the forest except in his dreams. Was this still punishment for his original curse? He couldn't fathom why they constantly invaded his sleep, but he listened to their high fluting voices, forced to concentrate or he wouldn't comprehend what they had to say.

"Her name is Elin," they whispered. "Elin, lin, lin," it echoed in the hollows.

"Who is Elin?" Yeolani asked, unsure he understood anything they were saying.

"The Green Lady, the Lady of the Forest, the Queen of Growing Things, your lady, the one you've prayed for," they piped, overlaying each other's words.

Had he prayed for her? "So, it isn't Rashel?" he replied, suddenly pained and felt like that bucket hanging from the snowy world had dropped like lead onto his gut, and he awoke in the pervasive dark, alone and grieving.

So, instead of a Talisman, he had found his lady's name, but now he did not want it. He had wanted to fall in love with Rashel. Nevai...could he leave the baby with a woman who would not be his mother? How was he going to visit the farm and help this woman while looking for another one, one that would supplant the other? Did he dare return to Rashel at all with these feelings? He squirmed with guilt and sudden frustration. Limits had been part of becoming a Wise One, and on the surface, he had accepted that, but now, more than ever, he wanted to rebel.

In his despair, Yeolani wanted to reach out to Nevai as a source of comfort, but he was too young to have insight, and Marit was even less so with her alien mind. Yeolani didn't dare reveal his inner turmoil to the likes of Honiea or Vamilion. They would chastise him and add new layers to his emotional quandary. How could he have fallen in love with Rashel in just a few days and not have that love justified by magic? He felt so sorely tempted to listen in and just hear her thoughts, not daring to actually speak with her. Could he just tap in to watch her as she did her simple chores? He would not invade her mind but, instead, find some solace there?

Without consciously meaning to, Yeolani's mind drifted away from him. Perhaps he fell asleep again, fairy hounded, and cast his mind into the winter night. Rashel was giving

Nevai a bath, washing him in one of her milk tubs, humming a gentle tune to him and wrapping the baby in a warm towel. Yeolani surveyed the cabin like he was a ghost, seeing Rashel's movements as she fed the baby and put him to bed. She dumped out the bathwater and then dimmed the lanterns. Each time she walked in front of the hearth, her bright eyes caught sight of the crystal on the mantle. Yeolani's heart leaped. She was thinking of him.

He watched her looking at the bed he had left empty. With a fascinated heart, he observed her prepare for bed. He couldn't resist watching her pull her braid free, brushing the luxurious wood toned strands and letting them fall loosely around her shoulders. It fell like waves of grain across her limbs and down her back, and he wanted to reach out and touch. She pulled it to the side, exposing her pale neck as she reached back to loosen the ties of her bodice, and Yeolani bit his lip. *What am I doing to myself watching this,* he asked himself?

With a tremendous wrench, he pulled his mind back into the cavern and sat up again in the dark. Numb, he walked blindly to the water's edge, and when he felt its chill on his bare feet, he stopped and dipped his hands in, splashing the frigid water over his face. That shock knocked him back to his senses but left him no answers. Yeolani wished desperately to forget Rashel's name, his attraction to her, and even that he had ever known the woman.

In his confusion Yeolani finally realized the only safe place was in forgetting. Witlessly he heaved himself to the surface in one of those ill-advised shifts. Then, retching and ill, he transformed himself into a tornado that sucked the snow from the prairie and raced across the night in boundless fury. He didn't care if he lost track of his well in the middle of nowhere. He cut across the Land like a knife, the knife through his heart, and all he knew was he ran south through the plains, away from his memory and every touch of civilization.

Two days later, the blizzard inside Yeolani left him tattered and on the verge of insanity at the edge of the Land, looking out at the Open Ocean with only a few steps of sand before he washed away. He stood at the base of a cliff, and he turned back to see the mountains he had come blustering through, covered in the snow from his passage. His eyes barely focused. He wavered, wondering if he could keep going out to sea, but that decision was made for him. Yeolani collapsed into darkness in the icy surf and didn't remember landing.

14

COMPASS

*S*ometime far later, the warmth of half-a-dozen blankets and a breaking fever woke him to firelight and soft voices. He looked blearily at the humble cottage of a family that he didn't recognize. They were gathered around the table enjoying their evening meal when the littlest girl, swinging her legs on the bench, spied him as she hopped up and down.

"Da, he's awake," the blonde toddler announced, and the entire family turned to stare at the stranger who abruptly wanted to sink back through the ground, back into a well of darkness. He couldn't even move, let alone use magic. Could he use magic? He couldn't remember.

The mother of the household rose to set water for tea while the father came to the side of the cot, escorted by a trail of six children, the youngest barely able to walk. "Well, sir, welcome back to the world. Can you understand me?" the father asked as if he wondered if his foundling could speak the language.

"I think so," he whispered. He had never felt so wretched, except he couldn't remember anything really. Where was he?

He put his hand to his eyes, trying to recall where he had been when he had fallen so sick. He remembered darkness and a single shaft of light. Was there a bucket swinging in the light? Where had he been? He recalled a blizzard and being bitterly cold, but that could have been the sickness. Where had he been before that?

The mistress of the house came to him with a cup of tea, and the stranger struggled to sit up to drink it, trembling with weakness, but it moistened his throat and drew a longing for more from his queasy stomach.

"How long?" he gasped after he had sipped a few more swallows and then fell back onto the bed, unable to hold himself up any longer.

"Three days," the father supplied. "Elin found you on the beach like you had been washed up wearing nothing but your trousers, but the storm was blowing out to sea. Very strange. You might have been there a few hours before she found you. What's your name, sir?"

The young invalid struggled to think. He couldn't remember anything except that darkness and the one ray of light with a bucket swinging in it. "I'm not sure," he had to admit. "I've been...been cold."

"I wouldn't doubt it, walking in a blizzard without a shirt, cloak, or even boots. You were lucky not to freeze to death, though how that could be, we cannot fathom. Well," the father shrugged that off, "I'm Everic and these are my children, my wife Emmi. You're welcome here, and I'm sure you will recover now. You have...have many people who must be looking for you."

"Many people?" the stranger asked, curiosity the only emotion he felt able to dredge up.

"You've spoken in your fever," Emmi came to his side with a more substantial soup. "You were asking for help: Honiea,

Rashel, Nevai, Marit, even our little Elin. Do any of those names mean anything to you?"

He shook his head and then realized that movement only scrambled his brains, and he firmly reminded himself not to do any more shaking. Instead, he applied himself to the broth that Emmi served him.

"At first, we thought you were speaking another language, but then we heard you say Vamilion. That's a name we know," Everic supplied.

"Who...who or what is Vamilion?" managed the younger man.

"You're just south of the Vamilion Mountains. Perhaps you crossed them?"

He looked across the room to the winter-filled window where night skies were lined with gray clouds. Vague memories of white-capped mountains teased at his thoughts, but from far below him, as if he were a bird passing over them, and it made him dizzy. He firmly refused to let himself think about these things and instead sipped at the soup, feeling much better with something in his stomach. He would learn to think again when it was daylight and he had rested. Perhaps then he would be able to bring forth some worthwhile memories.

The next day, with Everic escorting him, the recovering invalid went outside. He wore rags on his feet and a cast-off shirt of his host's, but the wind on the cliff where the simple home stood didn't seem to disturb him. Caught on a cusp between white-capped mountains to the north and the white-capped surf on the beach to the south, this little home struggled to survive. Neither the mountains nor the sea brought anything to mind for the struggling wanderer.

"How did I come to be here?" he asked aloud but to himself. "I couldn't have arrived in that storm dressed that way. I've seen mountains and ocean before, I'm sure, but I cannot remember when. What am I that I would come here without supplies? Where did I leave my boots?"

"Still no memory?" Everic commented. "There wasn't a mark on you, so you probably weren't in battle. You have no scars except long-healed rope burns," and Everic held out his hands so he could witness the scars of pulling fishing line. "You've been at sea, but it was years ago. You can't be much over twenty, so you were young to your calling and left it. Can you do anything else that might witness to your profession?"

Curiosity made the stranger look toward the shed that Everic approached and saw there all the implements of a farmer, a fisherman, a blacksmith, and a hunter. There must be no town nearby that would supply the family's needs, and so Everic and his wife must make do and performed every profession for themselves. Without asking, the stranger reached for the bow that leaned against the back wall of the shed and pulled it out, sensing the familiarity that went with the actions, as routine as breathing.

"Then you're an archer," Everic confirmed and brought out the quiver that went with the bow. "That's what we'll do today to fill the pot then. Around here at this time of year, there're plenty of birds; difficult to hit, but there also might be winter rabbits come out early and now are hungry after the storm. Shall we try your hand?"

They spent the day hunting birds and only had a few for their trouble, but they gained a sense of the stranger's skill. He made every shot, and Everic was asking him for his recommendations to improve his own skill.

"Make yourself a better bow," the nameless stranger suggested. "This one doesn't fit either you or me. I'm used to a heavier pull and less length. And better fletching. Try goose, not seagull feathers."

"You know your trade then, Archer, for that is what we'll

call you. Do you have any other inclinations you'd like to pursue before we go in?"

Archer...it wasn't his name, but he would use it nonetheless. He stopped on the bluff considering the question and looked over the edge to the beach several hundred feet below him.

"Can I see the cliff?" He didn't want to add to his reputation for being slightly off, so he would not tell his new friend what he actually was feeling. A compulsion to climb down and dig into that cliff face would not help their trust in his mental state.

"There's a path down to the shoreline over there." Everic pointed and then led the way west, and they climbed down carefully.

The rock face rose black and stark against the wintery sky. It stood riddled with rookeries of a variety of birds. The two men could have climbed for eggs, but Archer's footwear would prevent it at the moment. Instead, he walked the beach right up to the face of the cliff and rested his hands on it as if it were a door through which he intended to walk. He had touched stone this way, like a craftsman about to cut his way through the cliff, but he couldn't recall when or why he knew he'd done this before. The rock spoke to him, and it frightened him how much he wanted to reach his hand right through the solid stone.

"There are rumors of a man, old as the mountains themselves, who listens to the stone of the Land and it talks to him. They say he's a magician," Everic commented, and Archer shivered, pulling his hand back from exploring. He didn't want to think about magic. Something about the word chilled him more than the evening wind coming up.

And that magic haunted him for weeks as he struggled to remember.

Finally, one night beside the fire, Archer asked for and got the leathers that had been gathered for clothing. He also had to borrow a knife from Ellie to cut with and a mallet from the tool shed. Elin, the little two-year-old, watched him in fascination with bright, blue eyes. He expertly stripped the fur and worked the hides, rubbing in beeswax, and then began to cut long, thin strips as well as more carefully sliced pieces. The other children slowly gathered around him to observe the handiwork until their mother shooed them off to bed, and still Archer cut and then used the thin strips to start sewing the pieces together.

"You've got more skills than the bow," Everic commented as he came to fill in where his children had been. "Where did you learn to do leatherwork? You would be the handiest man out here on the edge. You don't have to leave."

Archer shook his head as he fit the next piece to his leg, trimmed a bit more off one side and then began sewing again. He thought carefully before he replied. "I remember a forest... where I've done this before. Tall trees with lights above my head."

"There's a forest on the other side of the Wall, but you don't speak like a Demionian. Your native tongue is that of the Land," Emmi commented. "I don't know of any other forest nearby.

"Up northwest, there's a forest," Archer commented and then startled, looking up from his work. "How can I know that if I don't even know my own name?" That conundrum brought a sudden ache behind his eyes, and he squashed the leather in his hands, gripping the knife like a weapon.

Then Emmi murmured something in wonder.

"What?" the men asked in tandem.

"The knife," she whispered and reached across the table to take the blade she had lent to Archer to cut and work the leather. "It was my butcher knife...but now it's got a curve...a leather knife. You're a magician, Archer," she declared with conviction.

Elin's bright eyes still awake in her bed in the firelight caught Archer's attention, and he wished that she would go to sleep. He didn't want her to remember all this strangeness he had brought to her family. How had he made a change like that to the tool without even knowing he had done it? He had wanted a better knife, had wished for it, but had resigned himself to awkwardly slashing and punching the holes he needed to craft his boots. But now, Emmi held the knife he would have wanted from the start – short blade, curved almost like a spoon and exquisitely sharp.

"An archer, a leather-worker, and a magician," commented Everic sardonically. "You are a very skilled man."

Archer looked over at the bed and noticed that Elin's wondrous blue eyes were asleep. Had he done that? If so, it frightened him. "What was the name of that old man you spoke of?" he asked as he took back the leather knife and resumed his work almost frantically. If he finished these boots tonight, he could leave in the morning and not bring ruin and magic on his hosts. If it frightened him, it must be terrifying for them.

Everic sat down on the bench beside him and rested his hand on his guest's arm. Archer paid him no attention and kept working. "I don't know, as he has a real name, but they call him the King of the Mountains, Vamilion. Is that where you're going to go? To find him?"

"I have to find answers or someone else who knows who I am," Archer replied. "If I stay here, I'll only bring a curse upon your house, and I don't want that. I'll finish this and then leave."

At dawn, Archer stood at the door wearing his newly crafted boots and bid his hosts goodbye. The comforting isolation and familial bond of the couple plucked a string of longing in his heart. He wondered if he had enjoyed this type of life before he lost his memory. Somewhere was there a wife and children wondering where he had fallen. Without thinking about it, Archer had somehow returned the leather knife back into the butcher knife. He gave it back to Emmi with his thanks. The children, who stood clustered around their parents, all smiled with bright eyes. Elin must have forgotten what she had seen the night before.

"You'll be fine, Archer," Everic reassured him. "Here is the bow. You made far better use of it than I could. Don't forget us here on the edge of the world when you've found your way."

Archer took the proffered bow and quiver, gave each family member a hug, and then turned away from the lonely cabin on the bluff. He walked to the west, into the morning mist toward the head of the trail down to the beach. He felt he must go that way, though he would only have to climb back the way he had come. Everic's family need not know that. He might have made himself invisible in the fog or maybe the bluff blocked his trail. He turned down the path to the beach as if drawn by a lodestone. Something there on the cliff face still called to him, and he wanted to seek it out before he went to go find some elusive King of the Mountains.

At the base of the cliff, he set his bow and quiver down and stepped up onto the fallen rocks to look more closely at the face than he had before. His hand-made boots, sturdy and utilitarian, allowed him to climb higher, to where his yearning had drawn him. It still pinged and itched like a frantic, far-off teapot demanding in its shrill voice to be heard. Unerringly, Archer reached to his left, to the very tip of his long fingers, and found a single handhold. He didn't dare question why he could do this. If he did, he'd fall.

As he hung from his single hand, his right palm reached out, and he set it flat against the rough stone. He imagined the opening he sought and abruptly felt no resistance to his pressing at the exact spot. The ringing in his bones only increased as a fist-sized hollow met his search. He reached blindly into the hole that magic cut, and he refused to think of what monstrous creature might dwell in such a den. Fear and his overactive imagination must be banished. This he knew. Archer stretched his fingers into the pit and felt something cool and metal. He grasped it and brought it out into the morning light.

Archer dropped down to the sandy beach before he dared look at the little gold box he had retrieved. How? Archer couldn't care less, though the magic of it all mystified him. If he regained his memory, would the magic not frighten him so much, or was this the key to that lost past? The box looked finely crafted, with a hinge and latch etched into the round lid that fit easily in his palm. The intricate patterns laced over the lid fascinated him. Horses, grasses, and a background of far-off mountains decorated the sides of the box. Carefully, he lifted the lid and peeked inside.

On a white, porcelain face, he saw finely crafted arms that spun around a central spindle of quartz crystal. The edge of the disc had been etched and then gold-filled, with marks and four symbols. Archer looked at them curiously as they teased at his memory. He'd seen them before, but like his name, the memory of their meaning washed away on the tide. Hopefully, his memory would return like the ocean's cycle again, but when worried him.

Instinctively, he turned to look back at the sea, but the arms on the disc spun erratically at his abrupt change in direction. Archer turned back to the cliff face and watched the arms in the little box move again. Experimenting, he watched as one arm always shifted toward one of the symbols. No matter how he turned, that arm always pointed toward the same mark. The other arm shifted more dramatically, spinning in both directions while he moved, but when he stopped, it stilled too and pointed up the trail toward the bluff.

Archer felt his breath leave him as it dawned on him what he held: a compass. It pointed toward the direction he was supposed to travel. He held memories of this type of device, but again, he had no idea where they came from. Were all compasses magic? Certainly, this one, with its hidden alcove in a sealed cliff, must be, but common compasses needed no magic, just a loadstone that would point north. Unlike those everyday devices, this one didn't point toward where he turned, but in another direction: the one he was supposed to take? He didn't doubt his instinct in this. Magic had guided him unerringly to finding the machine, so why would he question his understanding of its function? This was magic through and through.

Archer looked up at the cliff face and saw that the den where he had found the compass had closed. Its work was finished, and the stone remained solid, untouched. Well, then he had only to decide if he would follow where this new guide would take him. Archer retrieved his bow and quiver, hitched them over his shoulder, and launched out into the unknown, following a magical guide up the bluff and toward the west, away from the Vamilion Mountains as he had planned.

Instead, Archer chose to follow a stranger guide.

SIREN

*S*everal weeks later, crawling across the slopes
between the Vamilion Mountains and the sea,
Archer found his way to a river, wide and deep. It spilled into a
swampy area with vast marshes that threatened to drown him,
but the compass guided him unerringly the whole way, almost
step-by-step through the drier patches. He followed it
faithfully, for the device proved far wiser than he when it came
to hunting and shelter. It guided him to spring roots to eat, fresh
water to drink, a covey of doves to shoot, and windbreaks to
protect him in his travels.

Slowly, winter lifted as he trekked west, and spring rose up
around him. Mists, fens, and strange outcroppings formed a
maze he wandered. He half-expected the compass purposely
led him on tangled paths, for it meandered, and as the land
grew more sodden, he found himself stepping from island to
island in the fens. Now, if the river was the goal, he had arrived
and stood on a shoreline the compass could not help him
overcome. In the morning light filtering through the mists, he
saw the sun glare off the water, and though he wished for some

way to cross, the fog felt so thick he couldn't even see the far shore.

"What now?" he asked the compass, not expecting an answer. "I can't fly, can I?"

"No," whispered a delicate feminine voice in the mist. "Not unless you change shape. Can you?"

Archer whirled, pocketed the compass, and drew his bow in one swift movement, seeking the source of the shrouded human hidden in the fog.

"No need of that," the bodiless voice commented. "I'm right here. Follow the sound of my words."

Archer didn't know whether to trust it or not. He recalled the legends of the sea, of sirens that lured sailors to their death with the sweetness of their song. This voice might not be singing to him, but the allure of human contact after weeks alone across the frontier urged him on. He didn't lower his bow, but stepped carefully, leery of sinking sands and other mist traps towards the water's edge.

"That's right, wanderer. You've come a long way to find my home here. That takes guidance. What has led you here, wanderer?" the voice continued. She led him now, warning him of turns, reminding him how to make the subtle adjustments in his step.

Then the mist thinned magically, and he saw the Siren. She appeared like a ghost or part of the fog, and he could see the standing stones behind the wondrous, flawless visage of a woman. Her bronze hair flared in the morning light and flowed in a wind not found here in the marshes. Her alabaster skin seemed so translucent that he could see the rocks and reeds behind her. A spirit? She certainly could not be wholly human.

"I am the Lost; not a ghost, nor alive, but something in between. I am a seeker of those that made me this way. Are you one such as that?" she asked, her golden and green eyes flashing and beckoning to him. Archer kept his arrow trained on her, but somehow, he doubted that his bolt would have any effect on her. The mist formed her gauzy gown and blended into the morning. An arrow would do nothing.

"No, I'm an archer," he replied simply.

"Yet, you were guided to me. It must be fate," she replied. He felt his knees grow weak staring at her willowy form, fading around the edges as the sun began burning the light around her shape. "How did you find me?"

"I don't know." He felt his breathing grow shallow and realized his name of Siren could not be far afield. She was putting a spell on him, churning his curiosity, drawing him in.

"What is your name, wanderer?" she continued, with her voice sending shivers of warmth over his arms and down his spine. He found it difficult to keep the bow taut. Every word from her shimmering lips made him want to melt into the mud. Unwillingly, he lowered the weapon and felt the relief in his trembling arms. The blood in them began burning, adding to the sensation of melting. With an effort, he looked away, seeking the sun, and saw only a flat, white disc against the white of the sky; no gold. All the gold burned within the Siren's glowing form.

"Shall I read your fate, wanderer? I can tell you everything you've ever yearned to know with a look at your palm?" she promised.

The ragged ends of Archer's breath burned free from his lungs around a simple question. "Can you tell me my name?"

The Siren's head tilted to the side, curious, like the nods of the doves he had shot for his food. Her misty eyes glowed. "You do not know that? How strange."

Archer could not shake his head or speak any longer. He felt his skin begin to burn as the mist pulled in closer and his mind screamed for air. He was drowning in the shrouds of her hair, her arms, and the vapors. The Siren reached out and touched his cheek with her alabaster hand, and her caress burned as fire. He wanted to cry out and pull away, bring the bow back to bear, but he could not move. The Lady of the Mist had him completely under her spell. He would drown here on the edge of the Lara River and be lost forever. He knew it. The compass had led him astray.

"Then, wanderer with no name, we shall have to explore that indeed," she whispered, and her gentle caressing lips met his in an eruption of white light.

Rashel brought out a blanket and set Nevai on it to enjoy the first fine day of spring. She sat on the stoop beside the baby and noted the hens were pecking more urgently in the yard. She saw a faint haze of green on the trees just beyond the fence. The plum tree had grown red with potential budding overnight. Like magic, it must have struck, she realized and felt a pit of worry in her stomach. Yeolani, where were you? The plowing must begin soon, and he had not contacted her, not once in the weeks since he had left his dog with her. Marit frolicked with her puppies and enjoyed nipping at the heels of the cattle on this fine morning, forgetful of her missing master.

Rashel felt no such forgetfulness. She sought to distract herself by watching Nevai playing on the blanket, straining to lift himself and making the first efforts at crawling. She admired his determination. If only she could eventually do so herself. But no amount of hard work on her part would change the fact that she needed Yeolani, and he wasn't coming as he promised.

What will you do if he doesn't return? Could she be angry that he had abandoned her? What do you do when the villagers figure it out? They would start up where they had left off at the auction. A shiver of fear ran down her spine. She still had the crystal that she didn't dare touch. Her needs remained met, except for the plowing. She looked across the yard to the far field where the soil awaited, smooth and fine, needing the seed. Could she do that by herself? She had a horse now, but had she the skill and strength?

And then the pit in her stomach grew heavier for no fathomable reason. She sensed fear and danger, but nothing in the bright spring morning had come to alarm her. It was all in her head. Trying to comfort herself, Rashel picked up the baby and held him close, rocking him and tickling him, hoping the giggles and the rosy, toothless smile would make her forget her premonition of danger.

She was wrong. Norton tramped down the road toward the forest, carrying an ax and looking with covetous eyes at her farm. Without acknowledging him, as if she hadn't noticed him passing by, she rose with the baby on her hip, plucked up the blanket, shook it out and turned toward the door.

"Mistress Rashel," Norton called. "Where is your man this fine morning? I've not seen him about."

She paused at the doorway and glared back at the man who stood in the gate, just inside her property with his ax glittering and sharp on his shoulder. He was a huge man, half-a-head taller than Yeolani and probably a third more in weight. Her memories of Yeolani seemed fuzzy as if a fog had entered her mind. Where was he? she asked herself again. If she lied to Norton and said Yeolani was in the forest, would Norton go seeking him? Probably, and that would not be good. She would lie in another direction.

"He's sharpening the plowshare," she replied matter-of-factly and went in the door.

"And how are you doing all by yourself?" Norton continued, taking a few more steps into the yard.

"I'm not by myself, and I'm very busy," she replied coldly. She had already let him know she held him in contempt. His obvious possessiveness of both herself and her farm was unwelcome. Norton had not liked her defiance last fall, and now the widower seemed to have picked up his efforts at gaining her affections once again. "I've got bread to work and seed to set for my garden. Good day." And she shut the door on him.

Rashel had just put Nevai down on the floor on his blanket when the door rudely opened, and she straightened up in fright. Norton stood in the doorway with the ax still waiting on his shoulder. "I don't believe he is here," the man growled. "He hasn't been seen in weeks. He's abandoned you. He won't marry you. At best, you are a kept woman..."

Rashel felt herself blushing, and a gasp escaped her despite her determination to remain cold. How could he make that accusation? That had been the main worry of the town elders; that she would have to prostitute herself in order to remain on her farm. She would never have done that. The thought repulsed her. She had told Yeolani that she would rather walk away into the forest and die than face such a fate. The townsfolk were not so understanding. They had insisted the farm would go to the man who could pay for it. She would have to marry whoever paid for her so that she would not pay for it on her back. They would not allow such a woman in Edgewood.

"I am nothing of the sort," she rounded on Norton. Where was her butcher knife? She located it with a flick of her eyes, but it was no closer than the crystal on the stone mantle. Could she reach the crystal without seeming to seek it out and alerting Norton to the magic of it? If Yeolani came to its call, would he come from the forest quickly enough to save her from Norton's rude suggestions? Would he come at all? Rashel decided the crystal would be a better bet than her butcher knife and pretended to go toward the wood box to bring up the fire for her baking.

Norton followed her, and she felt his rough, heavy hand on her waist. "Has he even made a woman of you? No, you're still a maid. He's a gelding, not worthy of such a fine creature as you."

Rashel rounded on him, her eyes snapping in anger. "You will remove your hand, sir," she demanded, backing up one more step and feeling her heel connect with the hearthstones.

She couldn't back up anymore. Norton pinned her to the wall, his weight crushing against her, his rough hands groping up her legs under her skirts. "You'll do, and any time I'm passing by, I'll pay you with plowing of another type," Norton growled as Rashel fought to get his hands away from her.

Her mind erupted in panic, and she strained to scream, but Norton's mouth was on hers, mashing his lips against her face, smothering her in his beard and his mass pressed against her. Desperately, she groped to her right, straining to reach the crystal on the hearth. She scrabbled for it, fingertips touching the cool shaft. She grasped it and, with waning strength, brought it stabbing down into Norton's back like a dagger. The crystal wasn't nearly sharp or long enough to kill him, but it did penetrate his flesh, and he bellowed in anger, wrapped his huge hands around her throat and squeezed, lifting her completely free of the floor. Somewhere far away, with the light before her eyes sparking and pinging, and the buzz of losing consciousness in her ears, Rashel heard the baby wailing. The dark pulled in toward a pinprick.

Archer felt fire and light. Every particle of his body began to separate, drowned in the fog and marshes. The Siren's breath filled his lungs, musty with swamp water. Drowning? While standing on land? Could he? The glare of bronze and reflections off the river blinded him, but he could not move or fight the Siren's magic.

Abruptly something else tugged him violently from behind like puppet strings. His guts roiled, and he could see only the light fading in from the sides. He felt like he'd been lifted off his feet by his neck and thrown through the air. The harshness of the movement after the Siren's gentle burning threw him sprawling onto a hard, wooden floor, and he retched, gasping on all fours and coughing out bilge water from his lungs.

He looked up and saw cabin walls. A baby's wild protests almost masked grunting and struggling gasps. Archer turned and saw a brute of a man lifting a girl off the ground, half strangling her, half raping her, pinning and choking the life and light out of her. It didn't take a moment, but it seemed eerily slow to his mind. Without thinking, Archer staggered to his feet, drew his bow, set the arrow, aimed carefully down the shaft for the point where the man's arm met his chest, just under the armpit, and then drew the string to his cheek, breathed out the last of the swamp gasses, and released.

His arrow flew true, and the grunt of air passed from both the girl as well as the rapist in the same sound as she landed shakily on her feet. The huge man sprawled dead on the floor. The shaft had pierced through his heart, and the wretched man didn't even have the dignity to bleed. Archer looked from his victim to the girl and tried to make some sense of all he'd just experienced. He couldn't connect the strands into a reasonable braid of a story. The girl held a bloody crystal in one hand that she now dropped and then scurried to pick up a baby who continued to cry, though more in anger than fear now that the stranger was down.

"You came," the girl commented with a tone he could not interpret. Relief? Disbelief? Irritation at his timing? Archer felt his legs trembling with reaction, and he staggered to a nearby bed. He had never killed a man, at least that he could remember, and he didn't like how it felt. He wanted to vomit, but there was probably little left inside him. The Siren had taken everything.

The young lady came and sat beside him wordlessly, still comforting the baby and rocking him until he stilled. Then she put the babe in the nearby cradle before she ever addressed what had happened.

"I'm glad you came," she reiterated.

Archer nodded numbly since he felt like another spell might be creeping in on him, this one crafted of the girl's sparkling eyes and sweet face. He didn't know if he knew this girl, but she certainly made him feel more human than the Siren had.

"Why haven't you come earlier, when I didn't really need you?" the girl asked.

"I....I...I don't..." Archer tried to explain, but words escaped him, and his voice sounded so harsh, full of mud and muck.

"Yeolani, are you well?"

Yeolani? Was that his name? He still couldn't remember, but his hands trembled, and he felt like he might faint in a mix of relief and fear. He managed to shake his head no and then leaned forward to vomit a swamp on the girl's floor.

16

HEALING

*R*ashel had hoped to never need this, but she reached for the white candle Yeolani had left her, and with her hands still trembling, she lit it with a taper from her fire, holding it high. As she waited, she looked around her house and realized that she would have to do a lot of explaining if this Honiea were to come. A baby given by fairies, a magician passed out on her bed, and a dead man with an arrow sticking out of his side. What would the Queen of Healing think on her arrival?

The flash of light was exactly like the one that had brought Yeolani, except hers was lavender light, whereas his glow shown golden, like him. And the Queen of Healing stood in the cabin looking like she was any other villager come to deliver honey or buy some cheese. Rashel blew out the candle and put it back on her hearth and then turned back toward the magical visitor.

The Queen of Healing surprised her: a commoner, not a queen, with a long braid of golden-brown hair and a dusting of freckles on her pale skin. She wore a brown smock bound with a bodice of linen and a stiff apron with several pockets, and she carried a haversack as if she traveled the road to get here rather than coming in a burst of lavender light.

"Welcome," she said hoarsely. "I'm Rashel. This is..."

"I know who he is, my dear. Please don't speak his name," Honiea said, and to Rashel's ears, the command seemed harsh. "Is the baby well?" the woman asked as she walked toward the bed, leaving her bag on the floor beside the dead body.

"He's just been frightened," Rashel replied, surprised that the magician went first to Yeolani rather than Norton who lay with an obvious wound. Yeolani could have been asleep where she had managed to pull him onto her bed before she decided to use the candle. "We've all been frightened."

"You may call me Honiea," the female magician began as she sat on the edge of the bed and picked up Yeolani's flaccid hand. "Tell me everything that has happened."

Rashel gulped but did as she was ordered. She began at Norton's attack and made an effort to explain how the crystal had called Yeolani and then how he came but had fainted dead away moments after rescuing her.

Honiea bent and picked up the crystal which Rashel had discarded. As she touched the bloody shaft, Yeolani twitched, as if he were being transported again somewhere, but then settled. Honiea's quick eyes caught the reaction, and she creased her brow in concern. "And how exactly did he meet you?"

"About two months ago, Yeol...he came to town looking for help with his baby. I needed help to keep my farm. It was an exchange of skills. He would repair and run the farm with magic if I would take care of Nevai. He left me the crystal so I could call him if I needed his help, and it has worked thus far. But then Norton came..." her hand shook as she pointed toward the body, "and I had to call for help."

"I wonder where he's been in those two months," Honiea murmured. "He's been sick, lost a lot of weight that he couldn't afford to lose, but there's something more. Something magical has...Well, let us see." She set aside the crystal and knelt at the bedside and pressed her hand against Yeolani's closed eyes. With Rashel looking on, Honiea felt uncomfortable as she focused on listening to the mind she sensed. She hoped to see into the past so she could make her repairs. She wouldn't actually make the fixes until Rashel was gone.

Meanwhile, with Yeolani's shields down, much became clear to the Queen of Healing. She saw flashes of his work in a dark cavern and then him blowing into a storm, but she could not see the cause of his disquiet. Why had he left the cave so abruptly and unprepared? She witnessed pneumonia that had kept him feverish and burned his memories from him. She saw brief flashes of Everic's family but little of the interactions there. The discovery of a compass as a Talisman surprised her. She thought without knowing who he was, he would not have continued Seeking. Honiea then followed his trek west, guided by the compass. She saw how he didn't use magic to aid his survival. Then, when he reached the river, she witnessed his amazing encounter with the Siren.

"Siren?" Honiea whispered aloud, and Rashel stirred restlessly as she looked on.

"What's a siren?" the girl asked.

"I'm not sure. I've never heard the term, but he named it in his memories. It's something he met made of magic and mist on the river, and it began to take him over. He was drowning in the swamp when your crystal pulled him here. That saved his life, I suspect. He has amnesia and has had it for a while. He doesn't know who he is and might not even know he's a magician, but the Siren knew and drew him in. He's lucky to be alive."

Rashel nodded with a bit of understanding. "So, that's why he didn't come to do the planting," she commented. "He forgot everything."

"He made arrangements to come again?" Honiea glanced up and for the first time truly looked at the young woman Yeolani had given Nevai to raise. "What type of arrangements?"

"He had to be seen about the farm or the townsfolk would think he'd abandoned me and...and things like Norton thinking he could have his way with me would start happening again. Yeolani...sorry....he said he wouldn't marry me. Instead, he let the townsfolk think that it was because he was devoted to Nevai's mother, but I knew it was because he's a magician. I thought he would come more regularly just to let the town think that I had a man about the farm and that I was off-limits, but then, if he has amnesia, he might have forgotten Nevai and me completely."

"So," Honiea murmured mostly to herself, "you're what prompted that conversation. He and I had a little chat after he left Nevai with you. He wanted to learn how to travel quickly because he had an obligation to you but didn't dare stay long."

"I'm sorry, I don't understand," Rashel sighed with frustration. "Did I do something wrong in calling him? In calling you? What is wrong with him? Can you cure him?"

Honiea rose to her feet again to reassure her hostess. "You've done no wrong, and as I said, using the crystal to call him probably saved his life. He's very new at being a magician, and he probably has been foolish in even giving Nevai to you, but he's done nothing technically wrong. However, something is afflicting him, and I must break through that amnesia to help him. This will take some time. Do you have a chair?"

Honiea sat at Yeolani's side for several hours, and Rashel went about her chores, working her bread, setting her seeds, fixing a meal for three in hopes that there would be some change. She reluctantly went out to deal with the milk for the evening and forming her cheese. Once Rashel left the cabin, Honiea relaxed a bit. She had waited until that time when they would be alone to finally bring Yeolani out of his coma.

"Good evening," Honiea began in her most gentle voice, keeping the lanterns low in case his sickness remained sensitive to light. "Welcome back to the land of the living."

"Where am I?" Yeolani asked weakly.

"I'm glad the question wasn't who am I," Honiea replied. "Do you remember who you are now?"

Yeolani took a moment to consider. He looked around at his surroundings, at the simple bed and a screen to block the rest of the cabin from his sight, considering his options. "I am a magician who hasn't hidden my name. Yeolani? After my mother and father...I killed them, didn't I?"

"No, you tried to save them, but it was too late. Now, what do you remember doing last?"

Yeolani rolled his eyes and considered the problem. "I remember light burning on the river and a siren. I...a compass. And a blizzard. It was so cold. I was someplace dark and cold."

"The cavern," Honiea provided, making the connection to what she'd seen of the cave in his broken memories. "It's under the plains, beside a lake and the single shaft of light. You were working underground on something. Do you remember that?"

Taking the imagery she had seen earlier, Honiea shared it back into Yeolani's mind so he could match it with the memories that came flooding back inside. "I left my boots, everything there and became a blizzard. I'm an idiot," he groused. "That's why I was so cold. What happened?"

"That's what I'm trying to help you fit back into a whole,

not a scattered mess. Do you remember Vamilion and I discussing how you could learn to travel magically?"

He again had to work to make the connections. "I remember being sick every time I tried Vamilion's way. I was out looking for a Talisman that would help me travel."

"You found one, a compass?" prompted Honiea.

Yeolani restlessly drew his fingers through his hair and down over his eyes, trying to concentrate, to remember. "Yes, at the base of the cliff. But it didn't help me travel. I came as a blizzard. I found the compass and that family helped me. I used magic in front of them. They weren't frightened, but I didn't even realize I was doing it. They named me Archer...and the Siren, she drew me in using the compass."

"No, I don't think so," Honiea objected. "That compass is a Talisman. It cannot be misused if it is truly yours. This Siren, as you call her, hunted you because of your magic. You weren't even using your power to survive, but she sensed it in you and lured you in."

"What was she?" he asked, trying to get the mesmerizing image out of his mind by looking up at the simple ceiling of split beams in a humble home. He didn't remember arriving there quite yet.

"The Land is full of pent-up magic waiting to be tapped or harnessed. It is part of our Seeking to confront and explore these things....like that cavern. Where did you find that?

"Halfway to nowhere, out on the plains. I ...I think I dreamed about it when the fairies ...what did they tell me?"

"That there was a cavern under the plains?" Honiea prompted.

"No, the lake, they showed me the lake. Once I saw that it actually existed, I realized that people didn't live out halfway to nowhere because there had to be water. If I could tap into the lake beneath the prairie, I could bring people away from the rivers. So, I dug a well. That's where I found the crystals."

"Were the crystals part of a Talisman then?"

"No...." he strained to remember. "Were they a dream, real, or something in-between? I saw them in a dream, but they were really in that cave."

"So, what did you learn in the cavern then?" the Queen continued to help him build his memories backward. "Something drove you out into the night as a blizzard, so upset you left behind your boots and erased your own memory."

Yeolani closed his eyes over the unremembered horror. Flickers of light dancing in the dark. "Fairies again, flying in where I didn't need them. I dreamed something.... something I didn't want to hear. Fairies gave me... They gave me Nevai... Nevai!" He sat up in alarm, frantic that he'd forgotten the boy, but the blinding flash of pain across his eyes made him halt and Honiea pressed him back down into the bed. He collapsed back into the pillows and didn't fight her insistent hand on his chest.

"Go easy. You're still not well, Yeolani. Nevai is perfectly fine. You left him with Rashel, remember?"

"Rashel....?" And the air went out of his lungs in horror again. "The man was trying to rape her. I left her alone. That's why....Oh, what have I done?"

"Yeolani, did you fall in love with her?" Honiea demanded in a voice that would not allow him to equivocate. She didn't invoke name magic, but she came close, barely containing her disapproval.

Yeolani closed his eyes over the agony of remembering. "That's why I left the cavern under the plains. The fairies came to me there. They gave me my Lady's name, and it wasn't hers. I couldn't help it. I care for her, and I wanted...I wanted...I don't know what I wanted, but I wanted to escape from my own heart. That's why I can't remember. I wove a spell on myself to forget. And then I found Elin. She's a two-year-old girl on the edge of the world. And ...and you brought me back and made me remember anyway," he accused.

Honiea gently shook her head in regret. "No, your promise made you return. You gave Rashel a crystal that works like my candle. She used it out of desperation, and you couldn't help but return. Vamilion warned you not to fall in love."

"I had already met her, given her Nevai, and...and I think I loved her before we ever had that conversation. I've done nothing since except try to escape it."

Honiea dropped her head in regret. "Well, what's done is done. There probably was nothing you could have tried to prevent it. The Siren's song isn't the only thing you will hear for the rest of your eternal life."

Rashel's arms trembled with delayed shock as she pressed the moisture from the cheese curds, and she found herself bursting into tears. The rough hands that had violated her left their impressions on her flesh but more so on her mind. She ran to the well, desperate to wash away the memory of the attack. She poured a bucket over her head and then sputtering realized she would never feel clean this way.

And there was still a dead body in her house. Norton's children would expect their father to come back from the forest this evening. He wouldn't come. The magistrate would investigate and find Norton's blood had stained her floorboards, and Rashel shuddered with horror. What was she going to do? Yeolani would be accused of murder, and he would have to flee. No one would believe he was only defending her honor. How would she deal with this?

Unable to concentrate on such mindless work, Rashel left

the cheese molds and turned away from her chores for the first time in her life. She couldn't think and needed terribly to have answers, answers only to be found inside her home where two magicians hopefully had some way to reassure her. How could they deal with a dead rapist?

She stepped into the cabin and saw Honiea at the table. Rashel's eyes flicked toward the screen that shielded her bed where presumably Yeolani was still resting. Then she saw that the magician hadn't touched the body that now blocked her path to the hearth. The Queen's eyes did the speaking for her. *Come, sit and talk,* they demanded. In a witless haze, Rashel obeyed and sat across from the healer.

"How are you?" Honiea asked simply.

"I'm fine," Rashel began, but her hands gave her away, trembling.

"You were almost raped, or was he successful? Either way, you are not fine. You've bruises on your neck that I can see and probably somewhere I cannot see. How much did he hurt you?"

Rashel let her eyes break away from the Queen's so that she could answer a bit more easily. "I was more frightened than harmed. Norton always implied that he would have me and my farm someday. I couldn't stop him, just delay him. Now I'm afraid again for different reasons. What are we to do? They'll come after Yeolani for murder. He'll have to run, or they'll string him up, and nothing I say will change their minds. I can claim Norton was raping me, but they won't believe it...or they'll choose not to believe it. Then I will be turned out or the farm will be sold out from under me, and...and I am just frightened."

Honiea nodded her understanding, but she seemed unconcerned, even for the fate that awaited her protégé, let alone Rashel, who was a virtual stranger to her. "What if I could tell you that there was a way to make this all return back to how it was before? You could remain here at your home, raising Nevai, and Yeolani would not be wanted for murder. Even Norton would be alive."

Rashel couldn't move. She knew she must appear a fish, mouth open with surprise. "But he would....what is to keep Norton from coming after me again? You can turn back time?"

Honiea shook her head gently. "Not that I've tried, but I can undo much of what is wrong with what has happened, but in order to do that, I need your help."

"My help....what do you mean? I'm not magical."

"Not in the same way as we are. However, you hold a magic that is more powerful than you know. You hold Yeolani's heart, and that must be brought to bear."

"I hold...his heart?"

"Yes, he loves you. He cannot help himself now. It is as strong as our most grand spell, can topple empires, crack mountains, and break the Land. And Yeolani is powerless in it, even beyond what the Siren did to him. That's what drove him mad and brought him to his amnesia. He knows loving you is forbidden, and he washed away his own memory in order to forget you. And it failed. So, we must try a different strategy."

Rashel sat at her table for what seemed ages, watching the cold frankness of the Queen's words freeze in the air between them, hoping the doctor's medicine would go down her dry throat. Was the cure worse than the disease?

"And what is so wrong about falling in love with me. Cannot a magician make that choice for himself?"

"He will break your heart trying. You see, there is a Lady prepared from the foundation of the world just for him. He was given her name and it was not yours. He is bound, driven to Seek her out. He might love you, for he will come to love all those he serves like he loves Nevai and Marit. But that means that he will leave you or you will leave him in death. He will live forever, and you will not. He will be a slave to the magic's drive to find his queen. He should seek her freely, with no obligations or devotion to you. Would you want that for him?"

Rashel didn't answer. She thought instead. A seed in her mind grew into a tangled weed, strangling all other shoots that might strain up into words of possible solutions. She presumed Honiea would hear all her thoughts, but until she actually vocalized, Rashel wouldn't be rejected. This, on top of the other struggle, to see a future with a dead man in her path, made for a long wait. The dormant seeds of thought expected the light and warmth of being spoken to break through to them. Finally, when she had processed all Honiea had implied, Rashel came up with something to say that might allow one sprout to break her silence.

"You spoke of needing my help."

Honiea nodded, visibly relieved, for that meant Rashel could be reasonable. "There is a way to bring Norton back to life. Yeolani possesses it. I can heal Norton's wound. Together we can make it so that this man never will remember you and will never touch you again. But then you must disappear. You cannot cross paths again with Yeolani, and he must not be able to find you either. The cut must be clean, or it will drive him insane...and a mad magician is not a safe thing."

Rashel sat stiffly, not reacting to the harsh message, thinking numbly of how it would impact her life. There were loose ends and cold realities she must understand. For instance, "Nevai? Will he be mine or will he go with Yeolani?" Rashel fired at Honiea, now speaking just as clinically and coldly as the healer.

Honiea hesitated. "In that, I have no say. Yeolani has a voice on that decision as well. It is a problem. Nevai belongs to Yeolani, but there's no way he can honor his magic and be a father for a baby at the same time. He was right to bring him to you, but after....after this, you might not be able to raise him either. It is unfortunate that the fairies imposed this on you both."

"Unfortunate?" Rashel gasped. "No, I will never believe that. Giving that baby a chance at life, a family that loves him, that will always be magic. I might be homeless, but if Nevai needs a mother, I will do what I can to be that for him. You cannot take him away at the same time you tell me that Yeolani will also be lost to me." Her vehemence startled the queen.

Honiea's voice, humbled by the other woman, whispered. "So, you love them both, don't you?"

Rashel didn't have to admit to it; love wasn't a crime. She had no logical reason to love Nevai, and certainly not Yeolani. Right then she knew she would lay down her life gladly for both. "I barely know him, and I cannot explain it. If it's not love, what is this that I feel for him?"

Honiea shook her head with regret. "There is more magic in the world than any of us can comprehend. We learn more every time a new act is performed, a new spell imagined, a new mystery reveals itself. The Land ripples with potential waiting to be opened."

"Well, in that case, I am going to use my 'magic,' " Rashel insisted. "You say that I need to convince Yeolani that it is best if he leaves me. I want to talk to him first, to see how he feels. Is this a sacrifice he is willing to make? And then there must be a plan. I cannot survive without magic at this point. What am I to do with myself and Nevai?"

"I will think about that," Honiea reassured her, but Rashel interrupted.

"First, I speak with him, without your ...your...influence. Is he well enough to speak with me? Can you leave for a few hours so that we can talk privately?"

Honiea must be well-practiced at keeping her emotions behind a placid face. Rashel felt reasonably sure that the Queen would not like what the coming conversation might entail. Rashel knew full well that if she made the mistake of hurting Yeolani in any way, the wrath of the Healing Queen would not be gentle.

"I love him, remember," Rashel tried to reassure the magician. "I want him to make the right choices for us all, but I cannot do that if I do not speak with him."

Honiea nodded, agreeing, at least, in principle. "I am not his mother, but his teacher. I will not hinder you," Honiea replied slowly. "He should wake naturally. See that he eats something soon. Call me if you need me." And then the Queen of Healing stood up. "And one last thing. Ask him to remember the Life Giver."

"Life Giver?"

"He'll need to think about it, but he'll remember with a little prompting. It might help his decisions." And with that advice, Honiea disappeared in a rippling mist of lavender light.

17

GROUNDED FAIRY

*A*fter Honiea's departure, Rashel sat at her table a few minutes in a stupor, unsure if she could even reason through the quandary in which she found herself trapped. She instinctively knew that Yeolani would try to do what he thought was right, no matter how miserable it would make him. She feared that. Did she love Yeolani? If what she felt wasn't love, she had no other name for it. Why was she falling in love with a virtual stranger? She would lay down her life for this man after only a few days in his presence. She would weep if he left her and rage for the rest of her life at the magic that would separate them. Why? What was the magic that did this?

It wasn't all physical attraction, either, Rashel reasoned, though that helped. She loved the lean lines of him, his simple rangy wildness like he'd been crafted out of the earth and timbers as raw material, right from the Land. And when he smiled, which was often, his eyes twinkled, warm brown, and she felt an irresistible need to run her fingers through his hair, like the grain in a barrel or the freshly tilled soil of a field: magical. Yeolani's strange, self-effacing antics also attracted her.

He had an odd habit of humming at the strangest times: scraping moss off the roof, when he scratched Marit's head, or when he held the baby. It was simply charming to her. Why?

And Honiea claimed Yeolani loved her? Why? Again, the magic shouldn't allow him to fall in love with her, but yet he had. That wasn't fair to him. She sensed a low anger warming at the fickle decisions of their emotions. Fickle as fairies. She didn't trust any of it and wanted to rebel. Weren't magicians also humans and free agents, not pawns of God? Everyone else in the Land could make decisions of their own, and yet magic toyed with him. How dare it do so?

Oh, you're a fool Rashel, she told herself. *Life for everyone is fickle, and you know it. Your mother died young, your brother left home younger, your father basically sold you into slavery, and life just happens that way. No fairies to apply to any of it. The flighty passage of life also dropped feathers of joy and goodness into your life. You are a better person for having known Yeolani, for holding Nevai and seeing this magical world. It might only be for a small while, but you were happy in it.* Life Giver, indeed. Yeolani was a life giver to her.

Rashel still didn't know what to do or where her decisions would go, but she felt capable now of taking a step into the dark and feeling her way, as long as Yeolani was willing to speak with her. It would be a deep, honest conversation.

With trepidation, she looked over at the screened-off bed and rose to her feet. Rashel slipped behind the screen, leaving Norton's body behind, and saw Yeolani there on the bed, sprawled all over it, occupying far more space than was fair.

She knelt at his side and looked closely at his face. He seemed worn, haggard, but the faint freckles across his cheekbones, the blush of sun, even this early in spring, and the irresistible dance of his closed lashes attracted her. He looked younger than he should have. She gave into an urge and caressed his hair, drawing her fingers through the long strands that needed a trim. He stirred, and she snatched back her hand. His eyes flickered open, and she waited until he managed to get them to focus on her, and she smiled.

"Good evening, sir," she whispered as softly as she could, hoping Nevai would not wake any time soon.

"Rashel?" Yeolani asked with a huskiness in his abused voice.

"Water?" and she didn't wait for him to reply. Instead, she reached for the water bucket and helped him sit up to drink from the ladle.

He drank gratefully but didn't make eye contact with her while she tended to him. He looked everywhere; the roof beams, the screen, to Nevai's cradle tucked near the head of the bed, even the window above his head, anywhere but at Rashel right in front of him holding the water.

"Honiea said you were to eat right away," Rashel declared, trying to keep the tremor out of her voice. She hoped he wasn't listening to the chaos and fear in her inner thoughts.

"Honiea said...has she left?" Yeolani finally turned toward her, though Rashel wasn't sure he actually looked at her.

"She agreed that you and I need to talk. Do you want to come to the table, or should I feed you here in bed?"

Yeolani's manly pride wouldn't allow this, so she helped him out of the bed to hobble to the table. He straightened in alarm when he saw Norton's body still with the arrow sticking out of his side. Yeolani's eyes grew wide, but Rashel chose to ignore it. That man was nothing but an obstacle as she navigated Yeolani to the bench and then stepped over the corpse to get a bowl of her stew and to cut bread. Wordlessly, she served supper, smeared some of her soft cheese over the bread, and poured milk into mugs for them both. Neither of them really felt bad about eating with the dead. Norton deserved to be ignored.

"You're a wonderful cook." Yeolani finally found a voice after he had scarfed down two bowls. "Where did you learn?"

"My mother...and then when she died, I asked around the village for help. I was only six, and my father demanded...he was a hard man to please, but I did my best," she replied in a conversational tone, careful to avoid sensitive areas.

But Yeolani wasn't willing to do that. "I killed my own father. He beat my mother to death and would have me as well, so Norton isn't the first man I've killed...except for sorcerers. It seems to be my fate to kill men of that sort." He looked over at the corpse with a critical eye, judging the accuracy of his shot and the simplicity it had entailed.

Rashel would not let him dwell on what he had done. She wanted him to recognize it had been a service to her, and she drew his eyes away to focus on the good. "No, you're a life giver. Honiea wanted me to make you remember the Life Giver. Do you know what she was talking about?"

"Life Giver?" He looked away from Norton to Rashel and for the first time truly seemed to consider her again. "She wanted me to remember the Life Giver? Where did I leave that...my pack?"

Abruptly, he put down his spoon and then held out his hand over the table. With little idea of what he was trying, Yeolani sent his magical mind out into the night and over the prairie. He noted how the green grasses now poked through the winter dead patches and spoke of spring to him. He passed horses and great herds of buffalo and antelope, seeking an empty place in the middle of nowhere.

He found it after raising his mind's eye up into the sky and pressing down with his thoughts, seeking a depression in the earth. The well he had built, invisible except from high above, waited for him. Yeolani plunged his mind through the hole and into the crystal cavern. He avoided the water and strained for the shore in the pitch dark. And there he found his boots, his pack, and all his belongings undisturbed after weeks in the cave. He closed his mental hand over the strap of his pack and pulled it back to Rashel's cabin.

She lurched in alarm as the supplies landed with a thump on the table without Yeolani even physically going after it.

"I left my pack, but if it doesn't die of neglect, the Life Giver should still be in here." He began rifling through the things he carried with him. "I'd forgotten I even had it."

Rashel looked at his belongings in interest as he pulled items out: a wickedly sharp hunting knife, bow and a quiver of arrows, stylus to record his travels, a sack of desiccated apples, a change of leather trousers, a clean shirt, and wooden dishes. Finally, he upended the bag and out spilled three objects she couldn't identify: one furry little ball and two gently glowing marbles the color of the moon on a clear summer night. Her hand reached irresistibly for the furry thing, but unexpectedly, it rolled away from her and into Yeolani's lap. It chattered and yipped with indignity at her, and Yeolani absently began caressing the creature. As Rashel looked up, she saw a stunned expression on his face. He stared at the glowing marbles. He looked like he'd seen a ghost.

"Yeolani, what is it?" and she snapped her fingers in front of his eyes. He jerked as if he had just been slapped.

"Oh...um, um... it's a horrible trick, it is," he replied with consternation and then peered again down at the two glowing balls of light. "There used to be one and now there are two. I didn't realize that it came with the name."

"What are you talking about?" Rashel asked, forcing herself to be patient with his slowly returning memories. She knew better than to reach for the obviously magical orbs, especially since they seemed to have terrified Yeolani. For his part, he wasn't sure how much he dared reveal to Rashel, a non-magician. He knew one of the two Heart Stones was his, but from where did the other appear? How could he tell which one was his? And what was he to do with the second Heart Stone?

Then he realized who was supposed to have it: Elin, the toddler. The thought of waiting twenty years until that little girl grew into a woman... it overwhelmed him. Could he wait for that balance and love that he witnessed in Honiea and Vamilion? Could he endure the loneliness? And how would he explain this situation to Elin's parents?

With a trembling hand, Yeolani reached out and touched the Heart Stones. At the cool sensation of their glassy surface, he knew what had happened and how to resolve the mystery. One spoke his name to him and the other whispered the name Elin. The second one even pulsed to another heartbeat and breathing. It was Elin's, with her bright eyes the same color as the swirling light in the stone. He felt the compulsion. He must protect the child and the stone from all other interference, protect it more closely than he had his own life.

With a tremendous effort, he remembered that Rashel watched him and had asked him a question. "It's a Heart Stone," he whispered and picked them up. "It is what will turn my lady into a magician, once I find her. In the meantime, I'm supposed to protect them, although that's not gone well."

"The bottom of your pack is hardly a safe place," Rashel pointed out logically. "Bury it somewhere or make it invisible. It's a stone on your heart. Hide it there."

The words Heart Stone triggered an idea in Yeolani's mind, tickling at the magic at his disposal. He remembered how Honiea's pack felt weighty but was almost empty of anything except the exact thing she wanted. Everything else was invisible. He held up his Heart Stone to the lantern and then closed his eyes while he wished a spell of invisibility on it and then placed it in a space near his heart, small and undetectable, even by him unless he wanted to draw it back out into the open. Not even another magician would know where or how to find it. He could sense it if he wanted to, but he couldn't feel it unless he drew on it.

"That was an excellent idea," he complimented Rashel, but then he held up the second stone. "And this is my Lady's. Did Honiea tell you..." But he couldn't even finish the sentence.

You're a coward, he chided himself. *You barely know this woman and you are frightened to leave her to go waiting for a fairy's fevered dream to grow up.* And yet he did love Rashel, a lovely and compassionate adult woman. And what would this do to his magic? He had enough experience with the supernatural to know he could not ignore the impulses and compulsions being a Wise One would demand. More so, since he now knew where to find Elin. He would have to fight that contrary wind every step of the way. Would he come to resent these drives? Or would he grow bitter over the severed ties his magic imposed? It formed a scar on his life either way.

Rashel murmured from far away, "She told me you had a decision to make and that the Life Giver could help. She said you would have to leave me to seek your Lady. And that either way I would not be safe here. If you leave, the people would think...that they could do what Norton presumed. And you will have to leave. You've killed the brute, and the villagers will demand justice and you will be hung. And Nevai? Traveling in a magician's wake is no way to grow up, but neither is starving to death with me."

Yeolani found himself shaking his head in denial before he could reject that future. "It will not happen that way," he intoned. "I swear that will not happen to him."

Rashel's eyes blurred with tears, or so she thought. Then

she eased back and looked at Yeolani. She recognized his very appearance had altered before her eyes. He hadn't moved, but now his clothing seemed to glow. His simple linen tunic, too big for him, had shifted into a fine silk shirt that rippled across his body in an unfelt wind right there in the cabin. He wore a jerkin of fine, sage green velvet with gold stitching that shone in the lanterns. Over that rested a cloak of subtle suede, tawny and rich and also patterned with embroidery of gold that crafted imprints of wheat and horses running across a vast expanse. At his back, Yeolani had strapped on another bow and arrows, but these shone with polished mahogany wood, fletching of stiff white goose feathers and black arrowheads deadlier than she cared to guess.

Yeolani didn't look surprised at his transformation, just resigned. He took off the calfskin gloves that came with his changed status and placed them on the table as if they were a burden. "I'm sorry. That keeps happening. Every time I make a promise. Usually, I can stop it if I start cussing, but...but, Rashel, I find it very hard to use that kind of language around you. And I used to be a sailor," he laughed and reached toward her hand.

"What....what is this?" She managed to get the words out but only just. Her own hand instinctively pulled away from his reach. She watched the pained expression in his eyes as if she had rejected him. She really hadn't, but the stunning changes overwhelmed her.

Yeolani picked up his glove, muttered a curse under his breath and watched himself shift back into his simple clothing, worn, stained, and human. "It's the sign of my magic. I am the King of the Plains, just as Honiea is the Queen of Healing and Vamilion is King of the Mountains. We have charge of these gifts. I can travel as a tornado and am drawn to the open spaces. That, and I seem to be gifted with messing up things."

Rashel nodded and managed to relax at his snide remark. "And that globe, it makes someone else a magician?"

Yeolani had forgotten the second Heart Stone and picked it up again. "It belongs to the Lady I'm supposed to marry." Without more explanation, he made it disappear beside his own and hoped that would end her curiosity.

He had no such luck. "And what is the Life Giver?" Rashel asked, nodding to the contented furry creature still nestled in the crook of his arm, undisturbed by the magical transformations going on around it.

"It's another mistake I made. It is a way to repair the messes I seem to create." He looked down at Norton's corpse that had turned an ugly plum color where his blood had settled. "Honiea can heal him if I use the Life Giver to bring Norton back."

Rashel didn't argue that thought, though her strange eyes widened a bit in wonder. She'd seen enough in the last few hours to believe anything he claimed possible. What she did question was the wisdom of doing this. "I understand bringing him back to life, but is that really going to help the situation? He will still think he can have his way with me. You will still have to run for your life, and we'll be exactly where we were yesterday."

"No," Yeolani looked deeply at her. He had made up his mind, and now he had to convince her of what they could do. "No, I'll wipe his memory. He won't remember attacking you. He won't remember me shooting him, though I might give him some nightmares to prevent him from wanting to rape anyone else again. Norton will be easy."

"And what about Nevai?" Rashel asked frankly, her eyes moving past Yeolani to the cradle where the baby remained.

Yeolani reached out and touched her hands again, this time not letting her pull away. Instead, he almost begged for her peaceful eyes to settle him down. He could never be out of balance, he hoped, but he was willing to run this risk if she would simply help him. The fairies had given him Nevai, and so in a roundabout way, they included Rashel too. He had to put faith in that alternative magic. He might have to wait for ages to find Elin again, but he would be happy while he waited. He took one steadying breath and then spoke.

"Rashel, will you marry me?"

She stopped breathing for a moment, and if she could, her heart would have stopped just as suddenly. A thousand thoughts, like leaves scattering in the fall, flickered through her mind and then the branches of her mind were bare. She couldn't think at all. Spring in her thoughts took some time to arrive, and when it did, it came in a blossoming of buds that emerged and then faded before she even got them out of her mouth.

What about your Lady? What about when I grow old and die? I cannot follow you all over the Land. I won't hold you back. You'll be torn in two. What happens when you find the Lady? Will you have to break my heart and Nevai's? Honiea would never approve. I would be left behind. I would always be worrying every time you tore away in some tornado to battle with evil. A marriage should be between equals. I'm nothing, a dairy maid.

"So? I was a very bad, sea-sick fisherman," he whispered as a way to cut across her unspoken ranting.

"You were listening to my thoughts?" she glared, and for the first time, he realized Rashel had a temper. Yeolani thought she would be gentle and peaceful like she'd been with Nevai. Now, too late, he realized she was the mama bear and he had stepped in too far.

He nodded his guilt and admitted it. "I'm an idiot as well as a bad sailor. I've been bumbling through becoming a magician this whole time. What makes me think I will ever be better at it with experience? I'm a worse magician than I was a fisherman."

Rashel pulled back and looked surprised. "Don't put yourself down, sir. It's unbecoming," she ordered in mock severity. "You are amazing, and that doesn't include magic. You took on Nevai even though you never asked for him. You didn't for one moment try to avoid that responsibility. You tried to wipe your memory of me in order to spare us this problem. That took true courage. If you think I will allow you to sacrifice your magical destiny, pinned to the ground...it's not right. You're like the fairies. You shouldn't be grounded."

Yeolani lifted up the furry creature from his arm and held it out to her. "A grounded fairy. I cursed them by accident. My first act of magic. I actually killed them, but Honiea worked an amazing spell and brought them back in this form. She called them Life Givers because they will regain their wings if they bring someone back from the dead. I am going to give this one its opportunity with Norton. Will you give this grounded fairy an opportunity to love you?"

"I....I..." Rashel could not bring another thought to mind for a long moment, with his pleading eyes unhinging her. "You cannot be happy with someone like me. I'm just a simple person. I would never be able to keep up. This farm and Nevai, that's all I need. I'm rooted here."

"Then that's where you'll be. I could marry you here. My home is fine here. I know we can be happy here. I don't have to go Seeking. I could stay and love you and our child, and the world would grow old all around us, and I would be content. Please, Rashel."

She set her hand gently against his lips to stay his pleading. "How will you deny magic when it brought us together? When it brought Nevai to us? When we acknowledge that we love each other because the magic made it so? If you do not water your garden, you cannot expect plants to spring up with fruit. You will need magic like a plant needs water. It's in your blood."

Yeolani shook his head, unwilling to listen to that logic. "I've resisted using magic before, and with you in my life, it would be so much easier. Besides, too often with my magic I've made a bigger mess of things. It's better that I not overdo. I need you to balance me, keep me from foolish, flashy spells. No one should ever be a magician alone."

"Yes," she countered. "But I cannot be with you always. I will fade. You will last forever, like a great oak, and I am only a daisy, withering in days. All the Life Givers you have will not keep me from passing. And it will become obvious to the townsfolk. You will have to leave me before I look old enough to be your mother."

"I will never leave you," he promised and felt the shimmering of his clothing changing. "I will hold your hand until you cannot any longer...."

But unbidden, he saw in her mind's eye an image of them together in sixty years. He looked no different than he did now, still an exuberant twenty-two. And she, with silver and white hair, still in long braids, but with wrinkles on her weathered skin, hunched with age, and her eyes watery and dim. The older Rashel leaned her head in exhaustion against his shoulder and then slumped into a long sleep. He brushed his hand over her wispy hair in the vision and felt the breaking of his heart once again.

"Do not swear," Rashel whispered. "I will not let you break your heart twice. Once is enough."

Yeolani looked at this wonderful girl, so determined to set him free, and realized he could not win. She would refuse him for his own sake.

"Your answer is no?" he whispered in finality.

"I love you too much to let you make that sacrifice," sighed Rashel. She pulled back, trying to be clinical and cold like Honiea. "I will recover from the heartbreak. We only have to decide how we will take care of Nevai and the farm and...and how I will fare. It's best this way."

At those painful, truthful words, Yeolani felt an ache in the back of his throat. With all the magic at his disposal, he could not change her mind. That lesson of the coin had not prepared him for this bitter truth.

With a shuddering breath, Yeolani managed to match her detachment as best as he could. "I'll wipe Norton's memory and bring him back so you don't have to worry about accusations. We can sign over the ownership of the farm to you and insist that the town allows you to stay...stay where you're rooted. I'll leave you all the gold you need, and you can buy fodder rather than worry about planting each year. The spell to milk the cows will last as long as the barn is upright. See that it keeps mended. Eventually, if you find someone else, you might just make a habit of seeing that the cows aren't in their stalls at dusk. He need never know there's magic in the milking."

"And Nevai?"

Yeolani's voice almost broke, and he had to draw on the memory of the cold cavern's lake before he went on. "He's yours. You are right. Being raised by a tornado or in the middle of a herd of buffalo is no life for a baby. Perhaps, when he's old enough, I'll come and teach him some of the things boys need to learn, so he knows he has a father. And I'll look in on him...I will..."

"Please, do not swear," she interrupted him. "He'll need a father."

"Yes, and you can find someone and fall in love and give him a fitting father. Find yourself someone who can be your equal, though there cannot be another person in the world that is worthy of you. You are...."

"A milkmaid," she reminded him.

"Don't put yourself down, miss. It's unbecoming," he echoed, and she smiled sadly at his admonishment. Then he continued. "Shall I wipe your memory too? It would ease your way."

Rashel looked away from him, turning to Norton's corpse just to have some way to remain impassive. "No, I need to remember. You're a part of me now. How else will I know where Nevai came from. I need to remember because you are the most beautiful thing that has come into my life; a rose in a field of daisies. I want to remember that, and someday, it won't hurt. For those of us will die, the pain will fade too. All I'll really hold on to are the happy memories."

18

SWORN

*E*arly the next morning, they called Honiea to implement their plan to resurrect Norton. No one actually talked with the Queen of Healing about their other plans, and she had the grace to not ask about it either. Their reddened eyes and grim faces spoke enough, and Honiea knew they would not be happy with either decision.

"We need to bring the lecher back," Yeolani said without preamble. They hadn't bothered moving the body, but they finally had put a blanket over him the night before, if only to ease their consciences.

"Do you have the Life Giver?" Honiea asked, and when he held up the little furry creature, she nodded. "You'll have to remove the arrow first, and hopefully, we can fix the damage. I've never done this before."

Wordlessly, Yeolani flipped back the cover, and then, with little ceremony, he put his boot on Norton's shoulder to provide leverage and unceremoniously jerked the arrow out from under the arm. With a flash of magic, Yeolani made the offending shaft disappear; and then, as an afterthought, he made the pool of dried blood fade as well. No need to have a newly revived Norton wondering why he was lying on the floor in his own gore. He then magically lifted the huge man to one of the beds as the women followed.

"Now you must give the Life Giver to the corpse. It can only be a Seeking King. I can't do this," Honiea advised as she knelt at Norton's side, hands hovering over the man's chest, waiting for the promised soul to return.

Yeolani nodded, caressed the excitable little furball one more time, and then placed it right over the corpse's heart. They waited for some reaction with tense anticipation. What would they do if this didn't work? Probably bury the corpse in the forest, and Rashel could claim she'd seen him walk in but never saw him after that. She could lie convincingly, and she stood ready to lie about everything, to back up the story they had concocted to explain Norton's absence and why he was in her house.

Honiea sensed a thump from Norton's savaged heart and began weaving the sundered muscles, knitting them back together. One of the major arteries to the heart had been pierced, and she mended it with a thought. Norton had lost a lot of blood, but it had filled his chest cavity rather than spilling out of his wound. Honiea directed the blood back into the veins before she sealed them off, liquefied it again, and pushed down on the repaired heart in order to ignite the pumping motion. With her first push, a gasp of air tore down Norton's throat and he coughed. Norton's eyes flashed open in alarm. They'd grown milky during his time dead, and before he could try to focus, he collapsed in exhaustion and pain.

"Norton," Rashel began explaining to him through his groans. "Relax, you've been hurt. It's your heart. We've got a healer here. You'll be fine in a while."

Yeolani looked over at her and whispered, "You realize you didn't lie. Every word you said was true. That was amazing."

Norton spent the better part of an hour delirious and in pain while Honiea worked on repairing the damage of the arrow as well as the rotting process that had set in. Yeolani used that pain to link it magically with the thought of raping or even touching another woman, tying the thought to the agony he was experiencing. If Norton made it out of this alive and sane, he surely would never want to think of a woman again. It seemed to fit the crime, and with no overt magic to enforce the process, the man could live the rest of his life in peace and never know anything had changed.

While he was in Norton's mind, Yeolani wiped away the memory of what had happened on the day he tried to rape Rashel. Instead, he placed a vivid recollection of felling trees and having one fall on him, thus explaining the injuries and the need of the healer. It even worked as an explanation as to why he was in Rashel's house. Hers was the last one on the road to the forest, and anyone who brought him back in from the forest to town reasonably could expect to stop here to get help. While they worked, Rashel ran to Norton's house and told his children the lie they'd prepared and brought his oldest son back. Meanwhile, Honiea had covered the man with bandages, and he would have impressive scars to go with the perceived injuries.

The Life Giver had worked perfectly. The little fuzzy creature had moved on, now a dust bunny under Rashel's bed, lifeless and probably testing out wings once again somewhere else. By noon, Yeolani and Norton's eldest son had made a gurney to lug the man to his home to continue his recovery, leaving Rashel and Honiea alone in the cabin.

"So, what have you decided?" Honiea asked as she held

Nevai and entertained the baby while Rashel grimly prepared a lunch for her guests.

"He will be a magician and move on. I'll keep Nevai and my memories. Hopefully, we will both find someone else to love in the future," Rashel answered in a flat voice.

Unexpectedly Honiea didn't comment but stood up, bringing Nevai with her, and gave Rashel a heartfelt hug and handed the baby to his mother. "You are an amazing woman, my dear. Please, keep the candle nearby, and I will come if you need me."

With that Honiea left in her customary shimmer of light.

Soon after Yeolani returned from delivering Norton to his house. "He's settled and will make a complete recovery, unfortunately," Yeolani commented in much the same flat tone Rashel had used earlier. "Shall we go to town and transfer the farm? After lunch, I suppose, if I can eat anything."

"It's not a death sentence, Yeolani," Rashel reminded him frankly. "This is the best for us both. You're going Seeking again and will have many grand adventures. Do you know where you're going to go first?"

Yeolani hadn't thought about it. Indeed, he hadn't considered where he would Seek at all. Now, he needed some goal if only to avoid looking in on Elin. Without thinking about it, he fished the Talisman compass out of his pocket where he had carried it ever since the incident with the Siren. He had not even shown it to Rashel or Honiea. Now he wondered if he trusted the magic it held. The compass had led him to the Siren, a trap, and yet had also kept him alive. He sat at the table and opened it, briefly trying to explain it to Rashel.

"I found this when I had amnesia. It is a Talisman, a magical guide that I found, but I don't know if I should trust it." The one arm still faithfully pointed north but the second arm wavered and wobbled as if it couldn't make up its mind. It swung in a quarter arch and back again with no explanation.

"Why wouldn't you trust such magic?" Rashel asked as she placed sliced cheese, meats, and bread on the table and then turned to get a pitcher of her ever-present milk.

"Because the silly thing is following you," Yeolani muttered. He watched the magic arm swing back to the south as Rashel brought the pitcher from the sideboard.

She put down the milk and, while keeping an eye on the face of the dial, edged around the table. The compass moved unerringly wherever she shifted. "Maybe it doesn't follow what you should Seek but where your duty lies," she suggested.

"I didn't need to do some duty for the Siren, and it led me to her," Yeolani pointed out. "The deceitful thing led me into her snare."

"Not the compass. It kept you safe," objected Rashel. "The Siren's magic lured you in, and the compass expected you to confront her as part of your duty to use magic. It's still a guide. It guides you to what you should do, not necessarily what you should Seek. You have a duty to finish here with me, and then it will guide you somewhere else. Trust that."

Yeolani acquiesced to Rachel's logic, and they ate lunch without speculating more over the compass's use. Rashel cleaned up the dishes while Yeolani did some final preparations to leave her. He conjured a simple wooden box to sit on Rashel's mantle. Then he explained what he had created.

"It has no lock, but it will not open unless you and you alone are holding it." Yeolani demonstrated his own efforts to pry the lid open with his fingernails. Then he handed it to her, and she easily lifted it open. Inside sat a single gold coin. "This box will fill with however much you need to pay for whatever service you need. Hire someone to plow your fields or mend a fence. You can buy a cart to carry cheese to town or new clothes. You will never need as long as you have this box."

Rashel nodded and took the simple wooden chest, put it beside Honiea's candle, and there she saw the crystal he'd given her as a means of calling him. Her fingers brushed it, sending shivers down Yeolani's back as she picked it up. She brought it down, now numb with sadness. "I shouldn't have this then," she murmured. "I'd be too tempted...at least for a while."

With a sorrowful heart, Yeolani accepted back the crystal and made it disappear back into the earth from which he had conjured it. He then packed up his things and shouldered the pack made for Nevai so they could walk to town. Outside, the spring had settled into glorious bright warmth. They walked close enough to hold hands but didn't dare. It would seem wrong somehow now. The birds chattering and the light smell of plum blossoms mocked their solemn footsteps.

At the city hall, they found the gentleman who had officiated at the auction. Clerk, mayor, and magistrate all in one, Yeolani thought but greeted the man with a friendly handshake. "I'd like to take a look at the records of Rashel's farm. I want to make sure it is hers, no matter what happens to me," he declared.

"Of course," the mayor replied, but his suspicion evidenced itself with a sideways look. "You aren't planning on dying, are you, Master Yeolani." *Or leaving*, his thoughts continued loud enough for Yeolani to hear.

"You never know," redirected Yeolani, "so I want her to be taken care of."

"I would have thought you would come in soon to marry her instead," the silly man commented as he pulled up the carefully written deed and put it out on the counter. "Can you read then, sir?"

Yeolani assured the mayor that he could and made a show

of reading the official document while Rashel looked on. "Will putting it in her name ensure that she can remain on the farm if anything happens to me? No more auctions or some such nonsense," Yeolani wanted the man's promise. "I'll marry her when it's right," he added to reassure him.

The mayor didn't make the promise but instead brought out a pen. "I'll write her in as your heir and that should do the job. Now, Rashel, do you know how to spell your given name?"

"It's Elin, E-L-I-N Hokansdotter..." but she paused when she realized that the clerk had frozen with the pen hovering over the paper. She looked over at Yeolani who stood there with his mouth agape as well, but at least he was blinking. "What?" she protested. "Rashel's a nickname, and this document has to be official."

"How on God's green earth did you get Rashel from Elin?" he asked in near shock. Yeolani's mind wouldn't settle until he heard this amazing tale.

"My mother called me Rashel first. I was always climbing trees too high, falling in the well, riding the cows and bulls for fun, and otherwise putting myself in danger. She believed the fairies followed me to keep me from breaking my neck. She kept saying I was 'far too rash, Elin.' It became something of a reminder; "Rash El" every time I did something dangerous. It quickly got shortened to Rashel until no one knew me by my real name. Is that a problem?"

"No," Yeolani sighed, looking over at the clerk who remained in that frozen state like on the first day they had met the winter before. Then Yeolani shifted back at Rashel's intense eyes set in a perfectly sweet face. "It's just that when the fairies told me the name of my lady I had only two things to guide me: her name and the knowledge that I would love her immediately. It would be a compulsion. The lady I was to Seek was to be named Elin."

Now, it was Rashel's turn to have her mouth pop open in wonder. "You didn't know my name after all the mind reading you did? You mean..." and she reached out her hand and touched his chest where he'd hidden the Heart Stone meant for that lady he would leave her to Seek.

"It would mean you would become a magician, and there are a whole host of limits and strange things you'll find happening to you. You won't be able to lie anymore, and you'll find you have to..."

Rashel interrupted by reaching up and kissing him, making speaking impossible. That first kiss, gentle and amazingly light, as if spring finally had thawed him out after the terrible winter, made it all worthwhile. The torn priorities mended instantly. When she pulled away, Rashel's smile made him weak in the knees and he couldn't breathe.

"Ask me again," she ordered.

Yeolani put his hand against her cheek, twining his long fingers in her rich mahogany hair, hoping the spell on the mayor lasted a bit longer. "Elin, will you marry me?"

"Yes," she breathed.

"Even if it means leaving your farm and raising Nevai on the plains and fighting evil and living in that cave I found and..." She kissed him again to stop the litany of indignities he could foresee.

"Even if it means all of that. All I need is for you to be whom you were meant to be, King of the Plains. If it will not hold you back, then I will go with you anywhere in the Land."

The smile on her face was infectious, and he grinned back with a twinkle in his eye. "Then shall we?" He caught her nod of readiness, and he broke the freezing spell on the mayor. She took up where she'd left off.

"That's H-O-K-A-N-S dotter."

The official took down her name as Yeolani's heir and then

had Yeolani sign his name to agree to this change. If they seemed a bit impatient, or if Yeolani's hand shook slightly as he signed his name, the mayor didn't note it.

When the officer began blowing on the deed to dry the ink, Yeolani added, "Now that I've made that step, it's time. I think I will marry her, right here and now.

The mayor manfully covered up his surprise and gladly drafted out a marriage certificate for them. He called a passerby to come inside the office to witness for them, and they were married before the city official without much ceremony. This time they walked back to the farm hand in hand, traveling a great deal faster than they had come.

19

LOOKING DOWN

Yeolani made a tremendously stupid decision on the walk back toward the cabin. He felt so giddy with the wonder of having this woman actually agree to marry him that he needed to give her a gift to show his love. He stopped in the middle of the morning traffic in the busiest part of the path through town and gave Rashel a long, lusty kiss to prepare her.

"I want to give you the Heart Stone," he whispered.

"Here? Now?" Her eyes grew huge. "Won't it..."

Yeolani knew what she was asking and stopped her. "Nothing is going to happen. No one will notice. At least it didn't with me. It doesn't change you. It's a key to a door, and you have to walk inside."

"Very well," but the trepidation in her eyes spoke of her doubt. Loud in her thoughts rang dread of the villagers knowing she was a Wise One and throwing her out of her home again.

Yeolani did not share her doubts and brought the Heart Stone from its hiding place beneath his ribs. The fluttering of its light witnessed to the near panic pace of Rashel's pulse. Yeolani cast a blur of invisibility around them the same way Honiea had back at the inn at Simten. No one would notice them standing like idiots in the middle of the road, but he could not wait to see what Rashel would do with her magic. She reached out her hand to touch the globe between them.

Nothing happened, at first.

"Nothing," she whispered in relief, looking down at the orb in her hand and then back up at her new husband. "I feel nothing."

"That's right," he explained. "It does nothing until you learn how to do magic."

"What do I do with it?" asked Rashel.

Yeolani grinned boyishly as he replied. "You could club me over the head with it, or just put it in your pocket. Do you see the fairies are brighter now?"

Rashel looked up, and her face lit with the brilliance of the spring sun and the glow of fairy light that added to it. "It's so beautiful," she whispered.

"I couldn't agree more," Yeolani replied, but he had eyes only for his new bride.

Just then Nevai began to whine uncomfortably, and the spell was broken. The newlyweds began walking hurriedly on through town, wanting to get home. However, something strange began happening as they rejoined the flow of foot traffic.

"Look," Rashel muttered as quietly as she could, turning back up the road to show Yeolani what had caught her eye.

To their utter surprise, a trail of crocus flowers, bright purple and white, followed them up the well-pressed cobbles of the main street, squeezing through the cracks, and in some cases, sprouting right up out of the stones. Each upwelling of flowers was shaped perfectly like a footprint.

"Make them go away," she gasped, as people walking by them began to look at the phenomena with curiosity and traced them to Rashel who stood frozen in the middle of the track. She even lifted her foot to look, in alarm, at the sole of her boot.

"I can't," Yeolani chuckled, far less worried about this than his bride. "This is your magic. I remember now; the fairies said you would be the Green Lady, Queen of Growing Things. I'm just amazed that it showed up so quickly."

"Everyone is looking at us," Rashel hissed under her breath. "How do I make them go away?"

Yeolani grew serious and turned her to look her in the eyes. "First, tune out everything: the baby, the villagers, the traffic. Now, just wish the flowers to go away. They'll obey you."

Rashel followed his directions, closing her eyes in concentration. The crocus flowers faded like the spring sun scorched them and disappeared. She sighed in relief, but Yeolani could feel the tense set of her shoulders. "Now how do I walk home without that happening again. I wasn't thinking about flowers....it just happened."

Yeolani had no answer for her. Instead, he simply scooped Rashel up, baby on her back and all trekking toward the farm. When they had left behind the main gawkers and were on the final path toward the cabin, he put her down again and then advised her, using his Wise One instinct to try to teach her.

"Our magic is all about wishing and your thought process. For a while, you are going to have to concentrate on the fact that you are not walking on the ground. You are walking on shoe leather."

"Shoe leather?" Rashel's tone grew dubious.

"Just try it. You are not walking on earth, which will sprout just about anything to please you, oh Queen of Plants. You are walking on shoe leather that doesn't care about you at all. No barefoot in the fields for you, my love."

Yeolani's playfulness eased her tension, and Rashel tried it. "Shoe leather," she whispered to herself as she took a step into the farmyard and then looked behind herself to check. "Shoe leather, shoe leather." She made a few more tentative steps, and whenever she did not think strongly about shoe leather, daisies or dandelions sprouted up with abandon. "Go away," she growled under her breath, and they were obedient, but it was frustrating.

"I won't be able to go anywhere," she groused as they finally made it to the cabin door.

"That's fine by me," Yeolani chuckled and scooped her up again and carried her into their home. "I've no intention of letting you go anywhere for a while anyway."

That night, the dream came slithering. Rashel did not find it alarming at first, but the fairies plagued her, buzzing and whispering to her of crocus and ivy. She tried to shoo them away without actually waking, but their humming dissolved into a low hiss that shook Rashel's bones. The images with the dream remained dark, like she wandered a forest, only there were no trees, just the cold dark broken only by the feeble glow of her fairy escorts and edges of dark in shadow.

Then the hissing grew deeper. The fairy lights went out like snuffed candles. Rashel was plunged into absolute darkness. In her dream, she froze in alarm but felt herself drifting through the inky darkness as if she were on a barge, floating toward the danger. Something in her resonated; something here smacked of evil.

"You've come back," the voice slithered through her mind. "I've been waiting for you."

Rashel woke screaming in terror.

Yeolani took over an hour to calm the baby back to sleep and listened as Rashel spoke of the dark dream. "It cannot be real," she rambled. "There is nothing that dark. Why is it, the day I become a Wise One, I have such a horrific dream?" she asked, not really wanting or expecting an answer.

"At least you didn't kill any fairies in your dream," Yeolani replied as he paced the cabin floor with the baby while Rashel huddled under the blankets. "It's unfortunate, but dreams for a Wise One are important and about as useful as a barrel of fish. Apparently, you need to learn something from it."

Seeing the rejection on her face, Yeolani stopped pacing with Nevai, laid him back down in his cradle, and came to Rashel's side. "You've got an idiot for a husband. What can I do to make you...?"

"Can you make me stop worrying about my magic? I'm afraid of what I'm capable of, yet I want to be able to experiment. I've not even started to learn about it. It's haunting me already. Do you hear that?"

Yeolani could hear nothing except the rattle of branches in the wind. Was a late storm coming in off the mountains?

"No," Rashel answered to his unvoiced question. "That's me. The trees are responding to my eagerness and concern. They're coming closer. They feel like they need to come to protect me from exploring whatever is in the dark dream."

"Shall I call Honiea? Perhaps she can give you something to help you sleep."

Rashel shook her head and wordlessly curled up in Yeolani's arms, but in her unshielded thoughts, she defiantly refused even his aid. This she would have to face alone, and she knew it. The dark was coming for her and the bold defiance in her relished the challenge.

Dawn came late, and they all slept well into the morning. The cows' complaints at being penned eventually awakened Yeolani, and he looked bleary-eyed at the window, wondering where the daylight had gone. The cabin was still dark; no light came in to wake them.

"Rashel?" Yeolani shook his bride awake. "Look at the windows."

Overnight, the openings had been completely sealed with what appeared to by ivy leaves. Not a drop of light filtered through. Curiously, Yeolani walked to the door and tried to open it, but physical strength could not pry it open. "Don't you think you've overdone it a bit, my love. It's more root-bound than hermit's hair," he added before Rashel had even risen to see for herself.

"This is ridiculous," she declared in frustration. "Someone is going to notice if I don't get control of myself. Very well, let me see if I can bring this down as I did with the footsteps yesterday."

Rashel stood in her nightgown in the center of the room, concentrating on making the ivy withdraw. As she worked, a few beams of light made it through the panes of glass. However, Yeolani watched in awe as floorboards began to bud and stretch forth small branches like they were living trees again. Her efforts to stop the growth on one front only encouraged it elsewhere. Yeolani scrambled to retrieve the baby when his wooden cradle began rocking with the walls sprouting branches.

"Rashel, you've got to stop," he told her when a full blanket of grass began growing up to his knees. "You'll have us root-bound and buried like a corpse."

Rashel opened her eyes and dropped her arms in failure. "What am I doing wrong?" she cried.

Something in Yeolani's heart almost broke. He remembered

his mother's tears after she'd had to deal with his father. Yeolani could not bear a woman's tears, even those rooted in frustration. He thought hard about what he could do and felt a wave of relief as an inspired Wise One idea came. First, he needed to calm Rashel.

He gave Nevai to his wife and invited her to sit. He had no idea why her magic was so strong and coming without her wanting it, but he would follow the instinct. He let her rock the baby, and the leaves at the windows parted as if they now knew she had other interests. Next, he conjured a bottle for Nevai as well as a sumptuous breakfast for the adults.

"You don't need to do this," Rashel began, looking at the juice and bacon with wonder. "I'm the one who needs to learn how to do magic."

"You must be calm, or it won't work," replied Yeolani. "Either that, or I'll need to conjure a goat next to take care of the grass in here before we can get to the outhouse." He grinned at his joke, although she did not share his enjoyment at their predicament. Then he sat down beside her at the table and brought out his compass.

"It's your compass, not mine," she protested, but she sounded calmer as she began to feed Nevai.

"And it's a good place to start. I don't know if it works only for me, but we need guidance and to get away from here. You're right, someone is going to notice if the cabin is suddenly covered in ivy and the forest closes in overnight. It's worth the try."

He opened the compass and watched as the arms spun. The north arm stilled first and then the free arm turned to the southeast, away from them both.

"What's in that direction?" she asked.

"Thankfully, not the sea. I've no idea," Yeolani admitted. "I don't feel any prompting to go that way, not like I did when I was responding to the Siren. Here, you hold it. Do you feel anything?"

He transferred the compass into Rashel's hand. The arms spun again, helping them both feel that perhaps it was at least acknowledging a new person and would act accordingly. Then the arm settled again, pointing southeast.

"Do you feel anything?" Yeolani asked again.

Rashel concentrated. "I hear something. The voices...there are...voices of something... many somethings."

"Is it the same as from your dream?" he tried again.

"No, the grass...it's afraid. It is calling me. Grass? There are no other plants nearby. Just leagues and leagues of grass, and they...they all need me?"

"Can you sense where they are?" Yeolani asked as quietly as he could, hoping not to interrupt her focus.

Rashel's eyes grew dark with anxiety. Yeolani could sense her trembling, and the baby grew restless again, sensing her discomfort. "There is no way I can go there. I cannot even keep the plants here from going wild. I don't know what I'm doing."

Yeolani tried to smile, to make an off-hand remark in response to her obvious frustration at using magic, but only one thought came to him. "My father, such as he was, gave me only one good piece of advice. When I was nine, I was ordered to climb to the crow's nest, the very top of the mast on that boat, but I was too scared. He simply told me, 'if you're scared, then don't look down.'"

A strange expression came into Rashel's eyes. "I'm not afraid," she declared. "I want to try it all. I'm rash, remember? But the plants are out of control. Why won't they obey me?" She glared in annoyance at the grass growing up between the floorboards and the branches of newly sprouted trees tapping on the thin cabin door. The fierce, mother bear Yeolani remembered arose in her again.

Rashel stood up. "Here, take the baby." She then reached out her arm.

"Just don't look down," Yeolani called to her as she disappeared in a shimmering green light, the way Honiea often departed. His new wife already had a way to travel instantly. He was jealous, as well as alarmed.

"Rashel?" he called, stretching his mind toward hers. He wasn't surprised to find her to the southeast, but how far away floored him. He had to use his own sense of the plains to recognize his new wife had traveled five hundred miles from where he sat, leaving him to tend the hungry, stinky baby.

20

DEMON DUST

"What did I just do?" Rashel asked Yeolani instinctively across the distance. How far, she wondered but could not calculate. Instead, she looked around in awe. The sun shone down noon high, and she saw along the horizon no sign of the mountains, the forest, civilization or anything else she recognized. As far as the eye could tell, in every direction, she saw nothing but green waves of grass. This was Yeolani's world. He was the King of Plains. Why had she been called here?

"You went to where the call drew you – halfway to nowhere in the southeast," Yeolani answered, and she could have wept in relief at hearing his matter-of-fact reply in her mind.

"How far away am I? And how did I do that?" she asked in wonder.

"You handed me the baby and went to answer a distress cry from the grass. I'm very impressed because I've been doing this for over a year and still do not have a way to travel as safely as you just did. So, who needs your help in the middle of nowhere?"

"How would I kn..." but Rashel stopped as she felt the earth tremble beneath her feet. An earthquake? She had experienced them a few times before, growing up at the base of the Great Chain Mountains, but out here with no frame of reference, she could not be sure this was real. No trees swayed without wind. The dishes on their shelves were not there to dance about and topple down. Where were the voices that had called her to this spot? Was it the snake-like presence from her dream, shaking the earth?

As if on cue, Rashel heard again the wailing voices. "Help us!"

Rashel looked down at her feet in wonder. The grass? On the walk home yesterday, the crocus flowers obeyed her when she called on them to disappear. The trees and ivy grew up to protect her in the night. Now, the grass called on her to protect them...from what? From her dream about a voice in the depths? All she could do was ask.

She leaned down toward the ground, and feeling a bit self-conscious, she whispered, "What is harming you, my dears?"

The grass, the combined entities speaking as one voice, could only give her an impression, but she felt it like the many-toned voices of the fairies that hovered above her, invisible in the spring sunlight, encouraging her. If she wanted to understand, she must concentrate.

From miles around where she stood, the voices whispered. "The demon dust in the dark."

"The what?" Yeolani asked from far away, in an alarmed tone. "Demon....I've only encountered one. I haven't taught you about shielding. They'll take you over if you're not careful. I cannot come there. Someone has to look after Nevai."

Rashel nodded, trying to reassure him that she was safe, but her focus grew elsewhere. Her mind filled with an impression of sharp, edged stone in the dark and water below. Some cold presence poisoned the world above, seeping evil coming up from a pit. A noxious presence oozed through the cracks and seams below to kill the grassroots. She sensed it through this unspeakable link with the web of grass below her feet. For miles around her, she felt its terror at the demon dust.

Rashel always tried whatever she dared, all her life: riding a bull, running a farm single-handedly, raising a baby alone, even becoming a Wise One. She determined to live up to her nickname: rash. So why not confront a demon? She began walking forward, feeling every blade of grass below her bare feet. No crocus rose to greet her now. The earth out here on the plains could not support it, not with the terror lurking below. The hem of her nightgown brushed along the fresh spring blades, bowing to honor her as she passed. Rashel communed with the grass, lifting her face to the welcome sun.

And then she fell.

A hole in the middle of nowhere opened up below her. Rashel plunged down, involuntarily screaming as she went. With a splash, she landed in the chilled water and gasped as she bobbed back to the surface. Her underdeveloped magical instincts did nothing to help her. Instead, she tread water and tried to think. Hadn't Yeolani said something about a cavern, or was that Honiea? Rashel looked up in the shaft of light above her head and saw the edges of the hole through which she had fallen lined with crystals that she recognized.

Crystals? Like the one Yeolani had given her? Her first impression formed a guess that these must be the source of the poison. How could that be? Yeolani's crystal had been a tool and a safe one at that. Even as she watched, Rashel witnessed the crystals lining the opening grow to cover up the hole she had fallen through. The feeble light in the cavern disappeared.

It was her dream.

A dark, cold, and hissing voice celebrated the light's failure. Still, Rashel felt no fear, at least through the bitter cold. Her last glimpse of escape closed on the sunlight above, and she wished for the fairies' return. They could at least light her way to a bank. "Yeolani, which way to shore?" she called, hoping to hear his comforting voice again, giving advice.

There was no answer. This did not alarm her much; the excitement of falling and the cold seemed to combine into a numb carelessness. Perhaps she was too new to magic, not powerful enough to reach him from here below the ground. She was no longer officially on the plains, so maybe he could not hear her call. In any case, Rashel selected a direction and began swimming, grateful she'd learned that skill early in her life when her parents realized she had no fear of physical danger, especially of the river.

The frigid water began to soak into her bones as she swam. Her head throbbed with the rattling of her teeth, and her muscles began seizing up, making the effort to keep her head above the surface difficult. She coughed suddenly as she gasped in a mouthful of the bitter water. Was she going to drown? Her mind was not making sense as she swam in the dark.

Then the voice growled again above her in the abyss. Rashel couldn't think. The terror did not impact her, but the cold would shake her to death. Her magical mind reached out, found a patch of algae clinging to an unseen shoreline and pulled herself toward it. Thankfully, she reached some kind of rock where Rashel's frozen legs failed her. She collapsed on a bare rocky shore on the edge of the water.

What to do now? "Yeolani!" she shrieked at the top of her lungs, straining with mind and magic, while her voice reverberated around the chamber. A shower of loose bits fell on her head from the sheer power of her cry. Yet Yeolani did not respond.

Instead, something deeper and wilder replied. "?"

It didn't quite have sentience, not yet. Something in the dark stalked her, a sinister combination of snake and crystals. Rashel had come brazenly into its dark place, without a plan or even a kernel of training. She deserved what she encountered there in the lonely dark.

No, that's not me thinking. That's something else, she told herself. With the last dregs of her energy, Rashel forced herself to sit on the rocky bank and willed herself into warm dry furs. To her surprise, she got what she wished. Abruptly, she curled up in thick quilts and a wool dress with a cape and cap of some fur she could not identify, it was so soft.

How had she done that? Rashel had no idea, but obviously, someone was looking over her or she would have died of hypothermia within moments. It took even more time to fight back the exhaustion and desire to sleep that descended on her, but the rumbling of the demon dust shook her free from that.

"What are you?" Rashel called out to the essence she could only sense with her magical mind.

The tentative touch of anger and greed pushed back. It wanted her. She had a body made of more than dark and stone. It craved something more, anything more than what it possessed. Rashel knew she was completely out of her depth here. If Yeolani could not hear her or had not mounted a rescue, she would have to save herself, for this thing would find and consume her eventually.

Well, what did she know? The compass had directed her here, not unlike it had done for Yeolani, guiding him to the Siren, guiding into a trap. Rashel had some magic powers – to travel to where the plants called to her, to conjure something she needed, like the life-sustaining warmth of dry clothes she enjoyed. She had been able to call to Yeolani before the hole sealed up. What other magic had she witnessed from Yeolani? The healing of her rapist and the Life Givers brought to mind the fairies. They had been the very first magic she had noted, even before she knew magic existed. They had hovered around her all through her childhood.

Rashel lifted her head to the dark. Oh, for a fairy now, to show her a spark of hope and light. She wished, with all her might, for a fairy to come to light her way.

A flash of white light stunned her. It flickered, doubling itself in the reflection it left on the water's surface. A fairy had granted her wish. It flitted frantically away from the water, squealing in alarm at its surroundings, but Rashel could have wept in joy at something existing beyond the dark.

"You have called me," it said into Rashel's mind. "How may I serve you in this horrid place, so far away from my home trees, oh Lady of the Green?"

Rashel rose to her feet to address the light that had begun to race in circles around her head, leaving afterimages of a comet's tail behind her. "I was called here by the grass above, and now there is something in the dark with us, and I am trapped underneath. Can you help me learn what I must do?"

The fairy did not hesitate, and its tinny little voice cheeped in alarm. "Shield yourself. There is demon-dust here."

"Shield myself...how?"

The growl of the demon-dust in the dark rattled the crystalline ceiling of the chamber, and Rashel felt as if something crawled down her spine. Without instruction, raging with nervous energy, she wove her thoughts into an ivy tangled shield. Whatever stalked her would hopefully become pinned and never actually reach her. Unfortunately, this bound her as well. She sensed the vines creeping up her body and hemming her in. She felt trapped, even with the great yawning cavern echoing around her. In a fit, she again used her wishes for light.

And the light came. This time, an entire flock of fairies stabbed the cave with bright flickering, blinding her to all else. Gradually, as her vision cleared, Rashel finally saw the entire chamber she had discovered and gasped in awe.

The cave glittered with the spangled fairy-light glancing of a myriad of glossy crystals embedded in a ceiling of dark glass. These, in turn, reflected off the black water below, doubling the light and filling the shoreline with illumination. Rashel found she stood on a black rock shoreline, and other than an abandoned blanket, a pair of boots, and a long-dead fire ring, she could see nothing to witness any other life had been here.

She laughed at the irony. This was Yeolani's place before it was hers. She had found where he had left his boots. This cavern was the spot where he had learned about the muddy crystals and been given Elin as the name of the person he would marry. She wasn't the first one here...or even the second. The angry presence of an unknown thing cringed away from the light of the fairies. Rashel squinted into the well of darkness beyond the frantic efforts of fairies flitting above her head. The demon dust could not be seen.

"You!" she called and then had to wait until her echoes settled. "You must leave this place."

Laughter, wicked and jarring, rippled the water and air back at her. The ivy protecting her filtered the fear a bit, and Rashel was not intimidated by it. How had Yeolani battled the Siren? No, he had not defeated her, and this was a creature of the dark, not the burning, searing light as Yeolani had described. How about the sorcerer demons at East? Yeolani had forced them into a tornado and swept them out to sea. What could the Queen of Growing Things do to battle demon dust?

An idea, out of nowhere, came to Rashel's fertile mind.

Wise One inspiration? She was not sure, but she would act on it. She thought of a tree, growing here in the dark. She would feed it with her magic, rooting it in the water and pushing it up into the light above. The cavern ceiling wasn't particularly high. She could almost brush her hands against the ceiling here at the shoreline. She could do this, bringing light permanently to the cave. And the tree she would craft would drink the demon dust from the crystals, from the bitter water, and grow stronger with it. The tree would act as a filter and a well, siphoning up the demon dust and expelling it from the cistern.

Rashel eagerly put the idea into action. She sat back down within her armor of ivy and began to concentrate. The fairies and their light encouraged her. Her mind slipped under the water, to the roots of the well, so cold and dark. Deeper still, she found in the stone the energy she sought. She must ground this tree beyond any on earth. She imagined a seed that sprouted and drank from the magic of the Land. It reached out roots as vast as the cavern itself.

Then Rashel grew it up, widening the stalk, swelling and drinking in the demon dust that lurked within the cavern. As the vast tree rose, it pierced the water, sending ripples to her shoreline. It's diamond-hardened bark glowed green and blue in the fairy light. She pushed it toward the ceiling where she had fallen and then let it burst through. The reaching boughs sought the remains of Yeolani's original hole and scraped through it, seeking the sunlight.

As her massive creation broke through the surface, onto the plains, her connection to Yeolani returned. "Rashel! Where are you?" his voice reverberated in her skull, urgently and louder than the now drowned demon dust.

"I'm here," she reassured him, but her concentration focused more on the finishing touches of her grand tree. She launched it high into the air, stretching toward the nourishing sun. Next, she allowed it branches, worthy of the trunk that now spanned so wide it would take ten men to girth it. Finally, as the crowning glory, she encouraged glossy leaves to erupt, like a layer of snow cascading over a mountainside. An entire village could shelter under the shade of this magical tree that now drank away the demon dust.

21

TREE IN A STORM

*Y*eolani froze in horror. His wife had disappeared out of his mind, untrained and far away. He couldn't follow her, not with a baby to take care of. Yeolani strained to resist his impulse to turn into a tornado and rip across the countryside toward her, but there was no way to keep Nevai safe with him at the same time. Whom could he find to tend him?

Yeolani's mind switched to a different search. He debated whether to call Honiea and ask her for childcare. However, something in him knew Honiea would chide him for not teaching Rashel before she left him and make him deal with the consequences. No, that would not work. What about someone in town? The only person he knew by name was the neighbor, Norton, who was laid up in bed with deadly wounds still to heal. That would not work either.

Restlessly, Yeolani went to the door and used a little magic to tug the door free from the insistent ivy. His focus spun far away, using the clouds scudding across the sky to see across the plains, so he failed to sense closer to home.

To his surprise, the entire village, armed with torches and pitchforks, stood lined up around the fence. All across the barnyard, ivy and roses choked the path to the gate. The barn had completely succumbed to the forest which now had pushed its way to within an arm's reach of the door. The cows had escaped their prison when the trees had pushed through the walls and now ran freely in the just sprouting wheat. Yeolani stood on the stoop with Nevai in his arms and knew he could not go look for Rashel. He had his own battle to fight.

"Good morning," he called weakly.

Hodge, the old man who had bid on Rashel's farm, stood with a torch in his fist and a suspicious snarl on his face. "You ain't left, I see."

The mayor, also in the crowd but farther back, called out. "I just married you. Why would you do this....this black magic? And where's Rashel?"

Shouts from the frightened villagers of Edgewood rang through the trees. They feared for Rashel's safety and blamed him for the abrupt changes to the farm.

"I can pull back the forest," Yeolani promised, "but I need someone to watch my baby. Rashel's in danger elsewhere, and I need to go help her."

"Burn back the forest!" shouted one of the mob, and the rest of them murmured agreement. "Burn them out!" "Witches!" "Save the town before we're swallowed whole."

The rabble surged forward. Yeolani instinctively froze the mob, as he had done before. He needed to think. Rashel was on her own. Yeolani's problem was how to solve this impasse without magic, as that would simply frighten these people more. He'd not wanted to push away the forest and wild ivy growth, wanting to leave that to train Rashel. Not now. She was hopefully learning self-control elsewhere. With a wave of his hand, Yeolani made the trees disappear and the ivy withered to dust.

Now, how to deal with the mob that wanted him killed. Nothing flashy. Could he make them forget what they'd seen? Would he have to do each person individually? Resigned, Yeolani marched over to confront the frozen citizens of Edgewood. He reached Hodge and placed his hand against the old man's forehead. He was about to wipe the man's memory when he was faced with a wall, as Vamilion would have built. Something in the old man blocked Yeolani's touch.

Yeolani pulled back his magic and looked at the frozen man. To his horror, Hodge reanimated, snarling viciously, and threw his torch past Yeolani at the cabin. The poor building burst into flame. Hodge cackled in a fearfully familiar way. Demon possessed.

"Yes, King of the Plains," Hodge roared with more power than the feeble man should be able to muster. "I promised I would return."

"Roach," Yeolani snarled and wished fervently that there was somewhere to send Nevai so he would not be in danger in this battle. Before he could think of what to do, the other villagers also began moving again, demon-driven and throwing their torches at the barn and other buildings.

How had they found him?

The answers did not come, only the reactions. Yeolani shielded himself into his royal clothing and wove an invisibility over Nevai before he sent the baby into the forest with a thought. *May the fairies watch over you, my boy.* Next, Yeolani drew his bow and began firing into the surging crowd of raging townsfolk, all the while backing away from the flames that encroached on him. Those people struck by his arrows continued to stomp forward, unaware of the shafts sticking out of their bodies.

The cabin and barn went up with alarming speed. Even the stones of the well burned with a strange purple and green flame. There was nothing to save, Yeolani realized and gave up trying to simply stop these people. He needed to learn quickly how to battle demons, not humans. He had to save himself and not the farm.

Tornadoes. They came so easily to him. He felt his body torn from the earth and lifted gently into the sky. He swept through the village, leaving devastation in his wake. The shrieks of the demons blended with the roar of the wind as Yeolani sucked the fires up. The clouds he had invoked would put out any remaining flames, but there was nothing left now of Edgewood for him to want. Instead, Yeolani raced across the plains with his cargo of demons striking lightning across the whirlwind. He flew to the southwest, hoping to find Rashel.

"Stop!" the demons wailed. "Stop!"

"Why? You came back when I warned you not to come. I told you that we would always fight you if you returned."

"Stop," demon voices plead. "We will teach you how to know us, how to thwart us next time, if you will only stop."

Yeolani's mind was elsewhere, thinking of his wife and where she might have been lost. With his body phased into the essence of a tornado, it was difficult to think about negotiations with lightning-struck demons that simply would not die.

"That's right, we cannot die once we have formed," the voices screamed over the winds. "But we can be harnessed. The one named Owailion knows us. He will bind us to one shape, to serve. You carry one with you now, a demon dissolved into mastered magic. We will not return if you will let us go into a form."

Yeolani could not concentrate on the inane babbling of legions of demons when he only wanted to hear the winds and Rashel's voice. He raced across the open plains, refusing to listen. If Owailion knew how to bind a demon, perhaps he would explain later, but not until Yeolani found Rashel.

With his mind's eye, he surveyed the prairie below, basking in the waves of grass torn and flattened in his passing. He would rip the world open until he found the hole into which his new bride had fallen. He could not remember where his well shaft had been, but it was reasonable to think she had gone into the ground as he had and landed in the cistern. He could think of no more fitting place than there to house the Roach.

The tornado named Yeolani scanned far and wide for a landing place and found nothing until something emerged like the largest mole he could imagine. It began mounding up just a mile or so beyond him, and he willed his storm closer. Yeolani hovered around it as it grew, and his storm swept aside much of the dirt, adding a darker cast to the green and gray of the wind and its debris. Then something broke through the surface and rose above the massive molehill.

A tree grew through the prairie surface. This had to be Rashel's doing.

"Rashel! Where are you?" the tornado called.

In relief, Yeolani heard the words he longed to hear. "I'm coming."

Yeolani watched and waited impatiently for Rashel to appear, but instead, all he got was more tree. The thing was massive, lifting up to the cloud height he maintained. He didn't dare go near Rashel's creation, but he also did not trust the demons he still had bound in his grip. Their lightning and repeated stabs at escape lashed out now at the tree they too saw emerging.

"Where are you?" Yeolani asked again, "And what on God's green earth is this you're making? It's never going to survive out here in the middle of nowhere."

"Oh, yes, it is because you are going to protect it, my dear."

Rashel's mental tone made that an order. "This is my tree to suck up demon dust. Last winter, when you dug that hole, something fell down inside and absorbed magic. It was about to become a demon. It was demon dust. This tree is grounded in the water of the earth below, in your cavern, and it will absorb the dust and make it powerless."

"But where are you?" he begged in a voice driven by the winds. He could not see her, despite the spectacular view of her tree, now branching and budding out in silver and green leaves.

"Up...er...down here, in the tree."

Yeolani lowered his awareness perspective, while not once dropping his demon passengers. He dared not. He now saw Rashel standing amid the still expanding branches of her glorious tree. From head to toe, she glittered and gleamed in a royal gown of green silk embroidered with leaves of silver and gold. Her walnut dark hair trailed with ivy and camellia flowers, held together with gold twine. She waved as her tree lifted her into the sky, higher than any tree in the Land.

"Where's the baby?" she called, smiling at the tornado as he spun around her. "We need to talk."

Yeolani was almost speechless at her beauty, but he gathered himself, nonetheless. "Talk, that's an understatement. I have some demons in here with me. Will your tree make them demon dust too?"

Rashel finally halted the growth of the tree and considered what Yeolani had asked. "I really don't know. The fairies told me that what I found there was demon dust, not a demon in itself. I know nothing about them."

"Owailion does," Yeolani replied, "but I'm afraid to ask him."

"Who? Oh, why don't we just try? Send them to the cistern and see if my tree will trap them there. The only way out now is through the veins of the tree, purified in its waters."

Yeolani's instincts warred within him. He recognized Rashel's penchant for reckless experimentation. That's what got them here in the first place, but the little he knew of Owailion led him to believe they would not get an answer from that quarter.

"Yes," cried the demons trapped in his tornado. "Put us there and see if we can corrupt the tree. You have no alternative."

"Who was that?" Rashel asked in bewilderment. "It sounded like..."

"Demons," Yeolani affirmed. "They aren't demon dust, and I'll trust a demon when the world splits in two. We do have an alternative. We could call Honiea and Vamilion."

Rashel did the work of calling, with Yeolani's patient explanation, conjuring a candle, holding it high into the tree and thinking of Honiea's arrival.

The Queen of Healing arrived at the base of the tree and looked up at the tornado in alarm. She never noticed Rashel above her head in the branches.

"What...?" Honiea began.

"Don't ask," Yeolani warned. "We've got a problem. I'm swirling around here holding some demons and need to know how to handle them. Rashel has mastered what she says was demon dust – a not-quite-yet demon. She did it by sealing it under this magical tree. Will this work for a few fully formed demons like I'm holding?"

Honiea turned to look up into the tree's impressive leaves as Rashel hopped off her branch and used magic to buffer her landing. "Thank you for coming," she smiled at the Queen's surprise. "It's a long story. Let's just say Rashel is a nickname."

Honiea gave a delighted smile and gathered Rashel into

her arms. "That's a relief. I don't know why, but broken hearts do not make for good magic. Yeolani loved you the moment he met you. I'm so delighted you've joined us. Queen of....?"

"Growing Things," Yeolani supplied. "Can we solve this problem now and save the small talk for later? I'm very tired."

"Well, I'm not the one who knows how to deal with demons. Vamilion has had some dealings. And Owailion of course." Honiea stretched out her hand, conjured her candle, and drew for her husband. The King of the Mountains arrived as startled as Honiea had moments before. He pulled his pick that sparked lightning, ready to fight a tornado, but Yeolani stopped him.

"It's me, old man. We need some help."

They briefly explained the situation with a mental conversation because of the tornado's roaring. Unfortunately, Rashel learned of the destruction of her farm and village that way.

"All the villagers? And Marit? Taken over? Will they survive?" she grieved, and ivy began growing up over her, trying to protect and comfort her distress. In disgust, she huffed, and they withered back into the ground before they could bind her completely.

"The only way to remove a demon from a person is to kill him. Then the demon will leave voluntarily, even if you cannot kill it," Vamilion explained. "There has to be a better way, but we've not found one."

"Unfortunately, the people are all dead now, and I've still got nineteen demons getting very dizzy but not any better controlled. Will it work to seal them under this tree?"

"One way to find out." Vamilion put words into action. He walked over between two of the roots of the massive tree, looked over to Rashel who nodded that it was an appropriate place, and then hauled back his pick. "I don't know if this will work on something not made of stone."

Vamilion sank the pick into the thick earth, and the topsoil, as well as the rock deep below, split with a clang. The King of the Mountains held it there, concentrating on the depth of the rift he had caused, and only when he was satisfied did he remove his pick. "It goes all the way down to a cavern there. Is that where you want to put them?"

Yeolani did not hesitate. He spun up into a tight funnel and squeezed the base of it over the hole Vamilion had caused. He pressed the demon essences through the gap and then phased finally back into his human form kneeling over the fissure. Then, with a final thought, he brought the prairie back together, sealing the demons in.

"Now, how will we know if that worked?" Honiea asked.

Rashel looked over at Yeolani, and they wordlessly agreed to stay. "We will watch over the tree and see what it can tell me. I need practice in some things, and this should help me learn how to control my magic."

"It seems a little too easy to me," Honiea murmured, but she agreed and went to Vamilion's side. "Very well. Call us if you need help again...and Rashel, welcome to the Order of the Wise Ones." Then she and Vamilion disappeared in the shimmering of the setting sun.

"She's right, you know," Yeolani sighed. "Getting rid of demons cannot be that easy." He sat down on the ground between the spreading roots and laid back in exhaustion.

Rashel joined him gladly. "I'm tired too, but where is our baby?"

22

GATHERING TREE

"We should leave here," Yeolani said, knowing his Wise One instinct prompted it.

But he couldn't persuade himself to actually do it. Their little family, without a home in Edgewood to return to, remained underneath Halfway Tree. They justified lingering by saying they must keep an eye on demons that lurked beneath it. Perhaps they hesitated because of the baby. Nevai had not suffered from his extended stay in the forest except he was very dirty and hungry. The fairies had watched over him but could not feed or change him. Yet Nevai's care also did not mean they should move on. Instead, Yeolani began training Rashel instead of launching her out into Seeking without a drop of guidance. He needed something to do to ease the guilt of staying there under that wonderful tree.

Really, they remained to mourn the things they had lost: Marit, their home, the entire peace of a village free from the invasions and stress that magic brought into their lives.

"I never thought I'd cry over not having my cows, but now,

who knows what's become of them?" Rashel commented. "I thought I'd be glad to have them gone."

"You're missing the routine and predictability, not the work," Yeolani added. It had been why he had stuck with fishing so long, and afterward, he realized how limiting it had been, relying on the mundane known instead of launching into the unpredictable open world.

Rashel looked at the tree above her head and agreed. "This is nice too. But if we're going to use this tree for something other than shade, it's going to need some additions." She put words into actions and conjured a giant spigot. She had crafted it of bronze and big enough around for her entire head.

"What in blue blazes is that for?" Yeolani asked.

"For water. If this tree is a siphon for the water below, then we need to bring it up and make it useful." With that, Rashel turned toward the trunk of Halfway Tree and drove the spigot into the side with a wave of magic. Then she willed the tree to bring up the water in a fresh stream through her opening. They were rewarded with a flood splashing down the bark and out onto the plains.

"Too much for us to drink, but it tastes wonderful," Yeolani announced as he sampled it. Then he conjured a cap for the spigot and sighed. "Maybe we should bring the remaining people of Edgewood here. They cannot have any fond memories of the forest burning them out of their homes. We'll have to check."

Although he had said the words, neither of them was inclined to do that. They simply wanted to remain in their seclusion.

At night, sleeping in a conjured tent, Rashel and Yeolani both found their dreams disturbing but could not remember them the next morning. "Is that normal? Not being able to recall a dream that seems to haunt you?" she asked.

"For a Wise One, your dreams are guides to what you should do. I cursed the fairies when they blocked my view of the prairie that first night. The dream of your name drove me out of the cavern. I even dreamed that I would be given Nevai. You dreamed of demon dust. Every time I've dreamt of something important, I had no problem recalling it after I awoke. Not this time though. I know I'm supposed to remember this dream, but I cannot."

"It is the same for me," admitted Rashel. "Could it be the demons underground are interfering with our receiving an important dream?"

Yeolani considered her theory. "More likely it is the tree interrupting our dreams. You made it to squash demon dust. It's more than likely squashing our dreams for good measure."

"How can we know what we are to dream?" Rashel mused aloud. "Perhaps one of us can sleep and the other listen to the dream while awake. If I don't shield at night as you've taught me, perhaps you can listen to my dreams and learn if they're important."

"I see you want me to be the one to stay awake," Yeolani grumbled as a tease. "Just when we got Nevai to sleep through the night too."

"Well then, I'll stay awake and use the time to practice breaking through your shield that you say you can hold even in your sleep," she challenged.

"Let's flip a coin."

"Magic allowed?"

"Of course. How else will you get stronger?" Yeolani conjured a coin with a fairy etched on one side. This game he had developed to help practice control. Originally, she was tasked to hold the coin in mid-toss, freezing it with the face she called up. This time, she used her magic to rip it from Yeolani's mental grasp and launched it into the labyrinth of tree branches and leaves above their heads. He, in turn, slipped into the sky with his mind, expecting it to come up higher where he could wrest it from her magical grasp. Rashel did not let it escape the tree. Instead, she disguised the coin as one of the many leaves and let it rest, sealed underneath the shade.

Well, if he could no longer break through her shields, Yeolani would attempt another tactic. He called up a tornado and began savaging the giant tree. The roar of the cyclone disturbed the baby who had been content to sit in the shade on a blanket, playing with the flowers his mother kept conjuring for him.

"Enough," Rashel shouted over the wind. "The coin landed on heads. You get to sleep first, and I'll haunt you."

But Yeolani did not respond to her surrender. Instead, he remained with his mind high up in the thunderclouds he had summoned. Up there, far above the muting influence of the tree, and perhaps the demons, he felt something. Down on the ground, he turned toward the west. He knew now his dream had been about the west.

The storm clouds faded like dew off the grasses, and Yeolani brought out his forgotten compass. "I think the dreams are about where we should go next. I've been an idiot, hiding away here. Just having a dream should have been warning enough to do this."

"What is it showing you?" Rashel asked, scooping up the baby and joining Yeolani as he walked out into the sun, away from the tree.

"Due west...is something, but I don't know how far. I think we need to dream tonight, away from the tree. It's blocking everything magical."

Rashel looked at her husband with a serious eye. Yeolani so rarely grew this pensive. It must be something dangerous he sensed. "You sleep first, and I will watch over your dreams."

Yeolani saw noxious green and bloody smoke. Overhead, the stars hid behind billowing ash. He heard shouts and the splash of water on fires obscured by the arcane fumes. A fire someplace burned and frightened the people who fought against it. He could not make out the place, but he knew how to fight the magical flames if only he could reach it.

"Then I will take you there, my love," Rashel's mind voice twined into his dreams. "When you wake, we will go."

Yeolani bolted awake, gasping. It was East and West, burning again, he just knew it. Nowhere west of the Halfway Tree were there enough people to be fighting that fire. "Those demons returned," Yeolani explained as he sat up and looked at Rashel who had watched over his rest. "They found me at Edgewood as well as the villagers at West. They're taking their revenge there since they could not get at me here."

"We need to go then," Rashel agreed.

"We need to plan first," he stalled. "They know me, but they do not know you. Let's go do some reconnaissance instead. Those fires...no water can put them out. It requires salt."

"Salt? I can conjure salt, but what should we do with Nevai?" She looked over at the baby who slept soundly at last in his cradle. "Do we want to take him with us?"

Yeolani put his chin on his knees as he thought. "I guess we must. We really need to find someone to tend him when we are off fighting demons."

"We'll cross that bridge when we get to it. Right now, we have another bridge to save. Let's go."

Yeolani looked at her with wonder. "You aren't afraid? I've seen these demons before, and I failed to save much. I don't want to fail again."

Rashel shrugged. "I want to see if I can travel there and

take you and Nevai with me. I know of a tree on the east side of the river, about half-a-league north of the towns. I will use it to draw us there. I've not tried to move more than myself that way. I need to learn if I can do this, that's all."

"And your dreams? Don't you get to sleep as well?"

"Not when people are dying and a fire is spreading."

Yeolani stood up and began gathering the blankets that they had conjured for their bed. "It might not be happening yet. We've had premonitions of where magic will be needed long before it actually has come. We've both been having dreams for several days. You're right, we should go."

Rashel stood up in the spring grasses of the prairie under the starlight, looking toward the west where they were headed. She felt the pressure of time to try her traveling gift. She sensed the place she wanted hundreds of leagues away. She had come to sense the plants all around her. That sometimes overwhelmed her a bit. If she learned to listen, she could control it, especially to the larger things like trees. She heard their thoughts and collected news from them. Smoke and fear predominated this particular tree on the Lara River. It whispered to her, and she knew she was in the right area. Then Rashel pulled herself toward it with a wish that she could be with that tree.

Her gift worked perfectly. Rashel stood next to an ancient oak that grew along the wide river just north of the towns that glowed in the just lowering sun. Thankfully, this means of travel did not leave her ill, as it had Yeolani when he had tried magical leaps.

"No problem," she called to him where he waited. "Now, let me pull you toward me, so you and Nevai don't get sick."

Yeolani sent her a wordless thought of enthusiasm and encouragement in response as Rashel reached toward the

Halfway Tree. She found him there carrying their packs and the baby. She encircled them in her mind and gently lifted them toward the tree on the river.

"I'm so jealous of that," Yeolani admitted as he arrived under the Gathering Tree. He put the baby down under this new shelter and dropped their bags. "Now, what can we see of the fires?" He had guided Rashel in observing a situation from a distance using magic. He used the clouds, but now, with the sun setting, he had little light except that emanating from the strange blue, green, and purple fires.

"I cannot see much through the smoke," he admitted. "Can you do better with your method?"

Rashel used the senses of the trees and other plants in the area to observe downriver. She now saw why Yeolani had felt such a premonition that urged them to arrive sooner. The bridge which he had conjured to ease the tensions between East and West now stood aflame, though it hadn't fallen yet. Beyond it, a tall black ship floated on the river. She could only spot two masts spearing the sky above the smoke and chaos.

"Invaders on ships are at the town. I suppose they're who set the bridge on fire, but I can see none of them. I need a tree on the other side of the river, beyond the smoke that...I see it. Three ships, probably with dozens of men visible on board. I sense sorcerers, or something magical. Maybe the men aren't magical, but...."

"Demons," Yeolani speculated. "Roach promised to return. The crewmen will be innocent sailors most likely, powerless to its persuasions. Can you see what's going on in West?"

"No, the smoke is blowing right over it and obscuring everything," she muttered, eyes closed against the burning fumes. "Can you do something about that?"

Yeolani didn't reply but instead felt the prairie wind and

redirected it shimmering off the plains and encouraging it to blow west, off the ocean. Meanwhile, Rashel worked at seeing through the clearing air.

"West is burning a bit. They're trying to put out the fires while arming themselves against the men. It's mostly on the bridge. The invaders haven't landed yet, but it's only a matter of time."

"I'll deal with the fires," Yeolani replied, looking up at the cloudless skies. "It's about to get wet...saltwater wet."

Rashel felt a little shiver of anticipation, and she conjured a little tent over Nevai's cradle and tucked it right under the tree.

Yeolani meanwhile pulled more wind off the sea to the west, escalating the building of thunderclouds all across the horizon. It would be obvious to the demons on the ships that this was a magical storm, but it couldn't be helped. The huge splattering rain came down as the last of the sunlight fell over the horizon.

"It makes me nervous to leave our son here, but it's the height of foolishness to take him with us into a magical battle," Rashel commented. For good measure, she put the boy into an enchanted nap and then wove an invisibility shield over the tent. "There, you're as safe as can be under this Gathering Tree."

"I'll check on the boats to find out why the demon-men haven't attacked yet. I'll go speak with Sethan too. He'll probably club me upside the head for not finishing Roach off the first time, but it will be good to speak with him again. Will you look around the bridge and in East? If someone sees you there, they won't know you're a magician. Just keep your shields up."

"Very well," Rashel agreed, "but let's meet here at the Gathering Tree at dawn."

Yeolani made himself invisible and walked through his conjured rain to Sethan's inn, hoping the downpour would help the burning and obscure his bootprints. He noted how the cobbles of West had improved over the muddy gullies earlier last year. The warehouses that hadn't caught fire had people rallying to keep it that way with buckets manned mostly by the female population of the town. Meanwhile, the men barricaded the river's edge, carrying makeshift weapons to stockpile against it. Yeolani opened his mind to find Sethan had left his inn and was down, hefting a pitchfork, on the wharf.

"Sethan," Yeolani made himself visible and got the innkeeper's attention.

Sethan's grimace changed to a smile that disappeared into his beard as he caught sight of the Wise One. "I knew this storm could be anything but natural. You came back."

"I promised these outlanders that I would return any time they decided to make themselves obnoxious again," Yeolani commented as he surveyed the gathering of troops, most armed with farm implements and only a few swords. That did not bode well. Everyone here was a farmer, craftsman, or trader. Few were trained soldiers and probably most of those were the men that had switched allegiances during the battle last year.

"Obnoxious?" Sethan snorted. "Not the word I'd use. They're more direct this time, no mince-footing and making like they're all benevolent and going to fix things. They set the bridge afire three days ago before we even saw the ships coming up the river. I must say your bridge can take a lot."

"I aim to please," replied Yeolani. "I wonder why none of them have come ashore yet. I'll look into that. What defenses can magic provide? Weapons, shields, fireproofing?"

"A leader would help," Sethan looked over at his friend. "I

know you'll not stay in one spot long enough to give any directions, but someone with some experience?"

"Maybe," Yeolani sighed, "but I've got as much experience as a babe in arms. How long till they come ashore?"

Sethan shrugged and surveyed the townsfolk manning high positions or crouched behind the barricade. "That's just it. We don't know. They've been here two days and haven't set foot on our soil. It's like they're waiting for something. Your storm sure riled them up though. There was a great deal of shouting over in the ruins on the East side. They knew you were coming to spoil whatever they're doing over there."

"I'll try to ruin it, but not until dawn. This rain doesn't seem to put out fires. It needs pure salt, but my rain might beat down some. I'll get back to you."

And Yeolani disappeared, using the rain to obscure how he waded into the river and swam invisibly to the lead ship. He barely made a ripple as he parted the water and then climbed aboard. The deck was eerily quiet as he held his magic tightly tamped down in case the sorcerers here had means to detect unwanted spells. He listened for the conversation aboard, but there seemed very little. The crewmen all held swords and waited patiently on the damp deck, only shifting restlessly or working a line if it grew slack. They did not even react to the rivulets of rain running down their lax faces. Yeolani noted the smell of demon covered everything aboard, from the men down to the mast and oars.

Yeolani began feeling ill just being aboard but not so these men. That meant they weren't naturally magical but had been invaded by demons to provide them with their power. Good, that also meant they would be novices and far more likely to panic in an arcane battle. They were essentially pawns, brought here to die by overwhelming the city of West in sheer numbers of bodies thrown at the shoreline. Yeolani needed to find the leader of this invasion.

He walked carefully past the awaiting sailors and slipped to the wheelhouse to seek someone there who would have a plan. No one manned the wheel there. How strange, Yeolani thought. He saw the hatch that went down into the hold and wondered if he could sneak in. Carefully, he cast a scattering of sound to the aft of the ship, and every head turned to look. Yeolani used his distraction to lift the hatch and disappeared inside.

He didn't even have to go all the way down into the hold before he heard the leaders there in conference. The first voice, a gruff male, with clipped sentences continued a conversation that had obviously been going on for quite a while.

"We might never find it. I don't trust Muelker. We stand only to lose more bodies. I vote we look after everyone leaves."

"You're a fool," replied a female voice.

This surprised Yeolani. Demons seemed to occupy just about everyone. Perhaps these demons had just attacked a village of civilians, commandeering them all, man, woman, and child.

"We've come so far and only have a few more days to try this before they discover we're here. We must find it, or we might as well go back to Limbo. We'll never get bodies again."

That confirmed it for Yeolani. These were indeed demon-infested men, not sorcerers. Yet it still left him curious about this thing the outlanders sought. What was it? They had prior knowledge of its approximate location. They also knew that the Wise Ones would come to prevent them from retrieving it. Had they been seeking this thing ever since East had been invaded the first time, before he had come, banishing them. What could it be?

Yeolani recalled Vamilion's magic lessons. If demons were

seeking something here, magic had to be involved. The Land hid a vast amount of power, most of it encased in the earth itself and not accessible except to Wise Ones. No matter how demons and sorcerers might dig for it or try to manipulate others, they failed to tap into...what had Honiea called it? Well, Magic. Also, demons rarely could occupy a human from the Land, and so most of their interventions had been of this type, bringing in an invasion force.

Well, Yeolani could speculate for hours, but right now, the argument between these two possessed invaders offered no more food for thought. He returned to the deck and wove his way to the side, invisible still, before he slipped off the anchored ship into the cool water and swam away, his strokes obscured by his magical rain. He had just enough time to swim out of the river and walk to the Gathering Tree before dawn.

Rashel curiously walked the streets of West. She had never been in such a large city, and she worried about how West's citizens were faring. She discovered several healers hard at work: two women in labor, but most of the patients came with smoke inhalation. Should she call Honiea? Something in Rashel's mind resisted. These healers probably knew about her candle. They'd been dealing with the fire that had been ongoing for days and hadn't felt the need to call her.

Besides, Rashel wanted to resolve this problem, just she and Yeolani.

Slowly Rashel made it down to the bridge. The alien fires didn't seem to consume what it tried burning: the bridge. She couldn't get close enough to see the fire if she remained visible, so after she checked to see that no one was watching, she moved behind a warehouse. She then turned herself invisible, as Yeolani had taught her, and continued down to the base of the bridge. She wanted to see exactly what the demons were trying here.

The elegantly built bridge, stone piers, steel spanners, and wooden deck still arched over the river, but the smoke and blue flame tried to eat at the joints where stone met metal. The fumes obscured everything. The rain that had soaked the area did nothing for the flames and only added steam to the smoke. Why burn the bridge? No one lived or traveled on the other side anymore. What did the invaders have to gain by destroying Yeolani's handiwork?

Rashel looked diligently for magicians that might be poking around the bridge just as she was, but if they were there, they too used invisibility. The fumes burned her eyes, making it impossible to see the eddies of someone passing through. A smokescreen? If so, this fire worked perfectly. If that were the case, what were they hiding behind it? No one could see what was happening in East.

Finally, Rashel decided she had to go into the empty city. She disliked using the new magic of invisibility while she still needed to concentrate on not causing flowers everywhere she walked. She also worried about leaving Nevai at the tree without someone nearby to hear if he woke. She knew all along that having a baby while traveling and doing magic would demand these kinds of sacrifices, but leaving her baby distressed her. Unwilling or not, she was now a Wise One and had to do her part. She closed her eyes, latched onto a determined daisy that had shoved through the cobbles of the burned-out section of East and drew herself toward it.

When she opened her eyes, she looked over the desolation left behind from a year before. Scorched and crumbling footprints of buildings remained after Yeolani's tornadoes had swept them clean, all but a single broken tower. Why had that building survived? Magically reinforced?

Rashel picked her way through the streets that still had not recovered. In the rain, the ash only made for ink that clung to her boots and choked off anything that tried to grow here. East felt toxic and would refuse to allow the living world to come in. Unless she healed it. At the base of the tower, Rashel placed her hand against the stones and felt the efforts of moss trying to grow in the chinks and seams. The spores struggled, twisted, and were deformed by the magic that had built this place. She tried a bit to clear a space of the poisons to allow the growth, and she felt the relief of the tiny seeds immediately. Someday, she would have to come back here to heal this place so green could grow again, but not now.

Instead, she stepped away from the dead tower and brought her mind to examine the entire area, wondering if there was anything worth seeking that would draw the interest of invaders from other lands. She tapped into the awareness of the seeds that remained below the singed cobbles and down into the soil. It might have, at one time, been a rich land, but being so near the river, the rocks would have to be cleaned away. The toxic demon magic had seeped into the soil, and that too would have to go, dripping like poison.

Then she found something that puzzled her, not in the soil but in one of the pit basements left behind after the buildings had been swept away. Something human moved through the underground cellars and tunnels, away from the streets. Retaining her invisibility, Rashel walked through the avenues and found the cellar where these men had descended. In the side of the foundation wall, she saw a hole had been cut large enough for a man to crawl in. And it had been recently. The dirt from the original excavation had turned to a muddy mess in the rain, but not been washed away from a winter's erosion. Someone was digging through the ground of East.

What were they seeking? Rashel didn't dare follow them through the tunnel, but that didn't mean she couldn't explore. She was the Queen of Growing Things. She could reach out and sense everything the soil may hide. Deliberately, she lowered her thoughts, broadening deep and wide through the earth. She passed acorns and seeds incubated for a thousand years, only waiting to come to the surface once again to join the sun. She followed the roots of grasses long dormant and let their tendrils be her hands digging through the earth. Something magical must impinge on their awareness. She passed over stone and pebble until, finally, she found something worth her attention.

A small stone had been buried here, not brought by the river in ages past. It had been here long, but not as long as the pebbles. Also, it bore the tang of magic. She felt this stone's power not as a toxic blend of blood and greed, but of pure buried potential. The aura glowed green and brilliant, clean and striving to be patient. What could a simple stone, probably granite rather than the sandstone all around it, demand out of magic? And the men in the tunnels, while they were far away from finding the granite stone, they sought it. She knew it would take them days to reach it, for they drifted away from a direct path as if unsure where it lay.

Rashel dared not let them reach the magic encased in the rock. With a flick of her mind, Rashel lifted the stone up through the soil, through the cobbles, and into her hand.

She looked down at the stone and felt its pulsing magic, but didn't want to take the time to investigate. After being so distracted by the simple stone, she looked up at the sky, wondering how long she had been away from the Gathering Tree. A pink dawn lifted over the horizon behind her. She would look at the stone later. Instead, she drew her breath to reach back onto the magic of the Gathering Tree's memories, to pull herself toward it.

But an explosion rocked her back before she could tap into her gift to shift toward the tree. Rashel looked up and saw a fireball by the shoreline. Where once the Gathering Tree stood, now only a pillar of fire erupted.

23

PILLAR OF FIRE

The explosion tore through the wood and blew splinters and shards for a hundred yards around it. That much the tree acknowledged before it died in an inferno. Rashel's mind didn't register that. She ran the few feet from the grass stem she'd latched onto to the tree but could approach no closer for the heat. Nevai! That was who she really reached for, but she couldn't find his mind there at the base of the flames that shot out like a geyser. The fire pushed her back, but she fought her way forward with magic. She conjured a shield to press against the heat and forced herself into the flames but still could not find him.

He can't be dead, he can't be dead, he can't be dead.

Her mind began the chant, but she knew it for a lie. She could never get those words out of her mouth as she pressed her way at the flames. When she felt someone tugging on her waist, pulling her away, she fought the resistance and lashed out with her mind. Yeolani lifted her away, using magic to fight her, and she threw a wave of pure, grief-fueled power directly at his mind. He absorbed it into the cavern under the prairie and physically turned her to look at him.

Through her tears she saw he too was weeping, but also, he was covered with ash and had a myriad of nicks and splinters peppering his face and clothing. He must have been standing near the tree when it had exploded. She could read the memory fresh in his mind. She saw him being blown violently away from the explosion and landing in the river. He too had tried to find Nevai in the pillar of fire, but it was useless.

Rashel collapsed into Yeolani's arms, and they wept together just out of range of the searing heat of the fire that wouldn't stop. They barely noted when Vamilion and Honiea arrived, summoned by the needs of the Land. Their faces grew grim, and grief dripped off them as well, but they began battling the alien flames rather than disturbing Rashel and Yeolani in their loss.

"What triggered this?" Vamilion asked of his wife in a whisper. He didn't want to be crass, but they were all in danger if they didn't discover what was going on soon, despite this tragedy.

"I don't know," Honiea replied. "The city is burning. It's a smokescreen."

"It's not a smokescreen," Rashel snapped, for she'd left herself open, raw and hurting, to every stray thought around her. "I caused this."

"Rashel?" Yeolani whispered in agony. "You didn't do this, my love. Why would you say such a thing?"

"I was following the ...there were people digging in the soil under East. I followed them. They were looking for something underground, but I found it first, and the instant I had it, they triggered this reaction." She pulled away from Yeolani long enough to bring out the stone she had discovered. The others left the fruitless battle against the fire and stepped near to look at what she had brought.

"They know we're here," Yeolani whispered as he acknowledged there must be a connection to this search for a stone and the instantaneous lightning attack on the tree. "When I was on the ship, I overheard that they knew we would come. They're smart enough to recognize this rain is magical."

Accordingly, he let the clouds loose, and they began parting almost instantly.

Rashel lowered her head as if the rain still weighed her down. "The demons knew they couldn't challenge us directly, so they attacked the tree where we were meeting. Did they know Nevai was hidden here?"

Yeolani answered, now feeling like he wanted to go hunt something and kill it. "Perhaps. They've not really hurt anyone in West, just kept them on alert. I agree they've hidden behind a smokescreen so the people of West wouldn't get curious. The outlanders were looking for whatever you found, Rashel. Since they can't get it, they attack us as a warning or against the only one of us without powers, Nevai."

"Wait," Rashel looked at the burning tree, then at Yeolani, and finally at the rock in her hands. "What were they looking for that would prompt this kind of response? It's just a rock. I was led to it. They really didn't know what they were trying to find and would probably have dug for days in the passages underneath East. I knew instantly the moment my mind touched it."

Vamilion now peered at the stone and then shook his head in puzzlement. "Granite, here? No, it's not here naturally. That's not native to this river valley this far south. Is there something inside that's magical because, right now, it's not giving me any hints that it's anything but a simple stone."

"But I felt it, from hundreds of paces away...is it? What is it?"

"A Talisman?" Honiea guessed. "You feel something, and we don't. It's just a rock to us and probably to those demons, though they knew it was there somehow. None of us would be able to sense its power until we touch it."

"A rock? No," Rashel could not believe that. The rock wasn't the gift. "No, there's something inside the stone that is calling to me." Then without any explanation, she threw it with all her might at the pillar of fire. She ignored the shocked expressions of the others, but she was following her instincts the way Yeolani recommended. If it destroyed her Talisman, she didn't really care at the moment. She felt too much grief at not listening to her premonitions to not leave Nevai alone by the tree. She would follow those premonitions faithfully for eternity now.

They all heard the pop when the rock exploded in the fire, but like a geyser had been shut off, the fire died with that rock's demise. The inferno left just the charred trunk and a few of the hardier limbs still intact. The blackened trunk glowed like an ember for a few minutes, and then even the tree cooled. Before anyone else could approach, Rashel ran to the base of the tree, conjured herself a poker and began digging through debris among the roots. She wanted at least Nevai's bones to bury, though she would probably not go very far from where they stood to make a memorial he deserved. Surely something of him had survived.

But she found nothing. No skull, bones, or the two teeth he finally had cut. She wanted something, but she fingered through every chip of wood and stone, and nothing remained to prove that he had ever lived. When she found a ring in the ashes, she almost threw it aside in disgust, but Yeolani stopped her.

"No, that's what was sealed in the stone," he admonished. He took it from her trembling fingers and walked with it to the river to wash it off. When he brought it back to her, he knelt and put it carefully on her sweaty and ash-covered hand.

Numbly she looked down at the ring she had won with the life of a little boy. She would never look at that beautiful ring and think of it as anything more than a cheap trinket. Nevai was dead, and she couldn't help but realize that she had gone after this Talisman rather than protecting her baby. The gold glittered, and a faceted green stone nested in its weave. The filigree of the band looked like ivy twining about her finger, and while it sparkled beautifully, despite her dirty hand, she felt no compulsion to even be curious about its power.

"Look," Honiea whispered, long after Rashel had lost track of the world or time. "The fires at the bridge are out too."

They all peered toward the city and saw that, indeed, the blue flames had faded. As the sun rose, the wind stilled, refusing to blow away the remaining fumes of the magical fires. The boats on the river still stood just south of the bridge, but they weren't moving, and everything seemed to wait for the next act in this magical battle.

Yeolani looked at the other Wise Ones and said aloud the words that all of them at the moment were thinking.

"Shall we go to war?"

The four Wise Ones walked into East moving shoulder to shoulder, pushing a wave of power ahead of themselves that drove everything out of hiding. They all wore the most war-like version of their royal clothing. All of them wore shields or armor and carried weapons. Yeolani was grateful for his arrows rather than the sword or spear, for he actually felt he could use those, that and the tornadoes he called up in the warming day. Vamilion, for his part, carried two weapons, a sword in one hand and his Talisman pickax that could crack open the earth.

Even Honiea, the healer, had a bow and white fletched arrows and silver pikes woven into her hair.

Rashel wore a bronze bodice etched with ivy over a long silk tunic and deeper green leather breeches. Gold and silver stitchery lined every hem, and her hair braid had wrapped up into a bun in which finger-long thorns of gold emerged. She carried a spear and shield, neither of which she knew how to use, but that didn't matter at this point. She was the mother bear, and she would savage anyone that waylaid her.

Rashel didn't imagine she would or could kill with the spear she carried. At the moment, her thoughts were more likely to stop someone's heart rather than any weapon she carried. Her mind went before her, pressing through the ground and making note of where the outlanders had hidden. The demon-men scrambled to the surface, warned perhaps by their masters, but nothing would move them fast enough to get away from four angry Wise Ones bearing down on them.

"Drive them to the ships," Yeolani ordered, and his tornadoes moved in, pushing from the east and south. With angry Wise Ones coming from the north side, it drove them toward West and over the bridge, but Vamilion had that already blocked with a wall of stone and magic. The demon-driven men scattered about East's ruins, but really there was no way for them to escape. Some chose to hide in the blown-out basements. When faced with being speared or shot cowering in a corner of a pit, they elected to claw their way out and march toward the ships. Others tried to dig into the holes they had formed in the search for Rashel's ring. She drove them out, choking the passageways with swiftly grown ivy or oak roots that effectively thrust them back out. Tornadoes swept them up and deposited them unceremoniously on the ships that remained at anchor, awaiting their cargo.

"They're humans who probably didn't volunteer for this," Yeolani said grimly as they checked to see that no one was missing. "Someday, we need to find a way to seal off the Limbo world from the physical world so demons cannot pass through and do this to others."

"But not today," Rashel declared. "Bad things happen. They go."

"They probably won't be allowed back into Limbo," Vamilion speculated. "The human part of them will commit suicide, and the demons will try to find another host. They, unfortunately, cannot die that we know."

"Any more than the fairies?" Honiea asked with a curious comment. "I wonder if it could work like that."

"What are you thinking?" Rashel asked with an edge to her voice. She didn't want to consider any kind of mercy for anyone involved in Nevai's murder.

"If you're thinking that one of the Life Givers can bring Nevai back, there has to be a body to heal, dear. It cannot work on ashes. I'm sorry."

"No, that's not what I meant," Rashel replied impatiently. "No, if Yeolani can curse an immortal magical creature like a fairy and have it die, why can't he do that to a demon?"

Everyone looked at her with surprise. It hadn't occurred to any of them as a possibility. While Yeolani had almost no experience with demons, he did suspect they were more powerful than fairies. Could he curse the demons, leaving the possessed people free?

"These aren't magicians," Rashel replied to that thought. "They're just everyday people who didn't ask to be possessed. Don't we have to try?"

Everyone shrugged, unsure, but they shared each other's thoughts. Would it be possible to at least experiment? And what would happen to the demon once driven out of the human host? Would it be free to float about looking for another body? That would probably be worse than the present situation. Could they drive the demons out into a form less dangerous, like a fish?

"Roach!" Yeolani shouted out to the ships, verbally and mentally, calling to the one demon he knew.

"Are you insane?" Honiea protested silently into Yeolani's mind. "Are you going to try this?"

"No," Yeolani promised. "I'm going to find out what they think of that possibility, and I'm going to challenge him again. Last time, I gave him two options. This time there's only one."

On the lead ship, one of the men came to the side and shouted back. Yeolani didn't recognize the body of the man who stood at the bow to address him. "We are all Roach," the demon man shouted back.

"Then," and the whirlwind came up and sucked the one man off the boat and placed him in front of Yeolani. "Then you will come and speak with me. Last time I sent you home. This time I can put you in the ground, unable to leave or to occupy a body. Would being forced back to Limbo be better? Which is preferable?"

The man's face contorted as if he indeed had a horde of roaches inside him. With a thick accent in the Land's language, he seemed confident as he faced down four Wise Ones, but his compatriots on board the ship didn't look as comfortable. The sailors began running at the side, trying to bash their way through the magical shields and barriers set around each deck. All they managed to do was to rock the ship like a toy in a tub. Absently, Vamilion held out a hand, and the boat stopped shifting, but dozens of demon soldiers collided against his barriers with the abrupt stop of their rocking motion.

"You're offering us a choice?" Roach asked. "Go back to Limbo or sit in a trap. It's not much of a choice. And besides that, we know you cannot banish us without killing this body."

"Oh, that's where you are wrong. I've done it before. I have a way to bring back a person I have killed. I wonder how many of your compatriots, if given a choice, would remain trapped without a body with no escape or go back to where you came from."

Hands on board all three ships went up at that suggestion. Some here wanted the freedom to leave rather than to be trapped forever. Very well, Yeolani had learned something.

Very carefully, Yeolani closed his eyes and grounded himself to the prairie at his feet. Then, with all his will, he cursed the Roach demon before him.

Roach only cackled at him, as if the demon wasn't even aware of his curse. "You know there will always be demons trying to come here. There are also powers in the Land that don't answer to any of us and have no desire for a body. I could teach you about them," Roach suggested arrogantly, knowing he was correct.

Yeolani sighed but did not let on how he had failed. "Oh, I've met the Siren of the River," Yeolani replied flatly. "I survived her and will one day challenge her again. There are doubtless others as well. That is not an issue."

Yeolani's eyes burned with pent-up tension, frustration, and grief as he completed his interview. "Now, you are leaving sealed in that ship and never returning. Eventually, this Land will be sealed from you and your kind. The magic of the Land is not yours to possess and never will be."

And with that, Yeolani flung the body back onto the ship. "Do we have them all?"

Honiea nodded, for she had checked to see that no one in

West had been infected, and Rashel knew that the eastern shore had been cleansed of the scent of demons. Without hesitation, Yeolani unanchored the ships and sent them south on the river with a push from a looming storm just short of a tornado. And then, for good measure, he set all three ships afire with a blue-white blaze that burned nothing but the sky.

24

MEMORIAL FOR NEVAI

*Y*eolani left Rashel to follow the ships with his storm eyes on them for six days, using his compass to know he was going the correct way. He took the form of a cloud threatening rain the whole voyage.

Along the trek, he passed one of the palaces he had not seen yet, on the eastern bank of the Lara, out in the open, without any town built around it. Only a herd of buffalo enjoyed grazing in its shade. They stood so thick about the building that the ground had turned brown with their backs and seemed to move oddly. His home? Yeolani promised himself that he'd come back this way to investigate, but right now he had to monitor three burning ships.

He also got a bird's-eye view of the swampland where he had encountered the Siren. No one could imagine living there, he knew. In the middle of that river delta, another empty palace of the Wise Ones stood guarding the riverway. He felt no compulsion to stop there, and the Siren's presence nearby would make that dangerous for anyone investigating. He hoped not to encounter her again, no matter what he had to say to the Roach.

Once the ships drifted out to sea, he blew the vessels south toward open water and set a seal that would see that they never reached land again. It would also capsize them, still afire, if anyone tried to stop the ships. With those magical imperatives, he released his power over them and returned back from where he had come.

Yeolani still traveled as a storm, but with less contact with the ground and more control. As he turned, he passed very near where Everic and his family had settled and thought he might visit them. It could be ages before he could return to thank them for their hospitality. Also, he wanted to reassure himself that Everic's Elin was not harmed for him choosing to be with Rashel. He took human form on the beach at dusk and walked up the trail to the bluff and toward their house. As he approached, he conjured a perfect bow to fit Everic to pay him for his kindness.

Everic's children were still bright-eyed and Emmi was soon to bring a seventh into the world. It made the death of Nevai all the more painful to see what he'd lost in the future of Everic's humble world. Yeolani tried not to look too closely at Elin as she hid behind her mother's skirt. The girl remained completely forgetful of the stranger who had come to visit them the winter before. Instead of dwelling on that uncomfortable time, Yeolani assured them that all was well and that he had regained his memory. He warned them away from going anywhere near the swamp to the west and left them with one of Honiea's candles as well. Then he departed before supper so that their happy children would not bring him to tears.

When Yeolani finally arrived back at East he hardly recognized the place. He had only been gone a week and landed in the middle of his bridge rather than trusting what his eyes said to him. East had become a garden, cultivated and green, with food growing on one quarter, a miniature jungle in another, flowers and shrubbery in the third, and a full-grown forest of trees in the last, all with the magician's tower in the center, still crumbled and covered in ivy. Yeolani was about to walk down toward the garden to investigate when Rashel came out of the undergrowth to him.

"What's this?" he asked by way of greeting.

She looked tired but smiled to see him, wordlessly wrapping her arms around him and stopping his exploration. "I had to. That land was so sick with demon magic and then with all our salt, so I became a healer. The ring helps. I don't know if it was the ring or just my gift, but seeds come out of it, one at a time. The seeds it gives are unique and just right for the spot, hardier and able to grow on the poisoned soil. The ring knows. I think that's why the demons wanted it. They could have used my ring to grow anything, including demons."

Yeolani considered that disturbing thought and felt a chill. "No, the Talismans are for the Wise Ones. They might have tried for that, but I don't think a demon could ever grow something from your Talisman any more than the Siren could use my compass to misguide me. I just hope the demons don't continue to seek the other Talismans. We've got enough difficulty finding them for ourselves." Then Yeolani looked at the wondrous garden, knowing that none of these plants would thrive without Rashel's influence. "And the ring wanted an entire garden like this? I've never seen plants like these," he murmured, stroking her back and tugging at her braid.

"As I said, it only made unique, life-giving seeds, like no other," Rashel replied. "And while it's pretty, no one will really appreciate it. I might as well seal the garden like a Wise One's palace." She sighed with regret and then continued. "No one will ever live there. The people of West are afraid of this place.

I removed all the salt and toxins and made it a garden, but they still fear it. Honiea and Vamilion have been speaking to the people of West, and they still want to leave. The river has brought them nothing but misery, and they don't want to stay here, unprotected and vulnerable to anyone...anything coming up the river."

Her words made an itch in the back of Yeolani's mind, and suddenly he got an inspired idea. "Halfway. We can invite them to the Halfway Tree."

"Halfway? There's no water...oh, my spigot. I knew there was a reason I conjured that."

"There's more than enough water. We'll make more trees for homes. A town there will never be invaded because there's no river there, just your tree to watch over a village."

"I think you've got a grand idea," she laughed. "I'm glad you have a solution for them because we're going to have a mass emigration as our next responsibility. I bet your compass will even point that way."

With that, she tucked her arm around his waist and walked him back over the bridge with the sun setting in their eyes to go find Sethan's inn to discuss a migration.

A few days later, most of the people of West had gathered their possessions and had crossed the bridge to follow the river path to Edgewood. Once there, Yeolani would meet them to build the road needed to go on the less traveled path to the city he planned to create halfway between the rivers of the Land. Rashel would grow crops for them, as well as a forest so they could put up homes and stores for the coming winter.

However, they didn't have to travel with the setters just yet. Indeed, the compass advised them to stay.

They had one more thing to do. Rashel still had not decided how to break away from this place because of Nevai. She knew she needed to move on, but she also wanted to create a memorial for him. She at first had hoped the wondrous garden in East would fit that purpose, but it didn't feel right. Finally, two days after the people of West had departed, she gathered the courage to return to the dead Gathering Tree.

At dusk, Yeolani went with her to support her as well as to say his own goodbyes. He needed to mourn his child also. With summer beginning to bake the prairie around them, against the low fallen sun, the tree looked all the sadder there on the river's edge. Without discussing it, they both used magic to lift the charred oak from its roots and threw it into the river. Then, as she half expected, Rashel addressed her Talisman ring and opened a little chamber beneath the gemstone. In it she found a seed, one she had never encountered before. She placed it in the hollow left by the dead oak and then covered it with soil.

Yeolani watched her as she worked, finally feeling some peace. Rashel used magic to draw river water to soak the ground well and then lifted her arms slowly. A sprout emerged from the bed of earth. In a matter of a few heartbeats, a strong sapling grew up with leaves that shown silver on one side and a velvety green on the other. Its clear bark shimmered gray as an aspen but thicker and more rugged. Neither of them had ever seen such a tree, pale and willowy.

"A ghost tree?" Rashel named it.

"A memorial tree," Yeolani amended. "He's not a ghost. He would have moved on, as we should. I'm just very grateful to the fairies for giving us the time we had with Nevai."

As if his words triggered something, the branches rising above their heads lit up with fairies.

Against the dusky sky, the glow warmed their aching hearts. The fairies dipped and swooped as if in celebration of the leaves in this wondrous tree. Yeolani strained to understand their fluting voices and heard so many at once that he began to tune them out.

"No, don't push them away," Rashel corrected. "They say they have a gift for us as well."

Suddenly, a cranky, teething cry cut through the air from the far side of the tree. They both bolted around the trunk to find Nevai in a fairy-crafted basket wearing the same type of swaddling in which he had first appeared to Yeolani. They scooped him up with wonder, crying and laughing at one time, squeezing their baby until he protested that too. He appeared perfectly sound and had not aged at all during his time away from them.

"Thank you," Rashel called to the fairies in the tree. "This gift is so beautiful. We cannot ever thank you enough. I'll try to plant more of these memorial trees for you if you wish."

"No," the fairy voices seemed to say. "We took him only when we knew he was alone. We kept him safe from all magic. We only want to watch your son from time to time. If you will let us."

Yeolani almost burst out laughing. "Babysitters?" though the word didn't actually make sense when it applied to fairies.

"We are going to have to find someone who can watch him when we're going about the Land. I will not leave him alone again." Rashel's words formed an oath and put her into a glorious silk dress with honeysuckle woven through her hair. She looked glorious and far less deadly this way, but her oath was to be taken seriously.

"Yes, ma'am," Yeolani replied obediently and kissed her. Then he looked down at Nevai who squawked in protest at being squished between his parents. "What's this?"

He found a pendant tucked under a layer of Nevai's wrapping. Yeolani brushed his hand across a gold and silver pin and felt an embossed symbol he'd seen when he wore his own regalia: waves of grass, a horse galloping across the scene with mountains in the background. The elegantly etched pin symbolized the King of the Plains, and yet Yeolani had no idea what it meant.

"It is your pendant, King of the Plains," the fairy voices chimed. "It is for you, given by your doorkeeper so that when you find your home, you may open the gates."

"Doorkeeper?" asked Rashel. "What does a doorkeeper...? How did Nevai come to have it? Did the fairies give it to you or to Nevai?" asked Rashel. Surely he would have told her if he had found something more in his Seeking.

"No," Yeolani replied in a wondering voice. "The pendant is meant to be given to a Wise One by his or her door steward. Door stewards aren't magical people, but they live forever and have the.... I wonder."

Now, Rashel was beginning to understand. "Forever? Is Nevai going to live forever? As your door steward?" Rashel gasped. She couldn't bring words to how that delighted her. Yeolani read her thoughts and grinned boyishly. Nevai was going to be part of this wonderful family for an eternity.

EPILOGUE

*V*amilion walked through the winter above the mountains and pounded on Owailion's door with a fist. He alone would make this trek, for someone had to do it. Someone had to get through to his old mentor that the world still needed him. And besides, he had a gift to bring the hermit of the north.

He should have known better than to believe that Owailion would open his door for him. Vamilion crafted his own door through the stone wall and walked into the warm environment on the other side where the King of Creating did his magic tinkering. Vamilion wove his way through the growing mess of broken projects and then to the inner door of the palace and let himself in. The cold, icy world was reflected in the gray and misty inside of Owailion's palace. No one met him here either, but that didn't matter. Vamilion had only come to deliver good news. The King of Creating probably didn't keep an eye on the rest of the Wise Ones or the Land, and this kind of news should be delivered in person.

"I care," Owailion snarled into Vamilion's mind but didn't bother actually making an appearance.

Vamilion had expected some reluctance, so he didn't anticipate his old mentor doing more than ignoring him. "Well, then I have news. We have found the King of the Plains, and the Queen of Growing Things. He is going by the name of Yeolani, which is his real name. He's an idiot for doing so, but I can't talk him out of it. Maybe he'll use another name with regular people, but with Wise Ones, he insists. She is going by Rashel."

"I heard."

"They're going to go slow with magic for a few years, build up a town they have founded called Halfway. It's out in the middle of the plains. There's a great big tree there now, made like the Talismans. The two of them will stay there to help the settlers until their son is raised, but they have already helped us repel two invasions. You should come out and meet them."

When that news got no response, Vamilion sighed and finally turned to leave again, not looking forward to a long walk back to the mountains from this summer-forsaken land nearly at the top of the world. Then he added one more piece.

"And the King of the Plains has encountered something he has named a Siren, a lady made of the mist, with coppery hair. The Siren lives in the marshes of the Lara River. She magically lured him in and almost drowned him."

For the longest time, Vamilion let his message hang in the chilly air, knowing it would have special meaning to the first Wise One. When Vamilion turned for the door, he finally heard a comment from the King of Creating.

"A son? And a Siren? Perhaps I will come."

GLOSSARY OF PEOPLE IN THE WISE ONES
SERIES 1-3

Arvid – Logger, Rashel's brother
Bowdry – Leader of a wood crew in the Fallon Forest
Demion – Kingdom directly east of the Land
Drake – sorcerer from Malornia
Elin – Evric's daughter
Emmi – Evert's wife
Enok – EE-nok – Priest in Malornia, Owailion's Door Steward
Evric – A settler on the southern coast of the Land
Evert – EH-vert – Honiea's Door Steward
Gailin – GAY-lin – Original name of Honiea
Gilead – GIL-ee-ad – Original name of Vamilion
Goren – GOR-in – Door Steward at Vamilion
Hodge – A settler in Edgewood
Honiea – Ho-NEE-ah – Queen of Healing, wife of Vamilion
Imzuli – im-ZOO-lee – White dragon, Mohan's daughter
Jonis – JON-is, farmer who loves Gailin
Jonjonel – JON-gen-el – Volcanic mountain in the northwest of the Land
Kail – KAY-l, draftsman in Gailin's village

Kreftor – Sorcerer of East
Lani – Lahn-ee – Yeolani's mother
Malornia – Ma-LOR-nee-a - Kingdom west, across the sea from the Land
Marit – MAR-eet - Yeolani's dog
Marwen – MAR-wen, Kingdom south and east of the Land
Mohan – MO-han – Golden Dragon, mate to Tiamat, guide to Owailion
Mohanzelechnikhai – Mo-han-zeh-LECH-nik-HI – Mohan's true name
Neeorm – NEE-orm, original name of Drake
Nevai – Nev-eye - Changeling child
Nevia – Ne-VAY-ah - Yeolani's sister
Norton – A settler in Edgewood
Owailion – Oh-WALE-ee-on King of Creating, husband of Raimi.
Pajet – PAJ-et – Non-magical first wife of Vamilion
Raimi – RAY-mee – Queen of Rivers, wife of Owailion
Rashel – Rah-shell - Queen of Growing Things
Sethan – SETH-an - Innkeeper at West
Stylmach – STEEL-mak – Outlander Sorcerer
Tethimzuliel – Teth-im-ZOO-lee-el – Imzuli's true name
Tiamat – TEE-a-mat, three-headed dragon.
Vamilion –Vah-MI-lee-un – King of Mountains, husband of Honiea
Yeolani – Yay-oh-lahn-ee – King of the Plains, husband of Rashel
Yeon – Yay-on – Yeolani's father

Dear reader,

We hope you enjoyed reading *Life Giver*. Please take a moment to leave a review, even if it's a short one. Your opinion is important to us.

Discover more books by Lisa Lowell at https://www.nextchapter.pub/authors/lisa-lowell.

Want to know when one of our books is free or discounted for Kindle? Join the newsletter at http://eepurl.com/bqqB3H.

Best regards,

Lisa Lowell and the Next Chapter Team

You could also like:
The Swordswoman by Malcolm Archibald

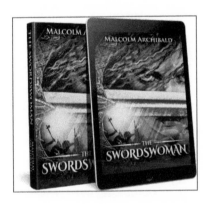

To read the first chapter for free, head to:

https://www.nextchapter.pub/books/the-swordswoman-scottish-historical-fantasy

ABOUT THE AUTHOR

Lisa Lowell was born in 1967 into a large family full of hands-on artists in southern Oregon. In an effort to avoid conflict, her art of choice was always writing, something both grandmothers taught her. She started with poetry at six on her grandmother's ancient manual typewriter. By her teens, she moved on to pen and paper and produced gloomy, angst-ridden fantasy during adolescence. Her mother claims that Lisa shut the door and never came out until she left for university. During this time, she felt compelled to draw illustrations throughout the margins that helped supplement her neglect of adjectives and consistent storylines.

A much-appreciated English teacher, Mrs. Segetti, collected these moody musings and sent them in to scholarship foundations. Lisa got a scholarship for that rather poor writing, escaped Oregon, and went to university. While she loved her family, her only requirement in a school was anywhere too far away to come home on weekends. She got as far as Idaho, Utah, and then even Washington D.C. before she truly launched. She traveled to Sweden (Göteborg, Lund, and Sundsvall) for a year-and-a-half during college where she also reconnected with her heritage.

During college Lisa also fell in love and then had her heart broken. Suddenly she had something to write about. Every story written since harbors a romance and a tangled journey, a *saga* as it were, where the tale comes back to the start. She started to tap into Scandinavian myth and overcame fears of writing conflict. All her earlier failed starts and fascinating characters now molded into an actual story. Completing her degrees in Secondary Education and Masters in English as a Second Language at Western Oregon University, Lisa continued to travel and read favorite authors: Lloyd Alexander, David Brin, Patricia McKillip and Anne McCaffrey. She graduated with a teaching degree in 1993.

Then, when she came back to Oregon, like a fairy tale, she met Pat Lowell. They met on Sunday, played racquetball on Monday night and were engaged by the end of the date. The sense of peace in meeting someone with the same goals and values made it right. Four months later, they were married. Lisa began reworking childhood manuscripts into credible stories, and this was when *Sea Queen* began. When children did not arrive as expected, the Lowells adopted three children, Travis, Scott and Kiana. At that point, Lisa chose to ease off writing actively for a time to focus on her family. However, she kept all the ideas and honed her skill while teaching Middle School English. Storytelling remained her true talent and made her a skillful teacher. In 2011, she was named VFW Oregon Teacher of the Year.

In 2012 a friend asked for manuscripts so he could learn how to get a book onto Amazon in e-book form. As she had several half-finished works she could contribute, Lisa gave him one, and when she saw how easy that seemed, the idea of publishing snuck up on her again. Her children were moving on, and she felt she could again begin to write. She reworked the first book in the Wise Ones series, *Sea Queen*, and began sharing it with beta readers. However, her friends wanted to hear the back-stories of some of the other characters, so she started writing those into full manuscripts and realized that a series was born.

Publishing became more important when Pat had a terrible accident and developed Parkinson's. Lisa had to stay closer to home to help him, and he encouraged her writing. She continued to teach English in middle school (someone has to) and blogs on a Facebook page at https://www.facebook.com/vikingauthor/. At present she is maintaining a website at www.magiccintheland and tinkering with her next novels, Markpath, a set of sci-fi novels. She loves to write but also experiments with drawing, dances while she writes, sings when the radio is on, and reads a great deal of poorly written essays by thirteen-year-olds. She still lives in Oregon, near waterfalls and Powells, the best bookstore on earth. She is still in love with her husband, Pat, and still loves writing tangled journeys.

Life Giver
ISBN: 978-4-86750-307-2

Published by
Next Chapter
1-60-20 Minami-Otsuka
170-0005 Toshima-Ku, Tokyo
+818035793528

5th June 2021